PAGAN CURSE

by Sam Taw

Cover art supplied by Carantoc Publishing Ltd
First edition, 2019
ISBN 978-1-9160051-5-0
Carantoc Publishing Ltd.
www.carantocpublishing.com

Author Note:

Although there is archaeological evidence of Cornish tin found in former Phoenician cities and settlements during the Late Bronze Age, there is little to support a direct trading relationship. Some historians believe that it is possible that the superior ship building skills allowed Phoenicians to venture as far as the Cornish coast, while others theorise that overland dealing across Europe is more likely. With this in mind, the following story contains elements based in fact and also themes extrapolated from theories. The remaining parts are products of the imagination.

Please note that this novel was created by a British author. Except for Cornish words, slang and dialogue, spelling and grammar are corrected to **British English**. There are also scenes which may offend more sensitive readers. It is not deemed suitable for children.

CHAPTER ONE

The willow bark came away with ease, my blade sharp and comfortable in my hand. It was hard to find a tree along the river bank which had not yet been stripped, such was the desperation for pain relief in camp. For more than half a moon now, my family and new friends suffered the severest ague of the belly. It came with fever, headaches and vomiting, not to mention the trouble from their rear ends.

With young Jago out searching for calming sorrel, I had to carry all that I harvested back to the settlement without help. The leader of the mining community, Kenver rushed to meet me as I neared his roundhouse. His eldest daughter was the latest to be struck with the sickness. I gave him a handful of willow and some fresh peeled blackthorn, instructing him to make a strong hot tea and get as much down her as she would take.

It seems to pull the young ones down quicker than the strong warriors, but I admit to feeling worried that I might fall prey to the illness too before the worst was over. How then would I tend to those in most distress? I hurried back to the hut I shared with the former Ruvane, Cryda and her new babe. She seemed to have escaped the ailment thus far, thank the goddess. I slumped down onto my bunk exhausted by the whole affair. As soon as those suffering were treated, a new crop of people would appear at my door begging for prepared willow.

Cryda swaddled the babe and lay her down on the bedding at my side. The dear little thing gurgled and chuckled blissfully unaware of the turmoil all around her. As much as I wanted to bide a while and take my fill of what little happiness she offered, there were patients to see and tonics to boil. I heaved my old bones back up and sighed.

"Are many laid low with the sickness?" Cryda asked, pouring a little goat's milk into a beaker and warming it through with a handful of thickening grains.

"Too many. I just don't understand it. A few people in the same family is quite normal, but it has cut a swathe right through camp. The only place I have not yet been called to, are the tents at the riverbank where the Priest Sect have settled." That only struck me as odd as the words left my mouth. Until then, I had not considered the uneven spread of patients.

Cryda thought about my statement and raised a suspicious brow. "Do you think they have invoked black magic to protect their clan?"

"What, waving feathers and drinking a spot of chicken's blood while spouting great nonsense? More likely they are too addled to mix with those who have the ague." I drank a little ale from her cup and set to crushing the pith from the inner bark into the water boiling over the fire.

Within a short while, Jago returned clutching a few twigs and stalks. The moment he entered, he cast them to the floor and rushed over to check up on the babe. Cryda smiled at his obsessive care for the child. Anyone would think him the girl's father, not a lame slave boy from across the seas.

I glanced at the stems wilting at my feet. "Where's the sorrel I asked for?" I peered up at him, but he was lost in the carefree gurgles and splutters. Stooping to gather up the twigs, I flicked his shoulder on my way past. "The sorrel?"

"Ah yes, I am sorry, Fur Benyn. There was no sorrel to be found anywhere, but I remembered that you told me about this plant with the funny name…" He pointed to the broken stalks in my hand. "Purple loosestrife, is that right?" The boy had learned a lot since he came into my service, and I appreciated the tender way with which he insisted on calling me wise woman, but this was not the plant I needed.

"Loosestrife would help their problem bowels, it's true, but I needed something for the fever that wouldn't anger their bellies more." How could I scold the boy after all that he'd been through? The gods must have a plan for this painted child, or he would not have survived such hardships and still be able to smile. Cryda spooned out some of the porridge from the beaker and gave it to me in a wooden bowl. I was too tired to eat. Passing it over to Jago, I continued to pound and grind the bark shavings.

"You know what they are saying about camp, don't you?" Cryda said, touching my arm to stop my labours. Of course, I knew. Everyone in the mining community, all of Blydh's Hunter Clan and certainly all of the priests knew. They made it their business to cast the omen as wide as possible. The leader of the Priest Clan announced to all who would listen, that a great ague would lay low our people. The rune cast was made off the back of our tribal leader's death, and swelled the number of our clans flocking to his religion. I should say he was a clever man, bending the feeble minded to his ways, but it sickens me to praise such devious methods of control. It never happened while Aebba lived. Now his young sons lead us, but are too green to recognise such wicked ways. Cryda was waiting for my answer.

"Yes, I know all about his prophecy. The man shouted about it for long enough. He doesn't scare me."

Cryda lowered her voice. "But what if he really does have the ear of the gods? What if they hear us saying unkind things, and they strike us, or my child, down with the sickness?"

"Well, if that is the case, half the settlement has been bad mouthing him. Make an offering to the goddess if it worries you so. Cerridwen would not see your babe suffer." I watched her nodding vigorously, before picking up the swaddled child and laying him in Jago's open arms. I rolled my eyes, realising that I had lost the assistance of my slave yet again.

With the smashed bark steeping in hot water, I went in search of my nephew, Blydh. I knew where he'd be at this time of the morning. There was no real need to check up on his health, but the walk down the valley to his house near the beach was refreshing and it was about as far from the priests as you could get. The winter breeze funnelled along the river blowing salt spray and new life into my old heart.

Blydh was snoring under his furs when I strode into his house. One naked leg dangled from his bunk as though it didn't belong to the rest of his body. Other than the stink of ale, I found no evidence of the ague and breathed a sigh of relief. Just to be sure, I reached over and touched the back of my hand to his forehead. It was cool. All was well.

He must sleep lightly, as he stirred awake. "Aunt Mel, what's happened? Why are you here?"

"Pay me no heed, boy. I came to check that you were not taken by the fever." I walked to the central fire and poked at the embers with a stick before adding more wood.

He took his time to gain his bearings, sitting upright and rubbing at his face. "It's getting worse, I hear. Practically every hut has someone with the flux."

"I'm doing my best to treat them all, but they don't seem to be improving with my tonics. I really can't understand it. They are the same recipes that I've always used, and the same mixtures that my mother taught me." I sat on the end of his bed. He looked almost childlike. The hair on his face was so sparse, it didn't cover his chin. How is he and his twin brother supposed to lead such a massive tribe as ours?

For someone so stoic and calm, I detected a hint of panic in those big eyes of his. "Do you think the gods are furious with us? Maybe this is their way of getting back at us for killing the Lady Eseld?"

I swallowed hard. It was not something I had considered. She had powerful mystical friends on her side. It was my fault entirely that she was accused of our Chieftain's murder. They had all trusted my word. I was so sure that she had poisoned Aebba so that her son could become the new Metern of the Dumnoni Tribe. How was I to know that all the evidence was laid at my feet pointing to her as the culprit? How could I tell them that the Lady Eseld was sacrificed as a result of my mistake? I shuddered at the thought of her priestly father discovering the truth.

"No, of course not, Blydh." I blustered. "Someone probably ate some bad meat and now its spreading across camp. Gods wouldn't be bothered with anything so trivial." I stood up to leave. The discussion had taken an uncomfortable new direction.

"We all heard the rune cast, Aunt Mel. We can't say that he didn't foresee this outcome."

I peered at the floor, unable to meet his eye, then pushed through the skins covering the entrance. Slightly shaken, I walked up to the coastal path and sat on the cliff side watching the wind whip the foam from the waves. The tide was almost fully out, revealing the spot where Blydh and Tallack's warriors staked her to the low water mark. I had no love for Eseld, by Cernonnus, she was a constant stone in my shoe but she did not have to die. Her sins were minor compared to that of the real killer. She walks about the settlement as though she is the new Ruvane, despite the fact that she and Tallack are not bound together. Up until this last quarter moon, Jago and I have kept out of her way, but there will come a time for the truth. It always comes out eventually, no matter what attempts are made to keep it suppressed.

It was blowing a gale up on the cliffs. I looked about for any useful plants but the biting wind drove me back down into the sheltered valley. When I drew close to my hut, I saw her standing outside, taunting me.

"What do you want, Brea? I have much work to do this day." I bustled passed her into the house, keen to be among others for protection. Cryda had not returned from making her offering to the goddess. Jago stood with the babe still cradled in his arms. The boy looked positively petrified when he saw Brea follow me inside.

There was no way that I would let her intimidate me. I picked up my largest knife from the leather wrap and slammed it down on to the loosestrife stems. It made such a noise, the child awoke and bawled.

"I… um, just thought you'd like to know that the scout returned from the cliff path. Tallack's boats have been spotted. He should be here before nightfall." She loitered next to my shoulder. I couldn't decide whether she was trying to re-ignite the friendship we once shared or whether she just enjoyed putting people on edge.

I turned to face her with my blade held aloft next to my face. "Good." I waited. She didn't move. I raised a brow and pursed my lips. "Was that all?" Narrowing my eyes, I met her gaze with the confidence that only an old woman like me can muster. She flinched first. Turning on her heels, she scampered from our hut without another word. Before she could release the door flaps, I let the heavy knife swing and hit the chopping block again. I swear I heard her jump with a little gasp. I had to be on my guard with that one. She had a knack of creeping about unseen. To my knowledge she was responsible for at least two deaths and almost took my life twice. I doubt Cernonnus would spare me a third time.

Even still, it doesn't pay to anger the girl. It was a good thing that there were no long feasting huts in the settlement. There was no time for merriment in a world filled with long days beneath the ground, chipping out rocks for the smelters to turn into tin ingots for trade. I miss the old camp next to the River Exe further east. For one, there was a great deal more space to spread out. There was plenty of room for our livestock and for me to grow herbs. This valley was never meant for all the clans to over winter. It's probably half the reason for the sickness spreading so quickly.

My bark tonic had turned a deep yellow, almost brown. With a length of woven fabric stretched across a beaker, I strained the hot liquor ready to dilute for my patients. They would have to take it without the sweetness of honey. All my supplies had run out and there was no chance of more until the summer.

I could not get the memories of Brea out of my head. She was cunning and ruthless. I thought about how she had taken one of my knives for ill intent before. If she rifled through my possessions now, she would come across the long sword of curious metal I found at the lakes near to Stonehenge. Brea wouldn't think twice about running me or Jago through with such a weapon.

I hurried to its hiding place beneath my bunk and instructed Jago to wrap it with fur and place it in one of the abandoned mine shafts further up the valley. He seemed to comprehend my thoughts, since he did so immediately and without question. At least no one would ever find that and use it against us.

With my willow and blackthorn tonics in two separate jugs, I began to make my rounds of all the affected houses. My first stop was at Kenver's house. I called out to those inside and waited for them to move the wooden panel keeping out the worst of the draughts. Kenver's son was on the inside, looking gravely concerned for his sister's failing health. I craned my neck to see behind him. Kerensa, was doubled over a wooden bowl, emptying the contents of her stomach and groaning in between.

I recalled my instructions to their father about making her willow tea. It must have made her stomach sore. All I could offer her was more of the blackthorn, but that would only help with staunching the flow at her other end. Poor young woman was covered in her own mess. Her mother fussed about, wiping her clean and wrapping more furs around to stop the trembling chills. She shoved a large jug at her son and instructed him to fetch more water from the river.

There was nothing I could do to help. Kenver thanked me for calling in, but I could see that he wanted me well away from his family's pain and suffering. Picking up my tonics, I left their home for the next patient along the river bank. By the fifth hut, my arms were aching from carrying the jugs. I set them down and sat on a boulder for a rest, watching people go about their day all around me. Up the valley, I could just make out the miners' shelters. Few had permanent fixtures like Kenver's, using clay wattle over woven hurdles. These were people who did not make old bones. Their long days below ground left them with little energy to fix up their homes.

On the other side of the river, lay the priest's camp. Theirs was a collection of green timber framed tents to suit their nomadic lifestyle. They were easy to dismantle and carry to the next destination. I was starting to think that this was the longest they'd ever stayed in one place, but then their leader had recently lost his daughter at the low water mark on the beach. His warriors spent their days smoking hemp and communing with the gods, while their women folk did all the work.

I looked at their leader with mixed feelings brewing in my heart. The man had caused untold grief to my kin over the last few cycles, but to my knowledge, he was not responsible for any of their deaths. My mistake had left him without a daughter. He wore his grief on his arm; a black feather secured in a leather band. It must be another one of his new religion's ways. It was not how we marked the death of a loved one.

We of course also shared the mourning of his granddaughter, my niece, killed in her attempted raid of this mining encampment by her brother's warriors. I felt her loss as though she was my own child, but the manner of her attack made it impossible for me to voice my grief. I bore it alone and silently.

Rested, I picked up the jugs to continue on my way upstream to the miners, when something odd caught my attention. The leader of the Priest Sect left his tent carrying a water container and walked away from the river. Spurred on by curiosity and suspicion, I crossed the tributary over the footbridge and followed him into the woodland beyond.

The jugs felt heavier the longer I carried them. Tucking them behind a tree trunk, I was free to amble along behind the old man. At first, I thought his vessel might be full of something he wished to be rid of, but as he swung it by the rim close to his legs, I could see that it was empty. On he walked, deep into the forest until he came upon a spring, gushing clear water from the rocks. As he filled his pot, I crouched low so that he would not see me. For someone who delights in drinking chicken blood and smearing red clay all over his body, he was going to an awful lot of trouble to collect water, when the river flowed right behind his tent.

When his vessel was full, I watched him splash the cool liquid over his face and hands, fill his mouth and swallow, and then begin the walk back to camp. There is far more to this than just the sweet taste of spring water.

CHAPTER TWO

I waited in the woodland, sitting on a fallen log for the best part of the morning. Every tribesman and woman that passed by were marked by the tattoos of the Priest Sect. Each of them came to fill their pots with spring water. Determined to get to the bottom of this turn of events, I returned to my hut to find Jago and Cryda. With my slave tasked to deliver the tonics to those in need, I bundled my kit in my bag with my knives and grabbed my stick. I expected a long walk and it would be uphill all the way.

The slope was gradual at first, the river plain wide and soggy under foot. I stayed close to the wooded edges, where the rain drained through the sandier soils. I stopped now and then, gathering what provisions I found along the way, but there were slim pickings to be had in such a poor community. It made me wonder why the Alchemist's didn't take more tin for themselves. They could easily supplement their own wealth and we would be none the wiser.

Having spent a few moons with their leader, Kenver, I realised that his abundant kindness towards us, didn't necessarily extend to those in his clan. He cared for their welfare, so long as they maintained the quotas of tin production my family insisted upon. I vowed to speak with my nephews, the new joint Meterns of the Dumnonii about this state of affairs.

Picking my feet up, I trudged in a north-westerly direction, further inland and away from my kin. I had a notion about the devious priests, but I wanted to prove my theory false. The thoughts flitting through my mind that could explain their peculiar behaviour were low indeed. My fears were not based wholly on my imagination, but on the many times through which I had seen past their illusions. The old man had a habit for well-timed performances, ramped up with a little help from his warriors. He was a showman through and through. I was convinced that he would stoop to any lengths to prove his rune cast true.

Before a slow meander in the river, I found another small cluster of shelters. These lowland farmers and gatherers had many young, and all were sick. I could smell their suffering from quite a distance, their washing hung across willow hurdles bore the stains of their mess. These people were not miners and not part of the priest's warning, and yet they were stricken with the same fever as those in our camp. As I walked on, I found a fork in the river just passed their houses. The smaller tributary branched off to one side of the farmers, while the larger water course carried on around the bend upstream.

I dallied for a while, indecision halting my progress, before an idea alighted in my mind. Sitting on a tree stump next to a pile of chopped logs, I waited for someone from the roundhouses to come outside. As I predicted, I did not have to tarry for long.

"Ho, there!" I called out to a young lad carrying a piss pot.

He tipped the contents out onto the midden and wandered closer to me. "Who are you?"

I didn't answer him. "Where do you and your family collect your water, this ere river…" I nodded in the direction I had walked. "Or that stream yonder?"

"Mother gets it from the stream." He said, squinting up at me and letting the drips of piss splatter over his bare feet.

"Good lad." I heaved myself up, handed him a few grains of tin and some blackthorn bark. "Tell your mum to make a hot tea from this and give it to those with the squits." I left him looking up at me with a puzzled expression and wandered along the adjoining stream.

This water course was far narrower. It was too small to support boats, rendering it almost deserted. The banks were muddied with animal tracks and difficult to plod through. Despite the cold snap, most of the bulrushes were still tall, with a fair amount of silt and weed built up in the channel. It was hard to believe that anyone had trodden this path in an age, and yet there were footprints ahead of me. Following them through a small field, I came to the end of my search.

There in the stream lay a half dozen dead goats, tied to a post by their horns. Their swollen bellies lifted them high in the water and maggots crawled from their eye sockets. This was no accident. These animals had not slipped together from the river bank and lashed themselves to a stake in the middle of the channel. This was a deliberate act to spoil our water supply.

"In the name of Cernonnus, I'll see that priest swing from the highest tree for this", but as I spat my anger and cursed the man for all he was worth, I realised that I could not prove my claim. There had to be a way to make the slimy kyjyan admit this terrible act of vengeance on our tribe. There were too many carcasses to clear from the stream myself. I needed serious help to sort this out once and for all. Keen to be rid of the flies and stink, I hurried back to the farmers' houses and told them about my findings, urging them to find a cleaner source of water.

Stopping to rest a while, I ate some curd cheese from my bag and a couple of crab apples. My thirst was raging but I could not drink any water from the river or from the bladder I'd brought with me. Just as I packed away my things, ready to set off again, I heard hooves cantering along the bank ahead. Horse and rider came into focus as they drew closer, my anxious heart steadied with relief. It was young Derwa's new husband from the mountains.

"What are you doing all the way out here, Fur Benyn?" He asked, pulling up on the reins.

"We're family now, boy. You can call me Meliora if you like." From his frown and tucked lips, I figured that it didn't please him to be on first name terms with me. I have no idea why that should be the case, I have tried to be welcoming to the lad despite his parentage.

I gave him some pathetic excuse about needing a particular herb for my kit and couldn't find it nearer to our camp. "Where are you galloping off to without your new wife in tow?"

He looked uneasy, scratching at his beard and thinking about his response. "I um… thought I'd go and hunt for a bit, give Derwa a couple of days to herself. She's always so cross with me, I can't do anything right."

"Give her time, lad. She'll come around, just you see." I had to say something to soothe him, even if I didn't believe a word I'd said. Derwa had a special kind of stubbornness seldom seen in our family. It could be down to her being the youngest for so long. With another half-sister just born, I can only see her tantrums increasing in number.

The lad from the Ordoviches Tribe still looked sour. "Is she always so disagreeable about everything? I can't seem to make her happy whatever I do."

"That's what being bound to someone means, putting up with the good and the bad. Maybe a couple of days away will benefit you both." It was another statement of which I did not mean. If anything, their time apart would only give them an excuse to get close to other inappropriate people in the tribe. What worried me the most, was that in the Ordo's absence, Derwa could get re-acquainted with the father of her aborted child. What kind of trouble would that girl stir up now? If she lays with another and gets caught, it'll be more than our Ordo copper supplies that would be in jeopardy.

I let the boy go on, with my word that I would keep an eye on his wife. He cantered off smiling for the first time since his binding ceremony at the wooden henge of life. There was little point telling him otherwise. No one listens to the old lady of the tribe, despite her wise nickname.

Puffing and blowing hard, I reached our hut before the sun was low in the sky. I could see the masts of Tallack's boats pulling close to shore. What a relief to have him back. Dumping my kit in the entrance to our house, I instructed Jago not to drink the water, and to share the news with Cryda as soon as possible.

"Did you have any trouble hiding the sword?"

"No, Fur Benyn. It lies in a tunnel at the top of the valley." He looked pleased with himself.

"And no one saw you?"

He shrugged. "I can't be absolutely sure, but no one pays any attention to the comings and goings of slaves."

"Good lad." Without delay, I hobbled down the path to Blydh, who sat outside his house skinning a couple of rabbits.

"Nephew, come quick. The water is poisoned, fouled with rotting carcasses." At first, he thought I'd lost my wits, but as I breathed through the cramping pain in my weary muscles, I settled to tell him about all that I had found that day. This time, I did not leave out my suspicions as to who could have caused such an outbreak, adding my sightings of the priests at the spring head.

It was only then, when Blydh had sent a dozen warriors to rid our water of the rank odours of death, that I began to realise what I had set in motion. With more warriors at his back, and Tallack's crew hot on their heels, they set out to demand an explanation from the Priest Sect. In a fit of panic, I rushed to catch up with my nephews reminding them that I had no proof with which to accuse them. They paid me no heed, charging across the footbridge and into the heart of the priests' tents.

Blydh did not wait for permission to enter the leader's shelter. He thrust both fists through the opening and ducked inside, to return moments later with the old man bent low and held at the back of the neck. Cowering on his knees, the bony shaman begged to be heard.

"Speak." Blydh growled, throwing him to the ground at his men's feet.

The priest stayed low to the ground, trembling in an exaggerated manner. "Oh, great Metern, are we not family, you and I? Why am I treated in this vicious way by kin?"

"Pah!" I exclaimed. I couldn't help myself, it just shot from my mouth before I could rein it in. The whole of Tallack's crewmen and all of Blydh's hunters now stood silent awaiting my reply. "As if you don't know what you've done."

"Me, Fur Benyn? I have no idea to what you are referring. I have been tattooing a lovely young lady in my bunk all day, just ask her if you don't believe me." He gestured behind him, pointing to the glassy-eyed woman staggering from his tent, addled on hemp and ale. She trotted a few more steps and then launched herself at Blydh's half-brother, Paega.

"Not this day, but before. You claim that you foretold this terrible ague that spreads across our tribe, yet it was you who caused it in the first place." I practically shouted at him; my vitriol had been brewing all the way home. At this point, the crowd was swollen with people from the mining settlement and all of Kenver's family and friends, curious about the noise and those gathered.

"I swear by all that's holy; I know nothing of what you speak. I have been in camp since the funeral pyre of my dear granddaughter and the murder of Lady Eseld, both my flesh and blood." He hung his head and faked a loud sob. I wasn't taken in by the old fool and neither were my nephews. His clan though, were loyal followers. Their murmurs and mutterings grew in volume until a few began to shout of his innocence. He cradled his head in his hands for a moment and then peered up at me with tear filled eyes. "If this tribe has been laid low with the flux, it is not by my hand. All I could do was predict it happening."

There were more outcries of "innocent", and "he speaks directly with the gods."

Paega, who had brazened out his brothers' banishment, now stood to defend his grandfather's honour. "Our clan leader should not be disrespected in this way. Let him to his feet. How dare you treat those of us in mourning with such a heavy hand."

Blydh's face reddened. A vessel in his temple pulsed and his breathing quickened. He'd seen first-hand how the sickness took people, especially the young and the weak. They were his tribe's folk now, and his vow to protect them was uppermost in his mind. Paega had revealed himself as nothing more than a liar and a liability. Our Meterns had no time for his protestations.

"I can assure you, Fur Benyn, I am innocent." The priest said in a sullen voice.

"You say that, yet you walk all the way up the valley to collect your water, when the river here runs right past your tent. All your clan do the same. What do you have to say about that?" I blustered, jabbing at him with a rigid finger.

"A local woman told us of the sweet spring further up the hillside and I told a few others. There's no harm in that, is there? Of what are you accusing me?" He fluttered his eyelashes, trying to appear innocent. The ruse didn't sway me for one moment, but there was no actual proof with which to condemn him. I sighed and flounced away, growling to myself. As I neared the footbridge, I spotted young Derwa heading towards me. She was ashen in the face, yet she glowed with beads of sweat.

"What's all the fuss? I could hear the shouting from my hut." Her eyes rolled about in the back of her head, before her legs gave way beneath her sending her crashing to the ground. I took two big strides to her side, but I couldn't catch her in time.

"Ho, there!" I yelled above all the noise and clamour. "Tallack, Blydh, come help." I screamed it a couple of times before they heard me. Pushing through the crowds my nephews ran to my side, tapping their half-sister's cheeks and encouraging her to come to her senses. Nothing worked. They called to her, shook her and pinched her arms, but the best she could do was to roll her head around as though it was attached to her body on a string.

"Aunt Mel, do something. Make her better." Tallack whined. His fondness for the girl had never faded in all their years. She was the youngest and most spoiled of Aebba the Wild's children. The old priest got to his feet and scampered over to his granddaughter, cupping his hand over his mouth and nose.

"See what you've done, you meddling kyjyan!" I bellowed at him. "And all to prove that you could channel the gods and their will." My nephews widened their eyes at each other. It was seldom that I used such language, especially in front of them. I held my hand to the girl's forehead. She was burning up, just like the others. With her so feeble and weak, it would be almost impossible to get my tonics down her throat without choking her.

Blydh rose slowly to his feet and squared up to the priest, his fists clenched tight, his teeth clamped together in a snarl. "Admit what you have done and we'll go easy on you."

The old man looked at me and then at his granddaughter lolling on the ground and then back at Blydh. His trembling was genuine this time. He'd already lost all but Paega in his family, Derwa was the last female of his direct line. "It was never meant to get this bad. Just a few people with the squits, was all I expected. Then Paega suggested that we put more goats in to make sure." He bit at his nails and blinked rapidly at Blydh. "You said you'd go easy on us, if we told you."

Blydh's tempered melted into a disquieting calm. The throbbing vein in his head eased and his fists unclenched. "And that we will." Blydh nodded to Tallack who immediately grabbed the priest by the arms and twisted them behind the old man's back. Their warriors closed rank around them, blocking all but Paega from attack.

Tallack leaned over me. "Can you help her, Aunt Mel?"

"I'll do my best, if one of your men can carry her back to her hut." I knew that the quicker I could treat Derwa, the greater the chance of her recovery, but I couldn't tear myself away. I had to see what Blydh would do.

The priest squirmed and darted, trying to break free from Tallack's strong grip. His priestly warriors jostled against the broader and more powerful head hunters, but they could not claw their way past to rescue their clan leader.

"You said you'd go easy on us…please, be merciful." The priest whimpered. Paega made a grab at Tallack, scratching and mauling to lessen his grip on the old man. Tiring of his attempts, Tallack swiped him away with the flick of his arm. Forcing the priest back down onto his knees, Tallack took a length of rope from one of his crew and bound his wrists behind him.

"As Chieftains of the Dumnonii, sons of Aebba the Wild and rightful leaders of all the clans under our protection, we name you guilty. The punishment for this crime is death."

CHAPTER THREE

The crowds were hushed and still. I thought there might be time for reason and debate, an opportunity for the old man to make amends for his mistakes.

Blydh unsheathed his bronze sword, and in the last dying flickers of winter light, swiped it down across the man's neck. The cut was clean, severing the backbone in a decisive slice. Blood splashed in a great puddle with flying spatters showering the twins and those around them. The priest's head thudded to the ground, teetered on the flat of the forehead, before rolling into the blood pool.

Paega cried out and fell to his knees. It was a howl of desperation, and felt by their entire clan. Blydh acted by instinct and with a cool temper. He never gave his foes the opportunity to explain or retaliate. Now he turned to his half-brother, his sword still dripping with the old man's life force.

"You were party to this treachery, brother. You must also pay." Blydh drew back the blade, altering his stance to carry out another quick death sentence, but Tallack clasped his shoulder.

"No, Blydh. We have lost enough of our family this winter as it is." Tallack faced Blydh and urged him to sheath his sword. "Allow him to live in banishment as we originally agreed. The priests will live out their days on the bleak moorland, never to return here, or to the burned camp on the River Exe." Tallack's voice of reason was the only one Blydh would accept.

I heaved a great sigh of relief. My words carried more weight with my nephews than I had thought possible. If they knew about my mistake over accusing the Lady Eseld, I too might find myself without a head. Paega didn't move from his spot on the riverbank, his moans and cries replaced by a black stare of pure hatred. I had no need to ask what the young warrior was thinking, nor did I have to guess whether their entire clan thought the same. The twins had made powerful enemies in the priests, and Paega would make sure that their wrath would be bloody and vengeful.

Blydh stooped to collect the old man's head. With its shaved scalp, he had no hair with which to suspend it from his horse's bridle. Wandering off with his bleeding prize, Blydh left Tallack to scatter the crowd and make good on his promise of banishment. With orders issued to his crewmen and to his brother's hunters, Tallack returned to me and picked up the fevered Derwa, to carry her back to the hut.

"Where is her Ordo husband?" Tallack asked me, resting his half-sister down on their bunk and covering her with furs.

"He rode off earlier this morning to hunt. Said he'd be gone a few days." I wiped her brow with a cloth and loosened her clothes.

"Stupid kyjyan, didn't he know that she was sick?" Tallack walked to the door, pausing to hear my response.

"She hasn't exactly made it easy for the lad of late. You can't blame him. It wasn't his idea to wed her."

Tallack shook his head and blinked slowly. He rubbed at his brow with the heel of his hand. "I'll send your painted slave over to bring your medicines."

I did what I could for the girl, making her comfortable and cleaning up the messes she made. It wasn't long before Jago arrived, but he was not alone.

"Is there anything I can do to help, Fur Benyn? Tallack sent me over here. Isn't he just the most thoughtful Metern ever?" It was Brea, of course. Come to taunt me and make us uneasy. Why the girl needs to keep wittering on about her relationship with my nephew, I'll never know. If the boy meant to bind with her, I dare say he would have asked her by now. Although I doubt it would be considered a wise union among the elders. A Metern must wed for alliances with other tribes, and that seldom means binding with the widow of the previous Chief.

I did my best to ignore her presence, taking my healing kit from Jago and sending him off to fetch clean water from the spring further up the valley. Derwa thrashed about in her bedding, writhing with fever and sweats. She had no idea that we were trying to assist her, flailing her arms about fighting me off. Brea stepped forwards and held down her limbs. I must have given her a look of incredulity for she peered at me and said;

"You and I are not enemies, Meliora. There is no need for you to avoid me like you do."

Still I said nothing, focusing my attention on Derwa and the humours leaking from her.

"I bear no ill will for you or your slave…providing you both keep your mouths shut." She said it with a spite that sent a chill through me. How could we do otherwise without incurring the wrath of my nephews and quite possibly that of the entire Priest Sect too?

"And now that my Tallack is driving the priests from camp, we shall all breathe a little easier." She continued. "Don't you think?" Her grin was as malevolent as her intentions. I didn't answer her, but the reference to *her* Tallack was hard to ignore. Eventually, Brea tired of my inertia towards her barbed comments and left. My relief at her leaving was, however, short lived, for her threat lingered in my mind for the rest of the night and beyond.

It took all our efforts to get Derwa to drink my tonics, but it was all for nought. The poor girl couldn't keep them down long enough for them to work. Between the bouts of sickness, she tucked her knees into her chest and cried with the cramping pain. I sat with her through the night. Jago did his best to run all my errands for me and keep me abreast of the news in camp, but Derwa worsened as the night wore on. Tallack returned to visit, bringing me food from his own hearth, but I was too scared to eat his offering.

"Is she any better, Aunt Mel?" He said, leaving the steaming bowl of stew on the table for me and sitting on the bunk by his sister's side.

I looked at the meal and wondered how much hemlock or nightshade Brea had stirred into the bowl. "If anything, nephew, she's worse than before."

He held her hand, expecting her to respond to his touch. When she failed to notice his presence, his expression pinched into a frown of deep concern. "Is this likely to kill her?"

For a moment I was confused. Many lives had been lost over the course of half a moon, but I'd forgotten that he'd been away at sea. This ailment was all new to him. "It might do, Tallack. It's a nasty flux and has left dozens of families across camp in mourning." To that, he squeezed her hand tighter and looked to be wiping away a tear or two when he thought I couldn't see?

We sat together for some time in complete silence. He made no attempt to leave and seemed at ease in my company. I banked up the fire and took advantage of his presence to nip outside to stretch my legs. Snatching some food from my own hut, I returned as quickly as I could to my niece and nephew.

When I arrived in the doorway, Tallack was hovering over the bowl he'd brought for me. "You've let your supper get cold, Aunt."

"I have, but it's hard to rouse an appetite with all that's going on in camp." I lied. "Tell Brea I'm sorry for the wastage."

"Oh, she didn't cook it, Blydh's slaves did. I grabbed a bowl from them on my way over here. Brea does nothing these days." He looked glum, almost depressed at the mention of her.

I should have minded my own business but the temptation to ask was too strong. "Things aren't all meadow flowers and sweet ale between you two then?"

He chuckled at my phrase, raising an amused brow in my direction. "She was great fun at first. I've always known that she favoured me, Aunt, even when she was bound to father. She'd slip me parcels of honey cakes and fresh baked bread with a bowl of Gwyn's squirrel stew. Poor Gwyn…" He tapered off, remembering the slave cook from the Long Hut at our old compound, who was famed for her abilities with squirrel. I didn't dare tell him that it was his current bed fellow who sliced her throat to prevent her from telling me about Brea's part in his father's death. Instead I smiled, hoping that he would continue to the juicier parts of the story. He did.

"As soon as I let Brea under my furs, she took it as a given that she was the new Ruvane. She treats the slaves in camp worse than father treated her. She beats them if they cook the wrong dishes or if they use too much of my salt stores." He picked up a chunky stick and poked it into the embers. "I really didn't think she could be so cruel."

I cast my eyes to the fire, keen not to show my feelings about her. There was something about his tale that seemed unspoken, a wistful reluctance to cast her aside. I should have kept my mouth shut, but he's my flesh and blood. I have a duty to aid in his happiness. "Will you bind yourself to her?" I thought that asking him outright would hasten his decision one way or another. My hope was that he would banish her along with the priests.

He took a long, slow breath and swallowed. I squinted at him urging an answer. All he gave me was a non-committal shrug. Honestly, as Cernonnus was my witness, I could've throttled my nephew at times like these. Tallack could catalogue all the crimes and intolerable behaviours of this woman, yet while he could stick his pintel into her whenever the need arose, she could go on creating chaos in camp. I despaired at the ease with which this new Chieftain could be manipulated.

The best course of action was to change the subject. Any mention of that woman gave me shivers. "When will the priests leave camp?"

"At first light. Blydh's men are watching them right now, mine will take over later."

"And Paega?" I watched his features carefully, hoping for a clue as to his real feelings about his half-brother.

"He's already gone." Tallack leaned backwards, throwing the glowing stick fully into the flames. "And good riddance."

"Hmm." I made it sound like an agreement, but Paega's leaving without further complaint worried me. In actuality, He was now the new leader of the Priest Sect, being the only surviving male member of the old priest's family, and I knew him to be as underhanded and vindictive as his grandfather. We have not heard the last of Paega the Wily, of that I am sure. I kept that to myself.

Derwa murmured and shifted restlessly. I jumped up and dabbed at her face with a cool wet cloth, hoping that she would revive enough to get more tonic down her gullet. Tallack saw it as an excuse to leave, taking the stale stew with him.

Come morning, Tallack and Blydh drove the priests from camp. When they were sure that the wandering sect were far away, with no chance of them returning to surprise us, the warriors returned to fetch clean water for the sick and elderly who remained. With the menfolk occupied and the womenfolk tending the afflicted, we all got through the worst of the ague within a few days.

Derwa's fever broke on the fourth day of her bed rest, much to the relief of everyone, but she was still too weak to go about camp. Jago and I took her food and clean water, and emptied her piss pot. Not the nicest of jobs granted, but I was relieved to have her in the land of the living.

When she was well enough to eat a full meal and keep it down, she finally asked after her Ordo husband's whereabouts. He had returned from his hunting trip the same day of her asking, but he told me he was too ashamed to visit her. If he'd stayed, he could have raised the alarm about her illness sooner. His dereliction of duty weighed heavy on the lad from the mountains. I told Derwa as much, and that when I'd seen him, he was as glum as could be.

"Well that's just daft. Tell him to come home immediately." She commanded. At any other time, I would have chided her for her insolence, but in truth I laughed. She was back to her old haughty self, ready to give the Ordo a piece of her mind. She has a lot of her mother, Eseld in her that one. She's far tougher than she looks. I sent Jago to fetch her husband, who returned wearing a shamed face and carrying an odd-looking rock.

Derwa peered at him, sitting up in her bunk with her arms folded across her chest. “Well?”

“Well what?” He frowned, confused.

“Aunt Mel tells me you’ve been out hunting all this time. What did you bring for me?”

I stared at the young man, trying to figure his state of mind. He looked to me that he was undecided about something. It was as if he’d come to a conclusion on the road, filled himself with earnest haste, and then faltered upon seeing my niece. In all honesty, I was surprised he’d come back at all. No one would have blamed him for returning to the mountains having wed an obstinate girl such as Derwa.

He turned the rock over in his hand and stepped closer to her. “I have brought you this.” He held it out with an air of reverence and placed it carefully into the palm of her hand.

Derwa cupped the article. Her nose wrinkled up pulling her face into a sneer. “What would I want with a filthy lump of green rock? Where are the pelts and the meat from your hunt? I have a fancy for a wolf fur collar like Tallack’s. What did you kill?” She threw the stone down onto the rushes, wholly unimpressed. Her husband crouched low and scooped it back into his hands. It was clearly precious to him, even if Derwa felt otherwise. He didn’t answer her insistent questions. Instead, he left the hut and walked with haste towards his horse. It didn’t occur to me to go after him and ask why the item was such a prize in his eyes, or whether he was riding out of the camp never to return.

As soon as the idea popped into my head, the arrival of Tallack and Brea put paid to my mission. They blocked the entrance, bringing Derwa gifts to cheer her and provisions to keep her fed. By the time I had pushed past them both, the Ordo had gone.

Tallack brought a reed flute from his trip to Iwerdon and a mother of pearl necklace for his sister. He pulled the necklace from a pouch tucked into a pocket of his tunic.

Brea's face was soured with jealousy. She did not look happy with his gift. Perhaps she had seen it among his things and expected the jewel was for her. Derwa was delighted with her presents. She even gave the flute a little blast. It sounded like a pony being gelded to me.

I stacked more wood on to the fire to heat the cold air that had seeped in with their entrance. "Were you able to negotiate a trade, Tallack? Do they have a good supply of copper?" I was keen to get to the reason for his trip even if the girls were more interested in the presents and bounty.

"Oh, they have copper, Aunt, enough to keep us going for ever more, but they were less keen on trading with us."

"Why was that? Were they not eager to lay their hands on our tin? How can they expect to make bronze without us?" I was amazed. Tin was rarer than gold, and critical to make strong bronze weapons for defence.

"They'd heard about Wenna. It seems that the Durotriges have a history of trading with the islanders across the sea. News reached them that we had killed our sister. They were extremely upset, accusing us of being disloyal and untrustworthy."

I shook my head in disbelief. "Didn't you tell them why Wenna was killed? Surely, they cannot blame us for defending our own land, mines and people when she and her warriors attacked?"

"That's not the version they were told, and they wouldn't listen to the truth. In their eyes we are selfish traitors who are prepared to kill close kin when it suits us."

As we spoke, we all became aware of loud talking, followed by shouts and hollers outside the hut. Tallack moved the wooden panel from the entrance, allowing us to see outside. Two riders were hurrying into camp from the top of the valley.

I squinted but couldn't see far. "Who is it, can you tell from here?" I asked Tallack. His eyes were younger and better equipped to deal with the sea mists rolling in land.

"It's two of Blydh's scouts. I'll go and see what news they bring." He said, wandering in their direction. I wasn't going to miss out on the gossip from the east. It'd been many moons since our compound on the Exe was razed to the ground, and none of our warrior clans were near the borders to defend them.

Tallack had such long legs and big strides he left me for dust. By the time I'd caught up, the messages had already been exchanged. My nephew wore a long and grievous look across his features.

"What is it? What have they said?"

"Blydh has a man on the inside reporting back from the Duros. He passed on the urgent message that their Chieftain has called in all the horse lords and clans from across their lands and are forging new alliances further east. They mean to build and train an army."

CHAPTER FOUR

It was obvious that we had stayed in the mining community for too long. None of our borders were defended and with the compound on the River Exe decimated, we had no base from which Blydh's warriors could launch attacks on the Duros. I followed Tallack to Blydh's hut to listen in on their decisions. That is the advantage of being an old woman. No one pays much attention to my presence most of the time, and the warriors never stop me from passing into the Meterns' houses in case I stop healing their wounds and injuries.

Tallack had already told his brother the message from the scouts when I reached them. They sat together either side of a large fire, contemplating their options. I sat down on Blydh's bunk behind them. They knew I was there but made no attempts to evict me.

"We will need more weapons for the youngest warriors to join the clans." Blydh said, his stoic calm was almost unsettling. He was talking about shoving untrained, young boys straight into battle.

"They won't attack us during winter. By Cernonnus, they can't handle our rough terrain. They'll have to train their clans as much as we will. No…" Tallack announced.

"They're nowhere near ready. You should take the head hunters back to the borderlands and rebuild the compound. As soon as there are a few huts and a grain store, we can pull in the homesteaders and train up the young ones."

"What about the priests?" Blydh glanced up at his brother.

"What about them?"

"We need the numbers. They are warriors despite the hemp and poor discipline. They are part of our tribe."

"I wouldn't count on them joining us anytime soon. Paega leads them now. No, forget them brother. We'll make do with what we have."

Blydh stood up and reached for his sword as it leaned against the wall next to his bunk. "What will you do?" He asked of Tallack.

"We have no treasure left to buy in supplies, we have no copper to make weapons. I will take some of my men and what tin we have here across the ocean to Frynk and see what deals can be done. It'll be quicker than dealing with those slippery Ordos of the mountains."

The chieftains nodded at each other. It seemed like a sensible plan of action, providing Tallack was right about the preparedness of our arch rivals on our borders.

Their decision filtered through my thoughts and left me in a panic. With Blydh and the head hunters at our furthest eastern border and Tallack away at sea, Jago and I would be left at the mercy of that murderous kyjyan, Brea.

I couldn't see myself riding through the winter weather to the River Exe, with no shelter to rest in at the end of long days of travel. The hut I built with my bare hands I could cope with losing. I'm not so sure I would be able to hold in the tears at losing some of my most exotic plants and herbs. The seeds I bought at the midsummer gathering were still safely hidden among my possessions.

It would be some time until I was settled enough to plant them.

Considering all the options before me, I rose from Blydh's bedding and rested my arm on his shoulder facing Tallack. "I'd like to come with you nephew, if you have a mind to taking me? With the possibility of battle on the horizon, I'll need all the medicines and tinctures I can lay my hands on, and there is nothing but charred remains back at the Exe. I can trade for what I need in the Frynkish ports." The twins looked up at me, brows raised and gasping. The glow of the fire lit up the amusement in their faces.

Tallack reacted first. "That's a good one, Aunt. You had me fooled for a moment then." Both took a long drink from their ale, still tittering between swallows.

"I am perfectly serious, Tallack. I need to go. Jago and I won't take up much room and we'll carry our own dried meats and cheese. I can heal any of your crew that needs it and learn much from the Frynks when we get there."

Their laughter grew more raucous and humiliating. Hadn't I already proven my resilience, having survived a near death poisoning and being shoved down a cliff? I rested my balled-up fists on my hips and scowled at each of them. It was the same angry glare I gave them before whacking their behinds when they were small for using my goats as target practice. The laughter stopped.

"It's too dangerous, Aunt. And anyway, I will need you in the compound when it's rebuilt to tend to the wounded." Blydh said, softening his tone. He was humouring me. It was little more than a pity gesture for an old woman past her usefulness.

"You think that it's too dangerous, boy? I grew up with your grandfather. They didn't call him Cador the Cruel for nothing. You've never known danger like riding with him." I narrowed my eyes, daring them to challenge me.

"But, Aunt…" Tallack ventured. "You were a young woman back then. We can't afford to lose you."

It was a pitiful attempt at flattery, one tinged with an insult. "Just you make sure you leave room on your boat for me and my slave. You won't even notice we're there." I shuffled to the door before they could talk me around. We had to get out of the mining camp before Brea could silence us for good. Cryda was not at any risk in her company, and there were plenty of slaves to do her bidding.

When I got back to our hut, I was giddy with excitement. I'd always yearned to travel, but Aebba had kept me close by to manage his growing list of ailments. The few times when my brother, Cador, had taken me to visit allied tribes, it was to offer me in binding to a tribal leader's son. I thank the goddess daily that none of those meetings ended with forcing me to wed, but I sometimes wonder what might have been.

Jago was rocking Cryda's babe in his arms while she slept. He was singing a beautiful tune with lilting words in his birth language. The child grinned up at him, dribbling and making a grab for his nose. It would be a wrench for him to leave the infant, but our safety was my priority. He watched me gather together a few dried bundles of herbs and a few lengths of catgut, along with my knives.

Frowning at me, Jago followed me about the hut. "Has there been another accident in one of the mine tunnels, Fur Benyn?"

"No."

"But that is a lot of stuff to be packing in your healing kit." His jolly mood vanished, replaced by anxiety.

"It is. We are sailing with the Chieftain Tallack at first light." I stopped packing to take in his response. His furrowed brow and open mouth told me that fear was uppermost in his mind. His last voyage with Tallack and his crew, left him with a smashed ankle and half drowned. Sailors in Tallack's clan are not known for their tolerance or kindness. Jago lost more than his health and freedom, he lost close friends too. I knew it would be difficult for the boy, but it was preferable to the continuous worry of Brea's lethal actions. "It'll be different this time, Jago. I promise. For one, I'll be there to make sure you are treated well."

He nodded slowly, but I knew that he didn't believe me. His gaze fell to the child, swaddled and warm against his chest. "Will the Lady Cryda be coming too?" I understood his meaning. He was asking if the child would be on the boat alongside us. It was she he didn't want to leave, more than the former Ruvane.

I shook my head. "She must stay here, at least until the new compound is built, and even then, it'll be too dangerous for her and the babe to stay so close to the border. The Duros are uniting their forces and training, ready for attack." The whites of his eyes doubled in size; such was his shock. "So, you see we must go and trade for copper to make more weapons."

"They need you to make the trade for the tin?" He was a sharp one. Not much escaped his understanding.

"No, but I can't restock my herbs at this time of the year. Everything I had at the Exe compound was torched. I can trade for what I need at the Frynk ports, but I'll need your help. You speak their tongue." He seemed to accept that as a good enough reason to leave. He took the babe and lay her next to her mother, sighed and began rolling up my tunics and sorting my beakers of ointments.

A part of me knew the apprehensions looming in his mind, another part of me wondered if he saw the trip as an opportunity to make a run for freedom. It was certainly weighing heavily in my thoughts. My primary concern was his safety. His happiness was another matter. Until an opportunity arose to give him all that he wanted, he had to stay close to me. The moment he is no longer under my protection, he would be at the mercy of the likes of Tallack's crew.

I took out my secret store of tin and handed Jago a reasonable amount. "There's a trapper up the valley living among the miners. He salts and dries most of what he catches and trades the skins and furs. See if you can barter for everything he has." He looked shocked at the amount of tin I'd given him, but I didn't want to be unprepared for our journey, and there was no time to cure our own. As he removed the door panel from the entrance, Cryda awoke.

"Mind you hurry, lad. There's lots to do before we can sleep this night." I flicked my hands at him to speed his progress, and then turned to Cryda. We'd grown used to the arrangement of sharing a hut. Having another pair or two of hands to help with caring for the young one suited her needs and it was company for me on the long cold nights. She would need to fend for herself, now that we were leaving camp.

"But you can't go, Meliora. I have no one else here. Most of Aebba's slaves ran, were killed or taken during Wenna's raid and the rest came here with us and have died from the ague. Who will I turn to if my child gets sick?" There were real tears brimming in her lower lids. It was more emotional than I was expecting.

"You're stronger than you look. You'll manage. Kenver will keep you supplied with tin, so you can trade for a slave or pay some of his clan for help. You'll be safer here than near the border anyway. You think the Duros would let you live if they got hold of you?"

She let the tear fall down her cheek and shook her head.

"We can't keep calling your child, *the babe*. You must think of a name." I thought that changing the subject might lighten the mood. It didn't.

She sobbed and cuffed the sleeve of her tunic beneath her nose. "But no one will be here for the naming ceremony."

"Then give her a name, but have the ceremony when we are all back together at the new Exe compound." I tried to comfort her, but she is so tall next to me, the best I could do was to hold her around the waist and squeeze. The sobbing quietened for a moment, then burst forth anew.

"And we still haven't laid Aebba's long bones with the rest of his payment to the Summerlands." For all her golden prettiness, she was a mass of red flesh and running humours, quite a sight.

"Well, he's waited all this time to gain entry into the land of his forefathers, I don't suppose he'll mind waiting a bit longer. You can't go out to the moors on your own. You haven't even arranged for the stone to be taken to the tor, let alone gathered enough tribal elders to heave the rocks into place."

"So, you'll let him wander the Between Worlds for an entire cycle?" She looked at me as though it was all my fault. I may have inadvertently accused the wrong person for murdering Aebba, but I couldn't be held responsible for Wenna's part in the Duro attacks. The twins had to make battle preparations their priority, even if it meant leaving their father in a clay pot until the summer. I said nothing to Cryda. She had a way of twisting the blame to suit her needs. If she had let the elders have their way at the summer gathering, his entire skeleton would be among his ancestors in a long barrow at Stonehenge instead of only his head.

I kept my observations to myself and raked the embers with a stick. Resting my longest blade in the hot coals, I waited until it glowed with heat and then immersed it in a cup of ale. It fizzled and steamed. "Here." I said to her. "This'll warm your heart up, make you feel better."

She took it from me and sniffed. I put the knife back into the embers ready for my own cup. Sitting by the fire, we regarded each other.

"I shall miss you, Meliora." She said. The fact of her saying it was shocking since while Aebba lived, she wouldn't have given me the drippings from her nose, but after a few moons of close quarters and mutual support, we'd grown reliant on one another. Each of us saw a friendship forged through necessity and now driven apart by circumstance.

"Ah, give over." I grappled her knee and gave it a wiggle. "Won't be forever. You'll see. We'll be back near the Exe, with your boys having chased away the Duros and taken great tracts of their land from them and a few heads as trophies." Our smiles and momentary cheer faded. A lot can change during battles, lives lost, people taken captive, and there was no way of telling when they might attack.

I slept poorly that night, the evening's discussions had unsettled me, leaving my temper raw come dawn. Jago shifted in his bedding too, I could hear him rustling and moaning as though his dreams were tormenting him. Our last meal at the camp was of wild boar lard with a little salt, spread on fresh baked flat bread. I made sure that Jago got plenty of the tasty jelly and the largest hunk from the loaf. We'd have to eat on the hoof from now on.

When it was time to leave, Jago struggled to pull himself away from Cryda and the babe. He helped to bring her into the world, and had been her guardian and protector ever since. Her helplessness and cheerful smile dragged him from the extremes of grief after losing his wife. Without her as a distraction, he was in danger of falling back into a black gloom.

Cryda saw Jago's plight. She had grown fond of the boy and his enthusiasm for her daughter's care. Holding the child against her breast, she walked with us to the beach, where Tallack and his crew were loading up the boats. We were used to him coming and going whenever he liked, but this time the trip felt more final. Perhaps it was the urgency with which the journey was arranged, or the speedy turnabout required for a trade deal, but Cryda's tears extended to bidding her sons farewell. As Blydh rode off with his head hunters, Tallack kissed his mother's cheek before lifting me onto his boat.

Jago couldn't tear himself away. His pleading and excuses to stay tugged at my heart, but he'd be lucky to live beyond the next full moon without my status in the tribe to protect him. Tallack laughed. His attitude was markedly different towards my slave now that he'd proved himself honourable with Cryda. At any other time, Jago would have needed to wade through the crashing waves and climb aboard himself. This time, Tallack scooped him up like a sack of grain and slung him over his shoulder. A hop and a skip through the shallows later, and he hoisted the boy into the boat next to me.

We stowed our things in the small space at the bow and tucked an oiled cloth over them to keep out the worst of the wet. As soon as we sat down, Jago began shaking. I dare say all the memories of his last encounter with this vessel came flooding back to him. I patted his head with affection, but it did not seem to calm him.

The tide was turning, I could feel it tugging at the ropes, pulling us out to sea, and yet Tallack had not yet boarded. I stood up to see what the delay was, hoping that he was simply taking his time to calm his mother's fears. The low sun glinted from the water, dazzling my eyes. Against the bright light, I saw his silhouette, standing alone on the beach. All his crew had manned the other boats and had already begun rowing out to catch the current heading east.

"What's the problem?" I yelled to my nephew. "We'll get left behind." I swayed about trying to keep myself upright, hanging on to the side. Tallack neither answered me, nor turned around. I thought that maybe he hadn't heard me call to him. I tried again, shouting against the force of the wind.

It was then I saw the reason for our delay. Brea walked onto the beach, carrying all her belongings in a large bundle.

CHAPTER FIVE

I could hardly believe what I was seeing. A tiny part of me hoped that she was just delivering Tallack's things to the boat. In my heart of course I knew that was not the case. She had spent the night convincing him that he needed her on the trip too, or that she couldn't survive the winter in the mining community without him. Being the soft-hearted sop that I know him to be, Tallack caved in and agreed.

Her presence on board had nothing to do with Brea pining for Tallack. It had everything to do with me and Jago. She had to make sure that we would not tell him about my mistake in a moment of weakness. Like Jago and myself, Tallack carried her and the baggage on board and immediately unbound the sail to catch the wind.

Brea treated me to a smug smile of victory as she took Tallack's seat near to the stern. At least she was as far from me as she could get on this foreign ship of his. Jago froze when he first caught sight of her, fidgeting as though he was about to stand up and throw himself over board and swim back to shore. I pushed him back down with a heavy hand to his shoulder, muttering, "Stay calm, boy. We'll look out for each other and all will be well."

"But, Fur Benyn..."

"Shush." I growled. "We'll take it in turns to sleep. She can't do anything in front of my nephew." He didn't appear to be reassured by my words, and to be honest, I found them hard to swallow myself. She was beyond sly. I uttered a few prayers to the goddess to keep us safe. Jago sounded like he was cursing her rather than praying. It's hard to tell when he reverts to his native language. We stayed as far apart as we could for the first half day of our trip, letting the current and winds take us along the coast to a narrower crossing point.

All the time that we sailed, Tallack watched the breeze fill the sails and noted the distance from shore. He must have made the crossing more than a dozen times, but his crewmen were as apprehensive as he appeared to be. Perhaps all the tall tales and bravado are to mask the fear of making a poor decision, when to steer into a deep wave, or when to alter course avoiding sand banks and storms. I had no idea how he navigated, whether it was catching sight of a landmark or waiting for the first stars, but all our lives rested in the hands of this young Chieftain. I hoped he'd learned well from the elders of the clan.

When it was time to steer towards Frynk, Tallack ordered Brea to sit at the front of the boat next to me and Jago. I could hear her whining and arguing with him, but he would have none of her nonsense. He was Metern of the tribe, and the leader of the sea faring clan. He would not tolerate disobedience at sea.

"Do as I say, Brea, or I'll dump you in Frynk to live out your days as a foreign slave."

That seemed to put a hot ember in her leggings. Grumbling and pouting, she struggled over the resting oars and legs of the crew, and slumped down next to me.

There was no avoiding conversation no matter how much I tried.

"Meliora." She muttered through clenched teeth.

"Brea. I did not know that you were joining us."

"Nor I you until the last moment." The look she gave me could have scorched a hole in the boat.

I edged further away from her, yanking my furs over mine and Jago's legs. She could die from the cold for all I cared. There was no way I was going to share my food and water with her after all that she put me through. We sat like that for some time, refusing to exchange civil words or even look in the same direction as one another. Her animosity stemmed from me inconveniencing her by travelling to Frynk with her man.

Until this trip, she was content to strut about camp as though she owned all Dumnoni lands. I suspected that she had planned to work her magic on Blydh in his brother's absence, since Tallack was taking too long to secure their relationship in a binding ceremony. If she couldn't force his hand, then Blydh would make a good back up position and still give her the power she craved.

What was it about this Ordo that gave her such lofty aspirations? Derwa's husband, from what I could make of him, was a kind and gentle soul, who stood next in line to their Chieftain. Derwa would one day become the Ruvane of their tribe and her sons would lead after they were gone. It was the natural order of things since the beginning of time. I can't say that I blame these young women for wanting more, for craving the power that comes with the titles, but they also come with huge responsibilities. A tribe is more than a few scattered clans and a bunch of homesteaders. It had a name and a reputation to uphold. Without those qualities, a tribe would be overrun and wiped out by marauding neighbours.

In some respects, young Wenna was the closest woman to being a Metern. True, she was forced to wed the Duros' chieftain against her will, but she blossomed into a fierce and respected Ruvane warrior in her own right. She instilled loyalty and devotion in her tribe. They would have laid down their lives if she had commanded it of them, that I saw in the short time I was with her at the midsummer gathering. If only she had put aside the animosity from her childhood and forged a true alliance built on the foundations of our shared blood. Her ambition cost her the lives of many from her tribe, and hers too. I will never forget the look of horror on her face when the arrows from her half-brother's men pierced her heart.

Further away from land, the sea was more than choppy. It rose and fell with such force; it left my stomach in my mouth several times over. Jago looked green as he leaned over the side and emptied his gut into the swell. Brea seemed almost as bad, but she clenched her jaw and held onto her middle with both arms, willing herself to fight against the heaving.

To my surprise, I was able to bear the rolling without sickness, but then my father was a great sailor just like Tallack. While my slave and tormentor retched and moaned, I used the opportunity to stretch my legs. Turning to face the bow, I could see why Tallack's face had deepened from concentrated frown, to resigned fear. Ahead of us, the black clouds stretched from the horizon to further than I could see. They billowed up in a tall plume and were lit at intervals with spears of lightning. The gods were angry with us and who could blame them. We carried the great Metern murderer among us.

I looked back at Tallack who acknowledged my panic with a nod. The wind picked up and threatened to shred our sails. With a slick manoeuvre, his crewmen downed the cloth and tied it to the mast. Peering across the wide peaks of water, I could just make out the other boats ahead of us. They too followed suit, lashing everything that could be hurled from the craft down with rope.

My nephew caught my attention, pointing to the leather straps nailed to the inner edges of the vessel. He gestured for me to slip my hand through the loop and hold on tight. I nodded my understanding and grabbed Jago first, attaching him by the wrist while he was sick. He hardly even noticed. Brea couldn't fight the swell any longer, she stood next to my slave and together they heaved dry bile.

With my tin nuggets in my pockets, and my medicine kit containing my knives wrapped around my body, I clung to the leather strap and held on for dear life. The next dip in the waves tipped us on a steep angle to the left. A bundle containing our food slid across the planks towards the hull, where a disturbing amount of sea water gathered.

With fumbling speed, I unhooked my hand from the loop and hurled myself across the short distance, until I was sprawled on my belly. Reaching out for the parcel, I felt the sharp stab of my knives digging into my ribs. One wrong move and I would impale myself on my own blades. I tried to push my upper body up to a kneeling position, but the craft tipped further, crushing me against my kit bag.

Just when I thought I would have to surrender our food and water bladders to the ocean, a new wave caught us in an upward lift, thrusting me back towards the bow. The food tumbled back into my arms, allowing me to reattach my wrist in the loop for safety. Gods be praised I thought my gut would be ripped asunder. Sweating with shock and relief, I lashed my kit bag and food bundle to another loop away from my body. Providing the vessel stayed afloat, my knives and herbs will remain on board, even if our food is soaked in salt water.

Tallack barked more orders to his men, some of whom bailed the liquid from the hull. Every one of them pulled in the oars and stowed them along the edges of the long boat. It seemed to me that we were at a disadvantage compared to those in the smaller crafts. This great monster of a ship that Tallack traded for struggled to compensate for the moving peaks and troughs of the rolling waves, where the smaller vessels were nimbler.

Still, my nephew seemed to have its measure. He knew his ship's limitations well. With the weight of his whole body against the tiller, he steered us along the edge of the storm, keeping the lashing rain and forked lightning to the right of us.

How long we could stay in this position, I could not tell. The storm looked to be heading closer to us, with Frynkish shores at its tail end. One way or another, we would have to endure its wrath. If we stayed still, it would blow in our direction. If we steered into the wind, it could knock us off course and shatter the ship from under us.

As old as I am, I desperately needed to hear some reassuring words that my nephew had experience of such a vast storm, but he was against the breeze. I could barely hear him calling out to his men. Keeping my eyes trained on our leader, I hoped that he would eventually notice me in the bow, shivering and soaked through with the salt spray, and give me a sign that all would be well. There was none. He caught my eye for a moment, but his expression was grave. I held on even tighter to my leather strap, checking every so often that Jago was still aboard and attached to the side. With more hollering from their leader, the men slipped their ankles into more leather loops. The storm had arrived.

Thrown into darkness, the clouds blocked out the sun's weak rays, stopping us from seeing our reference points and preventing us from charting our course. For all we knew, we could be heading back to Dumnoni lands, or pushed out to the never-ending sea at the edge of the world beyond Iwerdon. Jago sat back down, having nothing left inside to hurl. Brea remained standing, clutching the side of the boat with white knuckles and screaming between retches. There was nothing left to be done but pray to the Goddess of Lakes and Seas to protect us from harm.

If our vessel capsized, we might lose more than our lives. Our entire tin supply extracted and refined over the last few moons were in these boats. Our tribe were relying on us to return with copper and possibly grain. I'm so glad that I hid the long sword from the midsummer gathering in a secure place within the mining community back on land, but I cannot help but wonder if this storm was sent by Cernonnus to punish me for not awarding it to our Metern as I had promised. How could I give it to one nephew and not the other?

Jago looked to me as though all his nightmares were revisiting him during his wakeful state. He shook so violently, he rattled against my legs in our cramped position. It was crossing this stretch of water where he first met the Frynkish girl who became his wife. Her sacrifice killed something inside him. The joy of life left him the moment her throat was slashed. I guessed that it gave him little comfort to know that those who took her life met the same fate.

More men bailed out the water from the boat, some with their cupped hands, others with beakers and jugs but it was not enough. The waves crashed against the front and sides in massive eruptions of white spray, covering the tin ingots and laying us low in the water and at greater risk of sinking. I should have untethered myself to help them, but fear froze me to my seat in the bow.

The roar of the sea as it pounded against the planking, coupled with the ear-splitting cracks of thunder over our heads, compounded my terror. How were we to fight against such angry gods as these? I was sure that the storm would continue to ravage us until it had taken at least one of our lives, if not all of them.

All I could do was fix on Tallack's face and wait to see a flicker of hope. He and one of his crew now wrestled with the helm, steering us into the oncoming force of the next wave. His expression did not alter once. His teeth gritted, he pulled back on the tiller while his crewman pushed against the force on the rudder. Every part of his crew and the ship were drenched in salt water or sweat. The wind howled, the thunder echoed and the lightning strikes were getting perilously close.

I had no idea whether the rest of the smaller boats were still afloat. With our tin spread across all of the vessels, there was still a chance that one or two would make it through unharmed. As it was, I feared for our lives more than theirs, since our mast was by far the tallest, and most likely to make contact with the light spears of Cernonnus.

"Fur Benyn, we are going to die on this wretched ship." Jago cried, grasping my arm with his free hand. I had no words of comfort for the boy, as I believed that he could be right. Was this a result of withholding the sword, or from my mistake over accusing the Lady Eseld of murder? The thought cast a new shadow on our plight. If I untethered my arm and let Cernonnus take me for my sins, would he let my nephew and his crew live?

My fears remained, but the notion that I could perhaps save them all remained. I unhooked my wrist from my leather strap, closed my eyes and sent a word of prayer unto the gods. "If this is truly your wish, god of gods, then take me but leave my kin alone."

The moment I completed my prayer to Cernonnus, I opened my eyes to see Jago's look of abject horror. His extended arm pointed to the spot where Brea had stood only moments before. She was gone. In the turmoil, no one noticed a giant splash against the side of the boat which knocked Brea off her feet and into the ocean. I threw myself against the side, and felt Jago clutching my ankle lest I should follow her over board.

"Tallack!" I yelled, but my voice was lost among the crashing noise. I could see him straining to hold onto the tiller as another swell grew beneath us, raising us high into the air. I stared into the depths at my side, looking for signs that she was still alive.

A tiny fraction of my mind rejoiced. She was gone from our lives and justice was served in a most violent manner. Aebba the Wild was avenged at last. He was free to ascend to the Summerlands, to sit by the side of his ancestors and greatest warriors of all time. Peace would come to our tribe and a new era could begin in earnest. As these and a few guilty thoughts crossed my mind, I saw her head bobbing beneath us, as she clung to a rope attached to the bow.

Brea lived, but without our help to bring her on board, it would not be for long. The question remained; should Jago and I save her life knowing that she would bring misery and further heartache to my kin, or let her drown in the storm? I turned to face my slave. "She lives." I said it in as quiet a voice as I could manage. Not that Tallack's men would be particularly bothered by her plight, for none so much as acknowledged her presence on board.

"Please, Fur Benyn. You must let fate take its course." He begged me, still holding my leg to prevent my own tragedy.

I peered down at her, coughing, spluttering and shouting for help. She was a pitiful sight. It was a wicked way to die, with lungs burning and fit to burst from lack of air. My indecision filled me with dread.

CHAPTER SIX

It was no use. My guilt over the Lady Eseld already kept me awake at nights, having Brea's death on my hands was more than I could take. Without thinking it through fully, I leaned across and took hold of the rope secured at the bow end. Kneeling against the furthest reaches, I began to pull in the line.

"You can't, Fur Benyn. She will not rest until we are dead. You must not rescue her." Jago pleaded, but there was one thing he failed to realise. Tallack would ask why we did nothing to save his woman. We had no idea if he or his men had seen her go over, and I couldn't bear the thought of his disgust at my failure. If Brea was to die, it would not be from my lack of trying to save her.

"Give me a hand, Jago. We are not killers. We will not sink to her level." At the time, I failed to see the humour in what I'd said. He sulked and cast his eyes down, but ultimately helped me to pull in the line. Brea dipped below the surface several times as we reeled her in. Choking and wheezing through the rough water, it took all our strength to pull her onto the boat and not get sucked up in the smashing waves ourselves.

Drenched through and coughing up ocean dregs, she lay on the planks of the hull emptying her lungs. Jago was beside himself with renewed grief. She was alive and seething with anger. We both knew where she would direct that force and how we might suffer as a consequence. At no point during the storm, did she thank us for her rescue.

It was some time before the black clouds began to fade and the thunder trundled away towards home. The pitching and rolling continued for quite a while. Tallack ordered one of his crew to take a turn with the tiller, while he rested in the stern.

Brea's mood failed to lighten. She glowered with ominous intent, and without a single word of appreciation to Jago and me. It was then I started to wish that I'd taken Jago's advice. The gods had every right to claim her life for all that she'd done to my tribe. I shouldn't have interfered, but my former good judgement appears to have left me of late.

By nightfall, Tallack clambered over his crewmen to the front of the ship to speak with us. I unwrapped my soggy food bundle and offered him a strip of dried rabbit. He declined, and instead threw his arms about me and squeezed tight.

"I saw what you did, Aunt. You never cease to amaze me." Pulling away he kissed my head, and then offered his hand to Jago in a forearm clasp of friendship. My slave was puzzled at first, misunderstanding my nephew's intentions. I demonstrated the hold on myself, folding my lower arms over each other and grasping above my wrists with each hand. Frowning, Jago moved with caution, until Tallack could complete his gesture of friendship and gratitude.

"You are both braver than I ever gave you credit for and I thank you." Tallack looked at Brea with a beaming smile, expecting her to follow his example. She looked less impressed by our efforts, returning his grin with something like a pout.

"I seriously thought we'd lost you, Brea. Are you fully recovered from your ordeal?" He said to her, frowning at her attitude.

"Not in the slightest. I am exhausted and scared. I think I should spend the night at the stern with you." She feigned weakness, allowing her knees to buckle underneath her so that she fell onto his torso. Tallack caught her and led her to the back of the ship. Before I could get another word in, she looked over her shoulder at me and narrowed her eyes in warning.

Hateful girl. It wasn't my fault that she ended up over the side. Now I wished she'd drowned.

To add insult to injury, Jago piped up with, "I told you so, Fur Benyn."

Rolling my eyes at him, I snarled, "Just eat your rabbit and mind your tongue," but I have to admit, the boy was right to chide me. Rather than using the experience to let matters drop, or to smooth over our relationship difficulties, she was intent on making things between us worse. I thought at the time that maybe Jago and I should run away together when we reached Frynkish shores and let the lot of them be damned.

The night under cold wet furs was long and excessively uncomfortable. When dawn broke, I was overjoyed to see that the other boats had made it through the storm alongside us. The wind had lessened so much, it was no use in moving us forward. Tallack gave the crew time to eat and then ordered them to reposition the oars and row. The waves still peaked, slapping us sideways for every length we managed to achieve in a southerly direction. Tallack did his best to correct our course, but against such forceful currents, even I knew that we would be much further along the Frynkish coast than planned.

When the sun reached its highest point in the winter sky, we first caught sight of land. The men cheered, breaking open the ale in an early celebration. I sipped at what was left of our fresh water, sharing the last bladder with Jago. The cheese we'd brought with us was little more than a milky fluid with jelly lumps stuck to the cloth wrapping. I emptied it overboard. It looked too much like the contents of Brea's guts for me to eat.

Finally, we were close enough to row into port. The sun broke through the clouds and thawed out my chilly bones. Tallack ventured to the front of the boat to speak with me before we made harbour. His fingers were interlocked in front of him and he wore that infuriating pleading look that I recognised from when he was a small child. He knew how to get around his old aunt, showering me with compliments and wild flowers to get me to sway Aebba's mind over something the twins wanted to do, but that he had forbidden.

From the moment I saw that face, I guessed what he was going to ask of me. I braced myself, sighing loudly in preparation.

"Aunt Mel, please can Brea come with you to the markets? She seems to think you don't like her anymore. That's not true is it? You haven't had a falling out over something daft, have you? Tell me it's all a big misunderstanding, only the men and I have to row to the next bay for metal trades." He said it all so fast, without even drawing breath. It was a cunning tactic, since he gave me no opportunity to speak. By the end of his little speech, everything sounded so trivial, and I could hardly tell him the truth behind our disagreement.

All I could say was, "Fine. Tell her not to dawdle, I have a lot to do."

"Great, thanks, Aunt Mel, you're the best." He dashed off before I could think of an excuse to be rid of her. At any rate, I expected her to behave while Tallack was watching, but after that, she would no doubt leave us at the first bazaar. Jago gave me a glare that could freeze hot embers. I hate how I am always left stuck in the middle of strife.

A smaller boat from Tallack's clan pulled up to ours. He explained that the larger vessel was too deep in the hull to row close to shore. With care, Brea, Jago and I stepped across a boarding plank and into the smaller boat. Brea waved and blew kisses to Tallack, as his men paddled us to the landing point and then returned to join the others rounding the headland.

Brea strutted down the jetty to the beach, leaving Jago and I to struggle with our things. She brought none of her own belongings, choosing to rely on Tallack's timely return. I started to wonder if she had any tin or trinkets to trade for food and ale, or whether I would be expected to cough up for her keep.

Jago carried my knife bag, telling me that it was less likely for any thieves to believe that a slave such as he could carry anything of value worth stealing. I could see the boy's logic. The pouch of tin stayed slung around my neck on a thick cord and hidden under my tunic.

"This way, Fur Benyn." Jago sang, suddenly full of cheer to see the merchant stalls and produce for trade closer to the settlement. It was lovely to hear him speak in their Frynkish tongue. I'd forgotten how lyrical it sounded. The last time he spoke in this language was to teach his wife, my slave girl a few of our Dumnoni words. I was glad that he was joyful. It worried me that it might bring too many unpleasant memories to the surface and send him spiralling back into doom.

Brea trudged after me whining one moment and then pouncing on metal necklaces and ear studs the next, badgering me to give her tin to trade for them. That girl had a nerve. I walked faster, leaving her behind. The bazaar was incredible. Jago was keen to show me all that this port had to offer.

"Come see this…" He gripped my sleeve and pulled me to a spice stall. The coloured powders stood tall in their pots, orange like the sunset, reds darker than clay and richer than blood. There were fabrics dyed a deeper blue than the summer ocean at Land's End, and so fine I could almost see my hand through the weave.

Further along the row of traders were great vats of spicy stews and strange looking vegetables from further afield. Entertainers played drums and pipes, strummed odd shaped boxes with strings pulled taught across them and danced about us as we walked past.

I wanted to stay and listen, but Jago pulled me along. "No, do not stop. That is when the thieves come and take your gold from your pockets." I turned around, and saw a collection of dirty children lurking behind those who were being entertained. They are certainly wily these Frynkish settlers. They know when to take advantage of unsuspecting visitors.

As Jago hurried ahead, I thought we'd manage to lose Brea in the crowds, but sadly I was mistaken.

She plodded along behind and came to a halt next to me. "This place smells bad." For the rest of the afternoon, it was all I heard her say, either everything smelled bad or tasted bad, or looked bad. Nothing was to her liking whatsoever. I on the other hand, revelled in the delights this trading station had to offer. There were people from all over the place, some from further lands than even Jago knew about. Skin of every shade, some with markings and men and women so tall it hurt my neck to peer up at them.

Eventually, Jago bartered for some food he deemed safe for us to eat. His command of their language was impressive, and his choice of food, inspired. I feasted like a Ruvane on very few grains of tin, such is their demand for our metal. I took great care not to show how much I had about my person, for fear of attracting the wrong kind of attention.

When our bellies were full and I had tasted wines from sunnier lands, we went in search of herbs and remedies. Jago asked a kind Frynkish woman selling woollen fabric where we might find what we needed. She pointed to a hut where yellowish smoke billowed out from the door. I frowned at the woman, questioning her sanity, but Jago assured me that it was the right place.

It did not smell or look like my hut back at the compound on the River Exe. For one, the thatch inside was one great mass of dangling herb bunches. The ochre smoke thickened in my lungs making me cough. The woman inside flicked yellow powder into the fire. It sparkled as it caught the flames, leaving the pungent odour to linger in the air.

I waved my hand in front of my face, clearing a path to the woman at a table. Behind her was a long dividing curtain, but from the shadows thrown onto the back wall, I could see three people were there. One sat on a stool, one leaned on a wall nearby and a third was gesturing with his arms.

The woman at the table took one look at Jago and tried to shoo him out of their hut. "Hey now. Don't you be treating him that way. Stop that!" I bellowed at her, but the woman did not listen to me. It was only when Jago garbled a whole string of Frynkish at her that she stopped, turned to me and gave me the benefit of her toothless smile. "What did you say to her?" I asked my slave.

"She thought I was a dirty bazaar child until I told her that I serve at the table of a great Ruvane from the wealthiest tribe in all of Inglond."

"Ah, yeah. That'll do it. Wealth will open any door." I sighed at her shallowness. All of a sudden, she produced a bench for me to sit on and tried to pour me a cup of her best visitors' wine, even though it smelled sour to me. Brea hovered in the doorway. When she saw my lavish treatment, she rushed in to take her share of the fine life. While the woman was fussing about Brea, I took a long look at the herbs and dried offerings. The way that they hung the bunches from the cross struts of the thatching was a brilliant idea.

When the woman returned to my side, I instructed Jago to tell her which of the plants I was interested in. He translated my list into Frynkish. It was quite lengthy. After a while, the woman's face altered to disbelief. She peered at me as though we were trying to scam her. I'd already slipped a few tin nuggets from my secret pouch and had them tucked into my fist ready to begin the barter. I could see that she did not believe us true to our word. With a careful sleight of hand, I moved one nugget from my fist into an open palm, displaying it for her to see. "Tell her that there's more where that came from too."

That seemed to do the trick. She skipped about the hut, bundling my order together and trying to tempt me with things that I can easily obtain from our own lands. There was one item that I was in desperate need for, and that was always difficult to obtain.

"Jago. Ask her if she has any poppy resin. I'll take all she's got, but don't let her know that I'm willing to pay whatever it takes. If there's to be a battle, I'll need a hefty stock." I waited for him to explain my requirements in her own language. She rattled off something in return, to which he tried again. Jago looked irritated.

"What's the matter. Does she have any or not?" I asked of him.

With a deep frown, he tried to explain what she had told him. "She's says that if we had come earlier in the day, she could have provided the resin at a fair price. Now, she says we are too late. Another has agreed a large amount of gold for her entire jar."

"Do you think she's scamming us now, trying to up the price until we're destitute?" Jago and I huddled together under the smelly fumes from the fire.

"I suggested that, but she got angry with me. She says it's true. The man who has traded for all her poppy resin is with her husband receiving treatment right now."

There was nothing to be done. Brea flounced out of the hut and wandered to another trinket stall, while I paid over the agreed value in tin nuggets for my bundle of herbs. We waited outside to catch a glimpse of the mystery man behind the curtain, in the hope that we could persuade him to trade for just a small quantity for me to take back home.

They were in there for a long time. Jago fetched ale and more food for us before the man came out. When he did, we were all filled with surprise. His clothes were of the finest woven linen, his skin was darker than Jago's and he wore more gold about his person than I have ever seen before in my life. He was accompanied by a young man of similar appearance, but where he was spry and healthy, the older man used a walking stick and his spine bent in the middle.

I found myself staring without shame. He was quite the finest thing my old eyes had ever spied. Jago began sweating with fright, expecting the young man to lose his temper at our boldness. It suddenly dawned on me how rude my behaviour was towards this wealthy man. Not knowing how to communicate, I bowed my head in respect to him. It made him smile. He looked us up and down and then smirked at his companion, before addressing us in Frynkish.

Jago kept his eyes down to the ground and translated for me. "The gentleman says greetings, and that he doesn't think you are from around here."

Pleased that he was open to discussion, I knocked Jago's elbow with mine and told him to reply with, "I am from the Dumnoni Tribe in the South of Inglond, travelled all this way for medicines."

I observed his response as Jago told the men my aim for travelling. My hope was to steer the discussion around to the jar his companion held in his arms. The faint glimmer of a smile kept my hope alive. He spoke once more to Jago, with more tenderness and respect than those from my own tribe do. Jago spoke in courteous tones, pointing to the jar in the young man's arms.

That was when the conversation took a turn for the worse. The young man snapped back at Jago, snarling his Frynkish words so that even I understood his meaning. The poppy resin was not for trade.

Jago hung his head in defeat. "Fur Benyn, I fear that we are wasting our time. The man says that the resin is critical for his father. He says that he is cursed."

CHAPTER SEVEN

Brea took one look at the handsome young stranger and sidled back next to me for introductions. "Tell them who I am Jago, and make me sound important in our tribe."

I scoffed at her assertion. She was nothing more than a murderous widow of a fallen Chieftain, who had her eye on his sons. From her coy poses and fluttering lashes, I figured that she could just as easily swap allegiances to this young bejewelled man instead. It would be a blessing to the Dumnonii if she did. Sadly, the man turned up his nose at her attempts to sway his affections. She was just a brash slave girl to him.

"Jago", I said, with quiet calm. "Thank the man for his time and wish him the blessing of Airmed in his quest for good health."

My slave relayed my wishes to the old man, stopping to explain that Airmed was our Goddess of Healing. They in turn, bowed to me and wished me good fortune and peace. I watched as the old man shuffled away, his upright and worried son following along after him with the largest jug of poppy resin imaginable. That amount of pain relief would keep our whole tribe half-baked for more than a cycle.

It started my curious mind to thinking about all the possible health problems the old man had, and why he would need such a quantity of resin. Inside my head, I saw massive communities of people coming to him for aid and relief, in much the same way that our tribe do with me. If he was a healer of far off lands, he would know about local plants and herbs. There is so much I could learn from a foreign medicine man.

"Did he happen to mention where they were encamped?" I asked Jago, hoping that we might bump into them a second time.

"No, Fur Benyn, but I don't think he would be welcome in paid tents or houses around here. The old man is cursed."

"Eww, better to steer clear of them then." Brea shuddered.

"What kind of curse? Is he talking underworld demons or some kind of religious invocation?" I said, ignoring the selfish Ordo and demanding details from my slave.

"I have seen this before. They say that it strikes when you least expect it, and that once it takes hold of you, it can take many winters to die." His voice hushed to a whisper as if just speaking about it would make him cursed too.

"Die of what? What happens to them?"

"Their fingers turned to stumps; bits fall off them while the curse spreads through their bodies. Then there are the rashes and big lumps on the skin." Jago shook his head. "Once the curse is laid at your door there is no escape."

This was something I'd never encountered before. The older man looked fine, except for his slightly bowed back and shuffling gait. I had to put my curiosity behind me and concentrate on the fading light of the day. Turning to the loathsome Brea, I said, "I don't suppose Tallack told you when the boats would return for us, did he?" She shook her head. “No, I didn’t think so. Come on, we’ll need to find a warm bunk each for the night. Any suggestions, boy?”

Jago pointed towards a series of huts. There were plenty of people sitting around fires, cooking what little food they had and bending green stick poles to make their shelters. I looked at them and my shoulders slumped.

“What is it, great lady. Are you ill?” Jago enquired after seeing my pained expression.

“No, lad. I’m fine, just too exhausted to make my own hut for a single night of sleep.”

“I will ask around. Wait here.” Off he scampered, his old injury giving him a noticeable limp. Brea and I stood back to back, refusing to speak. I was starting to think I was better off in the mining community than all the way out here in Frynk, when Jago scurried back with good news. For a small amount of tin, we could stay in one of the larger boarding huts close to a camp for foreign travellers. That pleased me no end. Even Brea seemed happy to have a warm hut for the night, out of the mud and with an indoor fire to dry out our clothes.

When we arrived, it wasn’t so different from Aebba’s Long Hut. It was large and had tables to one side, and bunks on the other. Being quite full already, we had to make do with two bunks furthest away from the fire, with Jago on the rushes between us. I gave the man running the establishment a little extra tin to serve us a bowl of hot soup and lend us warm furs for our beds.

Everywhere smelled of black mould and dog’s kawgh. Combined with the stinking travellers and steaming wet cloaks, it almost choked me. Leaving Jago with Brea and our belongings, I wandered back outside to catch my breath. The clouds thinned, revealing a moonlit sky filled with the stars of the gods.

To my right, an area marked out with large rocks, showed visitors where they could make camp. Most of the shelters were poor, made from what timber and leaves they could find locally, but one was enormous, made from expensive fabric and pitched all alone at the end of the field. It was surrounded by burning torches and strong guards, each of whom carried a sword at the hip and a spear in their hands. Next to the vast tent, was a wagon of exquisite design, with carved symbols and plush curtains at the windows. Their horses were tethered behind the tent. They stood eating the lush grasses in the growing darkness.

I'd already begun to guess who this incredible travelling cart and shelter belonged to, when the young man left the tent and walked over to one of the guards. I edged closer, hoping that he would see me and initiate conversation. The man finished speaking to the guard and then strode towards the wagon. As he climbed aboard, it rocked with his weight.

I took the opportunity to lurk even closer, so that he would see me as he got down from the cart. The guards glared at me, trying to warn me off, but I couldn't help myself. The young man climbed down to the ground. He clutched a bundle to his ribs. This was my chance, I called out to him.

"Ho there, neighbour." I waved, grinning like the possessed. Clearly, I was too friendly, as he nodded recognition and then hurried away into the tent. Foiled, I returned to the smelly boarders, ate my soup and bread and turned in for a fetid night of snoring and farting.

Come morning, Jago handed me a cup of ale and some delicious cheese with a chunk of bread. He gave Brea her share and settled back on the floor with the small piece that remained. My tin nuggets went a really long way in trading for victuals and shelter at this place. I looked at his measly portion of food as he sat cross-legged on the rushes to nibble at the cheese. It was as though someone had shoved a dagger right through my heart. He took his role as slave protector so seriously; he was willing to starve so that we may eat. I passed the rest of my food to him.

"You do not like what I found for you? Shall I trade for something else?"

"No Jago, it's very tasty, but my appetite isn't what it was. You eat it for me."

The smile that shone on his silken smooth face made my guilt all the more painful.

"How far away from here is your real home?" I kept my tone low so that Brea couldn't hear me. She was already flirting with a large Frynk man on the other side of our bunks.

"A very long way, Fur Benyn. More days walking than I could manage and then across the ocean to my homeland." He wouldn't look me in the eyes. His hand fell to his lap along with the bread and cheese. He didn't like to be reminded of all that he'd lost.

"If you could pay for your passage to go home, would you like to?" It was a loaded question. He understood why I'd asked and appreciation flitted across his face.

With a tender tilt of his head, he said, "What is there to go home to? My parents were both killed in the raid on our homes. My sister…" His voice broke. "My sister, was taken to the flesh markets near the coast where I was sold to a Frynkish slave master who'd travelled for trade."

I hadn't noticed that Brea had swung her legs around to face us and was listening to his sad story. I thought that she of all people would sympathise with his dreadful experiences, maybe understand his dilemma.

She snapped at him. “Well it sounds like you got the best deal of that situation, what are you crying about? Do you think Aebba paid my father a fair price for me?”

“Oh, Brea, it’s hardly the same.” I chided.

“No? Why is it more pitiful for a boy to be sold into slavery than it is for a girl to be forced to bind to a brute of a Chieftain against her will?”

“You were the wife of a great man. You were given every privilege, wealth, status, jewels…”

“Bruises, broken ribs, raped every other night…” She spat. “He was a monster and I’m glad he’s dead.”

In a way, I was pleased that she stormed out of the shelter at that point. I had no excuses nor reasons for Aebba’s dreadful behaviour towards his third wife. Maybe he did deserve all he got from her in the end. Only the gods can answer that one.

With Jago alone, I asked him again. “I can give you your freedom and a little tin to see you home, if that’s what you’d like.”

He thought about my offer for some time, swallowing back his emotions and formulating his reply. “I am grateful to you, Fur Benyn, truly I am, and if you are no longer happy to have me in your service, I understand.”

“No, I’m not saying that I want to be rid of you, child. I feel bad that you were snatched by slavers and then treated worse than vermin by my own people. I can set you free. You would not be a slave anymore.”

He frowned at me as though I was plain stupid. “For how long would I be free crossing Frynk, before I was taken prisoner again and sold to a cruel master?”

That was something I hadn’t thought about. His beautiful dark skin was very different from the local crowds. Those that were darker, visited from another land, possibly the same place as Jago. His freedom would be short lived indeed.

"Are you content to stick by an old woman with bad habits then?" I jostled his elbow and smiled.

A tiny hint of mirth crossed his lips. "If you are happy with a crippled boy from the other side of the world."

We both laughed and I was thrilled to see him chomping down on the cheese once more. I yanked my kit bag up from beneath my bunk and handed it to Jago. He slung the strap over his head and followed me towards the door.

Brea was not far away. She was talking at, rather than to, the young man from the exotic tent. I could see him shrugging his incomprehension at her and doing his best to walk away. She caught sight of us in her peripheral vision and called us over.

"Boy, explain to this man that we want to trade tin for that golden torque around his neck." She folded her arms and jutted out a hip as she stared at him.

In faltering attempts, Jago did as he was told, translating her commands into Frynkish. As soon as he learned of her demands, his hand flew to his neck in protection of his necklace. The response was clear enough to me without the need for Jago to tell me. The man rattled off a rejection in one long and fast sentence.

Brea was not satisfied. "Tin… you know, make bronze with copper, tin?" She shouted the last bit as if he was addled.

"Lady Brea, the man says that the necklace is precious to him. It is passed from father to son and never traded."

Brea took the hint, but was not pleased. She growled her annoyance and strutted back into the shelter. I offered another apology to the man through Jago, explaining that she was spoiled and did not know the value of such items. That seemed to help smooth things over, since he invited us to their large tent where he hoped to persuade his father to give me a little of the poppy resin.

I tried not to appear too eager, but the fascination with this man had me trotting across the damp grass almost faster than the cursed one's son. With a nod to the guards, we were permitted entry. The inside was as magnificent as the decorated outside. There were long sashes of fine fabrics slung from the roof struts, the rushes were strewn with soft cushions and furs, and the old man sat in a tall wooden chair in the centre at the end. His entire body, except for his hands and face, was cloaked in a long grey tunic. His head was wrapped in more of the same material and topped with a tall coned hat, and a large amber jewel above his forehead.

Upon seeing me, he smiled and gestured for me to step forward. Jago stayed in the doorway, too scared to move closer.

I peered over my shoulder at him. "How in the name of Cernonnus do you expect us to talk with you all the way over there?"

He slunk to my side, but kept his head bowed away from looking at the man with the curse. Little by little, and with Jago's assistance, we managed to converse. He told me that his people were from a land where sand is more common than water, sun shines all day long and the rivers were beyond value. There he ruled over more people than could be counted in a dozen moons. Before he got too deep into his tale, I asked Jago to give the man my proper name and to ask for his in return.

The reply came back, "He is Prince Suliaman, Fur Benyn, and his son is Maleek. Shall I tell them that you are a healer?"

I nodded. Prince Suliaman seemed surprised at this confession. I looked around the tent at his guards and servants, none of them were women. If I had to guess, I would say that his healers were not of my persuasion either. Jago seemed to be taking his time explaining my position within the tribe. It gave me the chance to take in all the finery and sniff at their rich foods and drinks.

"I have explained that you are the best wise woman and healer in all of Inglond. The Prince asks if you know of any cures for his curse?"

How could I know a cure for an ailment I'd never encountered before? Any cursing in our tribe would have been the priests' doing, and would take a lengthy ritual at the Seven Sisters' stone circle to break. Anything more sinister, would require the Black Rites Ritual, at a more powerful henge. I relayed my thoughts to my slave who passed them into Frynkish for the visitors.

I didn't think any more of it until I noticed the old man sit forward in his chair and look animated for the first time since meeting him. He spoke to Jago in hurried tones and flicked his hand at him to translate for me.

"He wants to know more about the Black Rites Ritual. How do you get there?"

"It's at the top of the world!" I couldn't contain my astonishment. "Only people from Skotek are near enough for the journey. It's a fearsome long way to travel."

More babbled Frynkish took place, while I looked on with a bemused expression.

"But it can be done?"

"Well, yes, but it'd take a fortune in tribal tributes to pass through so many regions, and you'd need dozens of guards and that's supposing you were young and healthy."

Jago conveyed my response and waited until the Prince had spoken to his son. There appeared to be a certain amount of disagreement between them. Maleek's raised voice and clenched teeth told me far more than Jago could. This was not what I had in mind when I went snooping for poppy resin.

At length, the son caved in to his father's command. They gave Jago their request.

"Fur Benyn, the Prince would like to pay you to lead his group to the stones at the top of the world, and arrange for him to receive the Black Rites Ritual to cleanse the curse from his body."

I did not hide my amazement. He could see my age and my circumstances, and yet he was still prepared to embark upon a journey that could well spell the end of him.

"Tell him that I cannot be bought. I have to get back to my own tribe and I am too old to go traipsing across the wilderness to the outer islands of Skotek."

Jago did as I said. "He says if gold will not persuade you, what would?"

CHAPTER EIGHT

I thought of our problems in obtaining a steady supply of copper, and how Aebba was always keen on expanding our trading routes for our tin. With demand so high for a metal that only we could supply, we were in a strong bartering position.

"I'm not making any promises on behalf of my kin, but I know that securing a trade route to your homelands, and all the destinations in between, for our tin would please my Chieftains no end."

The Prince listened to our difficulties with metal supplies and trading alliances, and a huge smile broadened across his face. I assumed that the mention of tin brought about his easy compliance, since it was rarer than gold and twice as useful.

We batted a few other issues about for a little while, until I thought I had a fairly decent deal on the table. My only problem was that I couldn't lead the Prince along such dangerous paths alone. I needed Tallack's help and it was doubtful that he'd agree.

We left the Prince's tent with a promise to return before nightfall with our answer. We were all the way back to the port jetty before I remembered the poppy resin. We would have to make do with willow bark. Brea was waiting on the dock for Tallack, his sails billowing in the wind and unmistakable among our smaller boats and the Frynkish vessels.

When he finally landed, leaving his men in the boats with the traded copper, I told him about the Prince's offer. Brea scowled at his indifference towards her as he gave me his undivided attention, listening to every detail I could recall.

"Are you addled, Aunt Mel? Have you any idea how long a journey like that would take even for a fit man on a horse?" He threw his arms up in the air at me. I could see what he was saying, and I understood his reticence. With all the good will in the world, it could take ten moons, maybe more to reach the Skotek stones and the same amount again to return.

"I hear what you are saying, Tallack, but can you not see the long-term prospects of an alliance with influential rulers in the southern lands? Their trade routes could ensure our tribes future for all time." We stood on the breezy strip of land next to the harbour. He didn't seem to care that people listened in on our discussion.

"We can't be away from home for that long with the Duros threatening to attack our people. Who knows when they'll strike?"

"Precisely. They may already have, for all we know. Blydh is well equipped to deal with it, and has all the hunters gathering the clans for defence. Let's take the copper back and sail along the coast and up to Skotek with just one ship. We could leave your men for Blydh to lead. The Prince has his own guards." That piece of information seemed to stop him from his blustering rant. He smoothed his tunic down and scratched his head.

"You know, he could die long before we even get there, or pass the curse onto us." He sucked in his lips. Despite the negative back lash, I could tell that he was coming around to the idea. "That's supposing that we aren't sunk crossing back over the Channel." He shifted his weight onto his other leg, sniffing and thinking. "Plus, there are all the necessary tributes to pay for crossing other tribal territories."

"The Prince is wealthier than all the gods combined." I raised a single brow at his dithering.

"Is he now? Good to know, good to know."

"And I can ask all there is to learn about foreign healing practices." I said, sensing he'd turned the corner in his objections. "And we'd return home with limitless copper supplies and new trading partners abroad." The half-smile on his face broadened. I wasn't about to let it falter. "And with your slick sailing skills and fast ship, we'll be up that stretch of water and home again in no time at all."

He started to nod. "You said he was likely to pay us in gold for our troubles?"

"I'm sure of it. We'd be little more than guides. We take young Jago here to speak for us, and we'd be done long before spring." I clapped my hand against his shoulder, moving him further inland and towards the exotic tent in the foreigners' camp. By the time I got to introduce Tallack to Prince Suliaman and his son, Brea was in a deep sulk. Tallack had barely acknowledged her presence, and when Maleek stepped forward to shake his hand, it was as though Brea had vanished from the world.

I could see the attraction, as old as I was. Maleek's fine features and slim build gave him a refined air. He reminded me of delicate golden jewellery, forged and worked into the most intricate of patterns. Tallack was smitten, I could tell, but I could not detect any partiality from Maleek.

We shoved Jago between each of our groups, and kept him busy restating the terms of our agreement. We drank hot teas of floral scented leaves with a liberal trickle of honey as the day wore on. Tallack wanted to be sure that the old man knew what the trip entailed. He laid out all the dangers and pitfalls, yet still he would not be deterred.

"You think that I am frightened of a little discomfort?" Came his reply via Jago. "No journey could be as bad as bearing this curse. I must endure to prepare my son to take over my reign. There is still so much left to teach him. It would leave a stain on him if I let this evil take me before my time." Satisfied that a deal was well struck, they drank wine and shook hands.

"Permit me to give your ladies a gift each as a token of my gratitude." The Prince relayed, clapping his hands together. I stared at his fingers as they moved, looking for signs of rot as Jago had explained the day before. As far as I could tell, they were free from any damage. I thought then, that perhaps my slave had mistaken the ailment for another, or maybe the old man was indeed cursed by some black evil arts. Either way, we were to spend a great deal of time together, allowing me ample opportunities to sate my curiosity and learn all I could.

Following his signal, the Prince's servants appeared from both sides of the tent. One moved to Brea's side, presenting her with a golden bracelet studded with amber beads. Its value was beyond measure. Her face brightened significantly, grabbing at the item with both hands and thanking him for his generosity. Her attitude abruptly changed from sullen to jolly in an instant.

"The Prince says that his son said that you took a liking to their family treasure. He cannot give you that torque from around Maleek's neck, but perhaps this bracelet will be sufficient?" Jago spoke out in translation. I could see the old man narrowing his eyes at the gushing Brea, taking her measure. He was far shrewder than any of us realised. He observed us with a subtle judgement, so that none suspected his actions. What a clever man.

A second servant stopped by my side, passing me a small beaker with a lid sealed by wax. I took it from him and looked to the Prince for an explanation.

"It is a small quantity of the poppy resin that you wanted. The Prince thinks it is not for your own use, but for those who use your healing services."

I blushed. The amount was huge by my normal standards. This little pot would set me back a quarter moon's worth of digging and smelting tin for a dozen men. Not that I could source that much resin in Dumnoni lands with which to trade. With careful administration, it would be more than enough to see out the battle wounds and injuries ahead. I was overwhelmed. I tried to convey all that I felt but the words would not come.

Jago guessed my intention and spoke on my behalf, while I wiped the fog from my eyes. Why anyone would want to lay a curse on this godly man is beyond me. When I could see again, and regained my composure, I found both the Prince and Maleek smiling down on me from their high chairs. It made me so uncomfortable, I handed the resin pot to Jago for safe keeping, and excused myself to step outside. It would not do to show the Prince my vulnerabilities.

The low sun tried to break through the building clouds and the light had already begun to fade. I couldn't see Tallack wishing to set sail in the dark in unfamiliar waters. It seemed to me that we'd be spending another night with the stinking travellers in the boarding hut. For a moment, I tutted at the prospect, and then remembered that I had just volunteered to spend the next couple of moons in cramped, cold and probably soaking wet conditions to secure new trade. I needed to forget my former life of privilege and stop complaining.

When I returned to the tent, the Prince's servants were laying out a massive spread of dishes. He beckoned us over to help ourselves to the exotic looking foods. I recognised the taste of rabbit and deer meat, but they were coated in sauces that were so filled with flavour that my tongue started to tingle. One red sauce gave me pain it had in it so much foreign spice. My eyes watered and I coughed, until Tallack handed me his cup of sweet wine to cool my mouth. It caused much amusement in the tent. I can't remember the last time I had laughed so much.

Only when my mouth stopped burning, and I was given a spoon of soured cream to stir into the sauce, did I realise that Jago was standing by the edge of the tent walls, looking down at the ground. Puzzled, I walked over to him and asked why he was not eating the foods.

"Fur Benyn. I am a slave. Your servant. It is my place to stand alongside the Prince's slaves now that we are to be in his company." He whispered this to me, with his head still bowed, not daring to make eye contact with me.

"Don't be daft. You're my Jago, not one of the Prince's servants. Come and eat with us." I grabbed his wrist and tried to pull him across the tent, but he wouldn't budge. I couldn't decide whether he was intimidated by the situation, or whether he was simply too frightened to be close to the cursed man. Defeated, I scooped up a bowl full of food and bread and walked to the doorway. With a flick of my head in his direction, he limped after me and out of the tent.

"What's all this nonsense about. You're not in the Prince's service, you belong to me." I thrust the bowl at him. "If you won't eat with us, then get this down you out here. I can't have you standing next to his servants at the side of the tent scoffing down his food in front of them." I gave him and exasperated sigh.

He tucked into the foods as if he'd not eaten for two moons. I was used to his picky ways, his nibbling on food and making portions last him all day. This was new to me. He rammed his mouth full and swallowed until he almost choked.

The moment he stopped for breath, I asked, "How come you suddenly have an appetite?"

The satisfied groans and moans halted. "This is the food of my homeland. It tastes the same as my mother's cooking." That was all I could hear on the matter, for he scooped up more with cupped fingers and crammed it into his maw. Far from being upset by the reminder of home, it was the happiest I'd seen him since his binding ceremony to the Frynkish slave girl.

"Don't wander off. You told me yourself how thieves wander these shores."

I glanced back to see him grin, with spiced sauce dribbling down his chin. Tittering to myself, I re-joined the party. Tallack and Maleek were using a made-up form of gestures to communicate in Jago's absence, while Brea admired her new metal, oblivious to his growing attraction for the young man. Prince Suliaman sat back in his tall chair, content to watch the young people take their fill. He ate so little, and drank even less. I assumed that his need for poppy resin, curbed his hunger or that he chose to eat alone in private. How different he was from our Chieftains, especially Aebba. This man was quiet and studied, thoughtful and kind. Aebba was loud and raucous, brutal and at times, a bully.

It made me think back to his childhood. He was a sickly child, always at my door asking for willow bark and blackthorn for the gut ache. His kindness extended only to a select few, and Brea was not among them. This Prince seemed the perfect host. Was he too hiding a more sinister side beneath that wry smile? I guessed that only time would tell. Perhaps I would discover the reason why he was cursed, and by whom.

Jago returned with an empty bowl and a massive smile. I called him over to resume his job of translating. This he did with much vigour, having filled his belly with tasty fare. Tallack and Maleek busied themselves discussing and organising the trip across the channel. More boats would be required, along with men to sail them. Maleek did not seem to think this would be a problem and sent one of the guards to the jetty in advance.

I moved towards Prince Suliaman and sat on a low seat opposite him. So many questions cluttered my thoughts about his condition. Whenever I thought he was not watching, I looked him up and down searching for signs of the ailment, but saw none. At length, the Prince summoned Jago to his side, speaking in their quiet tongue.

“Fur Benyn, the Prince thinks that you would like to ask him something. Is he correct?”

I knew he’d be a crafty one. Nothing escapes his attention. I was perhaps slightly embarrassed by my lack of tact, but I wanted to know more about him. “Please, ask the Prince, if I can do anything to ease his troubles. I have a few medicines in my kit bag and would be happy to assist him.” I waited for Jago to relay my message. It brought a warm grin to Suliaman’s cheeks.

“He says that you are a kind lady, but he has a healer in his service.” Jago stepped aside and waited for further instruction. I couldn’t think of a way to turn the conversation around and make him explain his curse. Annoyed with myself, I took a breath and smiled back feeling thoroughly thwarted. Suliaman’s face pinched tightly, his forehead furrowed and his eyes closed for just a moment. I could tell he was tolerating a serious level of pain. A servant moved closer and handed him a small cup.

It contained a milky fluid. My best guess was watered down poppy resin.

When Maleek's guard returned and whispered into his ear, Jago was required once again. The news from the harbour was that the best time to catch the tide would be before dawn. There was much to prepare, and the old man needed his rest.

I reclined on the bench, wrapping my cloak about me and watching the servants, guards and Jago rushing around packing everything away, until it was time to collapse the tent itself. Yawning, I slung my medicine kit over my shoulder and wandered outside.

Brea and Tallack were behind the boarding hut, arguing like they were already wed. I only heard a little, but the general thrust was that Brea felt he was ignoring her.

Tired of her games, he turned about and muttered, "No one forced you to come on this trip, and no one is forcing you to return. Maybe you should stay and find yourself a nice Frynkish husband to buy you amber and gold."

She screamed at him, hurling the new bracelet at the back of his head as he walked away. I could hardly contain my amusement. Hiding behind a willow hurdle, I watched her scrabble about in the dirt to find the jewel, before wiping it clean of mud and sinking it in her cloak pocket. At least she is not focusing on me and Jago anymore.

A little later, as the sun started to creep over the horizon, I found a clean spring to refill my water bladders and pocketed some of the Prince's bread and cheese for the return journey.

Tallack and Maleek organised who and what should be in each of the boats, ensuring an even load and an experienced sailor in all the vessels.

When at last it was time to board the ship, Tallack had to act the clown to persuade the sullen Brea to climb the gangplank, while I lingered on the jetty waiting my turn.

My nephew grinned at me, waving me over to the walkway at his side. As I stepped up, I heard fast footsteps on the wooden boards heading my way. I peered over my shoulder, unsteady on the bowing plank. Before I could make it onto the ship, a tall lad made a dash at me brandishing a knife and screaming in Frynkish. The blade was so close to my face I could almost feel its keen edge.

CHAPTER NINE

The youth swished the blade closer, making me jerk my head back. I could barely keep my balance as he reached over and grabbed hold of the strap on my kit bag. It had all my bronze blades that Aebba had made for me, plus the poppy resin jug from the Prince. I was not about to let him take it from me. I lashed out, catching his nose with my fist. Together we wrestled, while everyone looked on in disbelief.

"Just give it to him, Fur Benyn." Jago yelled in horror. "Don't let him take your life too."

I had no intention of losing either. The lad grew angrier at my stubbornness, jabbing his blade into my arm and drawing blood. The pain soared through my shoulder and into my spine. He'd cut a vessel. It poured with blood. Still I held on, desperately trying to maintain my stance on the narrow boarding plank. Before I could punch him again, he sliced through the strap, grabbed the bag to his chest and ran.

Desolate and in surging pain, I staggered to the jetty and slumped to the floor. The thief turned and sprinted around the corner of a trading stall. Maleek was waiting for him. He held out his foot and tripped the thug over, sending him tumbling to the ground. In one swift move, Maleek unsheathed a massive curved blade and slashed open the youth's throat.

The lad clutched his neck, choking on the foaming and gurgling red humours. Maleek stood over him, watching the life ebb from the boy's body. With one final cough, his arms fell to his side, his eyes glazed with the stare of death. Maleek snatched my kit bag up and strolled to the jetty, his blade still dripping with the thief's blood. He approached me, holding out the ragged item and explaining something for Jago to translate.

"He says that it should be easy enough to sew back together." Jago looked at me in utter shock. Maleek took that lad's life as though he was slicing bread for his supper. I hurried onto Tallack's boat, making room for him to board after me.

"Jago, make sure you tell him how grateful I am." I stammered, hugging my kit to my chest and moving swiftly to my seat in the bow. My slave translated my words and then rushed to staunch the flow of blood from my arm. He has learned my craft faster than I thought he would. He collected salt water in a beaker and soaked a cloth, before washing the gash clean.

"Would you like me to prepare some poppy water for the pain?" He asked me, hovering between my kit and the fresh water bladder.

"Willow will suit me fine, Jago. Pass me my best bone needle, will you. This will need stitching."

He fussed and tutted at me, soaking the cattle gut lengths and threading my needle in readiness. I didn't think he would have the courage to sew me up, but he set about the wound as though it was his calling. Such fine little stitches they were too. He had a steady hand and a careful eye. Even Tallack commended the boy on a job well done.

We were late setting sail after all that had occurred. The Prince insisted that he travelled on Tallack's ship, along with his son, his personal healer and a large guardsman. I was relieved, since there was no room for Brea who travelled in one of the smaller crafts with a few of his crewmen. I offered to swap boats too, but Tallack feared that I might need his watchful eye on me after my brush with the thief's blade.

The arrangements suited me well. I had good company, fine food and no Brea to put me on edge. Young Jago relaxed too, although he was still ill at ease in the presence of the Prince and Maleek. Perhaps his own beliefs gave him anxiety over the nature of the Prince's curse. I on the other hand, was desperate to discover more. Apart from his obvious pain, I could detect nothing wrong with him. At least, none of the symptoms Jago told me about.

Suliaman's guard adopted the role of manservant while he was aboard. I wanted for nothing, having all my meals brought to my seat at the front of the boat, and more wine than I could consume. By mid-afternoon, the warm drink dulled my senses so that I could feel no discomfort from my wound at all. Unfortunately, the more I drank, the less I could hold my tongue.

"So, this curse…" I slurred to the great man. "How did you come by it exactly?"

Maleek's gaze turned towards the open water, his forehead pinched into deep folds. It was as though he'd understood what I'd asked before Jago had a chance to translate.

The Prince was a little more forthcoming about his misfortune. He narrowed his eyes at me and made a contemplative moan, before giving Jago his answer.

"He says that he upset a powerful family from a neighbouring land. Before he could make amends for the trouble, they conjured a demon to give him the curse." Jago shuffled further away, sitting with his back up against the side of the ship. I wanted to know more, how did the demon appear to him, what did he look like, and many other questions slipped through my inebriated mind, but I had paused too long, the Prince had his own puzzles to solve.

"Fur Benyn, the Prince asks whether your nephew is um… a word that means bad man of the seas?" Jago stared down at his feet. The enquiry threw my kin in a poor light.

At the time, I didn't see the insinuation, my brain half pickled in fine wine. "Ask him why he thinks that?"

Jago did, taking time to frame his words carefully. The response was immediate. "He says that this is a Phoenician trading ship from his homeland. Tallack could not have built such a vessel. He wants to know if he killed the merchant and took the cargo."

That woke me up to his suspicions and his low opinion of our family. I sat upright and indignant. "Tell the noble man that Tallack traded a vast amount of tin for this ship in a fair exchange. We are not pirates." I huffed so loudly that it alerted the Prince's guard, his son and some of Tallack's men. They observed our conversation with a keen eye, alert to any discord. I have no doubt that one word from me, and several of those rowing would have leapt to my defence.

Jago relayed my words to the old man, who immediately softened to my distress. His response was an apology, coupled with a hand gesture whereupon he touched his bowed forehead in a form of salute.

"I should think so too." I blurted, assuming his mumbling was an attempt to calm troubled waters.

"He asks forgiveness, and says that he needed to know that his son was in no danger."

"Hmm." I harrumphed. The problem was that I could see his point. In his situation, I too would be wary. Tallack is a fine talker, and a brilliant trader, but for all the Prince knew, we could have overpowered his guard and thrown him and his son overboard and made off with all his wealth.

The waves were kind to us for more than half the journey back across the Channel. When the wind picked up it was against us, making Tallack's men work hard to tack in a zig zag path to harness its power. We were in a better position than the crafts behind us. They had the added problem of fewer oars, smaller sails and were sitting low in the water from the weight of traded copper.

When the day ended and the clouds blotted out the moon, we had no stars by which to navigate. I noticed that the Prince refused all the food brought to him, and had taken only a little fluid. The closer we got to our own shores, the more the swell lifted us high into the air, before allowing us to plunge down the other side of the wave. Jago moved so that he could stand at the boats edge once again, but managed to hold down his meal.

The Prince blew out his cheeks. His skin took on a pallid tone and he breathed erratically. His healer approached him, holding out a tiny glass jar of a thick liquid, but Suliaman sent him away. Before long, his guard was holding a bowl beneath his master's face, catching his sickness. I tried to give the man his dignity, scrambling to the rear of the boat to speak with my nephew.

"This will not end well, you know that don't you, Aunt Mel?" He said, keeping a weather eye on the sails and the rigging, while pushing the tiller to one side.

"You don't know that at all. If what he tells me is true, and that a wicked demon has laid down the curse, then the holy men at the Skotek stones will lift it for him." I steadied myself against my nephew as the ship lurched in the rising waters.

"If he makes it to the Skotek stones. From the look of him, he won't make it back to shore. Can't you give him something from your medicine kit?"

"He's just shooed his own healer away. What makes you think he'll take what I offer him?" I looked up at my nephew.

He shrugged. "Not sure, really. He seems to respect you."

"Hmm." I wanted to say, *you wouldn't be saying that if you'd heard what he called you earlier*, but I kept my mouth clamped shut. Suliaman didn't give me the impression that he respected me, but I couldn't see any harm in offering help.

Tallack had a serious frown as he studied our trajectory. I took that to mean that I was distracting him and returned to my seat at the front. The Prince had a bear fur draped around his shoulders and was shaking from the exertion of his seasickness. I nodded to Jago to assist with language once again.

"Ask the Prince if he would like me to mix him a tonic to ward off the nausea." While my servant spoke to the poorly man, I retrieved my kit and took out a handful of dried hops. I held them in my palm for the nobleman to see. He reached out and took one feathery green frond and turned it between his fingers. While he made up his mind, I found some kindling and dry sticks in the storage holds beneath the rowers' benches and nestled them in a metal basket hanging from a chain above us. With a couple of flints cracked together, I sparked a flame and nurtured it into life. Before long, I had a fire strong enough to boil a little water to make my hot tonic of hops.

Suliaman watched me crush the hops into the hot water and to my surprise, he held out his hand to accept my offering.

"Tell him to let it steep a while before drinking it down. I'm afraid I have no honey to sweeten it, but it doesn't taste so bad."

Jago did as I asked, and just moments later, his guard and manservant went in search of honey, handing me an entire jar for my kit. I observed as the Prince sniffed the tonic. He sipped a little down, and decided that he did not require the added sweetener after all. I suspect that my potion helped him, or at the very least it engendered trust between us, as he seemed to smile more from then on.

My slave slumped down at my feet, tired and rather annoyed. "Did you not think to make a tonic for me on our way across to Frynk?"

I had to laugh at his petulance. "I would have but I had no hops until the Frynkish market." That cheered him a little.

"Would you have given it to Brea?"

I thought long and hard about that question and chose not to answer him. If she was not sick on the boat, she may not have fallen overboard. Either way, she was safe and sailing behind us in another vessel. Given the chance again, I'm not sure that I would have pulled her from the waves even with my nephew watching my actions.

Suliaman finished the tonic and returned the beaker to me with his thanks. I kept my eye on him for some time, assessing the progression of his ailments. The sickness may have stopped, but he was in just as much pain as before. He barked out orders to his healer who dropped a large bead of poppy resin into more water and waited while the Prince guzzled it down.

The more the ship rocked, the more anguish showed on his face. It was as if the cold breeze and damp air was setting off all his bodily feeling and triggering an ache that would not be quelled. I've seen what happens to priests who got too fond of poppy resin. It took more and more of the stuff to have an effect, so that in the end, the need for the resin gave more pain than the original ague.

I thought ahead to the long voyage up the coastline to the Skotek Islands at the top of the world. This was a comparatively short journey, and he was suffering all the way. Stoking the little fire to keep it alive amid the vicious winds, I went to the stern with the excuse of needing more wood. Tallack saw my errand and pointed to a box above the water line. I found all sorts of treasures and cloth, trinkets and metals at one end, and more essential supplies at the other.

Sitting on the container lid, I spoke quietly to Tallack. "The Prince will never make the journey by sea. If we are to secure those trade routes and a copper supply, we will need to think of an alternative way to get him to the stones."

My nephew is far more observant than I gave him credit for. "You're right. He needs resin just to cross from Frynk. The highland seas between those islands will kill him."

"What do you suggest?"

"I really don't know. Perhaps this entire enterprise was a fool's errand. Maybe we can just explain the matter and let him decide. Blydh needs us back on Dumnoni lands. As soon as we make port, we'll have to part ways, and hope that he'll still want to trade with us."

That was not what I wanted to hear. This man and his new ways intrigued me. There was so much to learn from them, that I did not want the alliance to be over with so soon. I took my sticks back to the swinging fire and sat down with a bump. The ocean was growing rougher again and land was nowhere to be seen.

With stomachs calmed and the darkest part of the night yet to steer through, I propped myself up against the bow and wrapped my cloak about me. Jago stayed awake and alert, too frightened to close his eyes. I saw no point in mistrust. They were at our mercy in a foreign ocean heading for an unknown land. Safe in the knowledge that my nephew's men would protect me from harm, I slept.

Before dawn, Jago woke me with warm mint tea and some stale flat bread. He'd kept the little fire burning through salt spray and gusting winds to make my morning drink. "Did you get any sleep at all?" I asked him, worried about his jitters. He shook his head. I peered over at the Prince sitting high in his chair on deck. He'd barely moved a muscle, but his eyes darted towards every movement on ship. For an old man in pain, he missed nothing.

"Jago, ask the Prince if he would like more hops to brew."

The answer came back a polite and grateful thanks, but no. I could tell by his reddened eyelids that he was battling pain again, and was probably on his second dose of poppy for the day. For a curse as painful as this, he must have seriously offended his neighbour. It made me ponder over the true nature of his crime. I got the distinct impression that there was more to the story than he was prepared to admit.

Tallack and his men gnawed on some dried meats and flat bread before putting their shoulders to the oars. The sail billowed out once again in our favour, but the thick clouds still obscured our sight of the stars. Our course was a guess at best. With no further chance to sleep, I thrust a wedge of fabric in each ear to blot out the rhythmic drumming to keep the rowers in step with one another.

Maleek stood at the side of the ship, watching the lights bob up and down from the other boats around us. When, at last, the light of day arrived, it brought with it a new hope and a first sighting of land. We'd made it across without loss of life or limb and with all our passengers and cargo intact. Maleek almost smiled at the vista and then told his father that the journey was almost at an end. The relief on the Prince's face was obvious. He'd been holding all his symptoms at bay for the entire crossing. I strongly suspected that he too, had reservations about hopping around bays and headlands all the way up to the top of the world.

I looked over towards Tallack. His face was ashen and stern. Every crease in his young face seemed accentuated by the drying effects of the salted air. I dodged oars and legs and returned to his side.

"Something is wrong, I can tell. What is it?" I blustered.

"I don't recognise this part of the coastline. We must have been blown off course last night."

CHAPTER TEN

The land ahead was flat. Massive beaches stretched as far as the eye could see. Landing on any part of this coast line would leave us vulnerable to attack. Tallack ordered the men to drop the sail. We let the current pull us towards shore as Tallack ruminated on our choices.

"How much fresh water is left?" He asked one man. The answer was not good. "Get the plumb line over the side. I want to know how close we dare get."

I watched his first mate clamber over to the storage boxes and retrieve a weight tied to the end of a knotted length of fine rope. It splashed the surface as it sunk to the sea bed. The man counted the number of knots submerged and informed his leader.

"This is as far as we go in this vessel. Can't afford to strand my ship on a sandbank." He said, stepping to the port bow and looking out to sea for the rest of the boats.

"You surely don't expect us to swim to shore?" I said with a hint of panic in my voice.

Tallack snorted with a titter. "No, Aunt. Give me some credit. We'll wait until another boat comes alongside and use it to ferry passengers to the beach.

And wait we did, all the time swaying and lurching with the tidal flow. The Prince looked spent. His features drooped into heavy jowls, his complexion waxy and strained with pain. As I watched, Suliaman dig his thumbnail into each of his fingertips in turn. I thought perhaps his hands were his main site of discomfort. With Jago's help, I asked him if I could make him more comfortable, perhaps a sling to support his hand.

The response had me more perplexed than ever. "He says that he has no feeling in his fingers, although he still has control over them. The pain is deep within, branching out from his backbone."

Now I understood the need for such heavy doses of resin. He gave me a smile that conveyed his appreciation, but I was stumped as to how to help the man.

More time passed. The morning was dull but dry and the ocean no less rolling. At length, Suliaman asked for more hop tea, which I was glad to make for him.

Eventually we caught sight of the rest of our fleet. With a careful exchange of copper for passengers, we loaded into the smaller craft and let Tallack's men row us to shore. It just happened to be the same vessel that carried a sulking Brea. Tallack's head stayed on a swivel, fearful of attack from an unknown tribe. He ordered some of his men to stand guard, and more to scout further inland. The remainder stayed aboard the boats.

The Prince look mightily relieved to be on dry land. My fears for his health, it seems, were well founded. There was little chance of him enduring the long voyage to the top of the world. Maleek held on to his father's arm, holding him upright as the old man's knees buckled under his weight. His muscles could not support his thin frame. Was this too, part of the curse?

I spun around in search of my nephew. He was standing at the water's edge looking out to sea with Brea nagging him at his shoulder. "Shouldn't you be bothered about what might lie behind you?" I asked, confused by his behaviour.

"I am bothered, Aunt Mel. That's why I am looking out for Renowden."

"And who might he be?" Before he answered, his face lit up in recognition. He stuck his thumb and forefinger in his mouth and blew out a shrill but distinctive whistle. A clear wave came back from a man in one of the boats. They rowed closer, allowing an older man to jump over the side and wade through the shallows. Brea slunk off like a beaten dog. I have no doubt that it was some kind of ruse to illicit sympathy from Tallack, or the Prince, or maybe both.

Despite being past the bloom of youth, Renowden was strong and lean. The gnarly stubble on his face made him look fearsome but his smile showed his softer side. As he approached us on the beach, he gave Tallack a beaming grin. "You whistled?"

"I did. Where are we, Ren?"

Renowden craned his neck, surveying our position. "This is Canti land. Your mother's tribe."

Tallack's shoulders slumped with relief. He took a long breath and let it out slowly, balancing his hands on his head. "How is it that I don't recognise this stretch of the coast?"

"Because you normally moor up some distance away to the west. You never had a reason to come this far east before." Renowden shrugged.

"But you know it well?" I asked him, curious as to this man's background.

"Yup, Fur Benyn. I know all the beaches and all the headlands around Inglond. Bit sketchy with Frynkish landings but I find my way eventually."

"So, what do we do now?" I asked them both.

"Nothing." Tallack replied, walking away towards the Prince. "Canti scouts will spot my ship soon enough. They'll come out to us."

Suliaman's servants and guards collected wood from beyond the dunes and stacked them up for a fire. The Prince shivered despite his furs and warm clothing. He was accustomed to the warm dry atmosphere of his exotic homeland. I remember it taking a while for Jago to adjust to our damp climate. Suliaman's tall chair was delivered from the ship along with cushions, blankets and his trunks of jewels and gold. We would need every bit of metal the man had to pay our way across this great land if we were to make it to the top of the world.

Maleek pulled the bear fur around his father, before stopping abruptly. He'd noticed something on his father's skin. I moved closer to see what the commotion was about, for the quiet discussion was building into a frenzy of noise.

"What's going on, Jago?"

"Maleek has found a patch of sore skin on his father's neck. He is worried that the curse is growing in strength."

"Let me see." I shoved passed the healer and guards to get a closer look at this sore. It was pale and no larger than my thumbnail in size. I couldn't with any certainty say that it was part of his ailment, or whether the old man had rubbed a bit of his neck raw, but Maleek's reaction was extreme enough to warrant investigation. It clearly troubled the man.

I turned to Jago and instructed him to boil some fresh water. Digging into my kit back, I unwrapped my knife roll and took out a small blade. Suliaman's guards went crazy, each of them aiming spears at me in the most disturbing and threatening stance. Raising the small knife between finger and thumb, I handed it to the closest guard, and rummaged for a bundle of burdock roots.

When they saw what I needed the blade for, the guard returned it to me with a nod of permission.

Scraping at the thick rind surrounding the fibrous root, I exposed a fresh section laden with oozing sap and approached the Prince. "Jago, tell him that this stuff soothes skin problems. It'll take off the itch and help it to heal." As soon as the information was received, the old man pulled down the bear pelt and tipped his head to one side. With as gentle a stroke as I could manage, I wiped the clean root across the sore and allowed it to dry.

I handed another length of burdock root to his healer, who fumed at me from the opposite side of the Prince. It was hard not to judge that excuse for a medicine man, but as far as I could tell, he did not earn his keep.

Maleek turned to me, and in our tongue, he said, "Thank you, Fur Benyn." You could have knocked me down with a puff, I was so surprised. I found myself blushing from the experience. He'd picked up our words just by listening to us talking. I wonder if he knew that Fur Benyn was not my true name, but a compliment paid to me for my healing skills. He put us to shame with his mastery over new language. None of our tribe even attempted to learn another tongue, although how Tallack got by with his Frynkish trading I'll never know.

When the Prince was settled and refreshed by warm teas of crushed burdock root to clean his blood and a little food from their supplies, he ordered his men to go in search of clay. Curious, I stayed on the beach to watch events pan out. By late afternoon, Suliaman's men stacked the fire high with branches and one of his guards sat and moulded a large amount of clay from further inland.

Tallack and I ate dried boar strips and supped some of our ale, while a statue the size of half a man took shape before our eyes. The head was large with jutting out ears, the eyes were quarter moons and the mouth curved up in a grotesque smile. The strangest part of all, was the figurine's arms. They twisted about the clay body and were much longer than that of a normal person. The guard took most care over the position of the clay hands. One rested on the arm of the other, while its right hand touched the neck of the statue at the exact same place the sore appeared on Suliaman's throat.

When the guard was satisfied with his labours, he stood back and allowed the remaining guards to move it into the hot embers. With more wood to stoke the fire, the clay man turned into pot. Tallack removed himself from the fire side to speak with the crewmen on shore. I guessed that he was making arrangements for the boats to sail west to deliver the copper to our tribe.

There was so much to organise, but I trusted that my young nephew had a mind to take care of the details. Jago sat in the sand at my side and stared at the flames licking the clay man. He was more than mesmerised. It was as though he'd seen a demon. I offered to share my furs with him, to ease the shivers that coursed through his body, but he didn't respond. The statue held him in a daze.

I whispered to him, trying to break the spell, but to no avail. His mind was lost in thought. Wrapping the edges of my cloak about his back, I left him alone, figuring that he'd tell me his troubles in his own time.

Tallack returned shortly after and ignored Brea's attempts to entice him to her side. "Aunt Mel. Our ships will need to set off on the next tide. I've asked Ren to stay with us, but we must have a decision from the Prince soon."

"You aren't serious?" Brea scoffed. If you are thinking of riding all the way to the stones at the top of the world you are crazy. That foreigner won't make it past Canti lands, and then it will all be for nought. Cut your losses and return home. Blydh needs us all if we are to defend ourselves against the Duros."

As much as I hate to admit it, the girl was right. The chances of Suliaman succumbing to the curse before reaching the Skotek stones were high, and then Maleek was free to break the deal. His character was as deep and troubled as Tallack's brother and I suspected deadlier too. It was our last chance to cement the arrangement with the Prince, before sending the ships home.

I roused Jago from his fugue to assist with translation. Tallack began to explain where we hand landed in relation to the Skotek stones. We lay at the farthest reaches of the south-eastern shore, with the stones in the opposite corner of the island, in the north-western isles. He asked the Prince how he felt about the possibility of a very long sea journey along the coast before the Black Rites Ritual could be performed.

The old man did not speak. He cast his eyes to his son and swallowed back his pain. His eyes misted over, giving us all a clear idea of his thoughts. At length, Maleek answered on his behalf. He used his native tongue.

Jago listened and told us his fears. "The Prince cannot travel that distance by sea. He suffers more and more each day and the inconvenience of being aboard ship, even one as fine as Tallack's, is too hard to cope with. He says that they will pay you handsomely to take them over land."

Brea's ears pricked up at the sound of payment, especially since she knew the currency would have a golden hue. She moved closer to Tallack and draped her arm over his shoulder. "Maybe you should consider it, my love. Gold would help to feed all the warriors that Blydh plans to train."

"Why would you care?" He snapped at her. "The payment would be for our whole tribe. You wouldn't see a single nugget of it." What had she said to him to make him turn on her so cruelly? I should have been more circumspect, but I couldn't help but grin. Brea saw me and stomped away from the fireside. Something told me that we we're brewing up trouble with that one.

Tallack tried to convey the difficulties in travelling by land across numerous tribal regions in the coldest part of the cycle. Every amicable tribe would require a tribute in payment to cross their land, and that was under the banner of pilgrimage. Other tribes who were less than reasonable, would be more likely to attack, taking all the Prince's wealth and possibly lives too.

Maleek sneered at this statement. He unsheathed his curved blade and stood back into a cleared space. With rapid swipes, he swung the blade about his head with such skill and determination, he almost severed an ear. As impressive as this display was, we all knew that it would not stand up to an attack of head hunters mounted on fast steeds. Their sheer numbers alone would reduce us to slavery or worse within moments. I didn't doubt his courage, only that his number of guards were too few.

The conversation batted backwards and forwards for some time, neither side making headway. I could see both arguments, but I leaned heavily on the side of forging this foreign alliance with our efforts in lifting his curse. Tallack leaned towards returning to the River Exe to assist his brother in rebuilding the compound and training new warriors in preparation for the Duro attack.

We reached deadlock. Tallack rose from his cross-legged position in the sand and began walking away. He was just a few strides from the fire when a scout rode into camp. Maleek and his guards scrambled into action until Tallack gestured for them to lower their weapons. The rider was his kin.

"Whoa!" The rider said, pulling back on the reins. "Are you going to have me butchered by your friends?" It was Tallack's cousin, Cade. He dismounted and hurried over to him, grasping around the back of his neck to pull their foreheads together in greeting. "We did not expect to see you so soon after your summer visit. What are you doing all the way down here?"

"Blown off course." Tallack smiled. "Good to see you, Cade. What's the news from camp?"

"You heard about grandfather?"

"We did. We are all sorry for your loss." I chipped in, for I could see that my nephew was desperate to empty his bladder but held off out of politeness. Cade wandered over to me and greeted me in the same manner. It was a touching gesture, usually reserved for close family.

"Fur Benyn. How fortunate that you have come. My grandmother will be keen to hear all about Aunt Cryda." Cade nodded through the obligatory introductions and then sat in the sand by the fire. The Prince extended his hospitality to him, ensuring his cup was filled with wine and food offered from a cedar wood bowl. Cade looked at the thin fabrics and tall hats coloured an unusual purple, and was keen to hear of our quest. Jago had his work cut out for him, standing a respectful distance between us all and keeping up with each translation to the foreigners.

"You got yourself a good slave there, Fur Benyn." Cade announced, accepting more spiced meats from Suliaman's servant. I was on the verge of insisting that he should call me by my given name, but realised that it would do no good. These youngsters either forget, or feel uncomfortable in its use.

"So, let me get this straight," Cade said, with a forefinger stuck in mid-air. "This one over here, is your painted slave from far beyond the Channel, but these painted men are noblemen from a Phoenician colony?"

I thought for a moment and nodded. That about summed the situation up. Poor Jago was simply in the wrong place at the wrong time when he was scooped up and sold into slavery. I had no idea about his life before then. He may well have been of a high social status himself, much like the Prince, who had the benefit of guards and wealth to protect him.

Jago opened his mouth to translate Cade's observations, but I gave him a tiny shake of the head to dissuade his attempts. It wouldn't do to upset them with his casual talk. Jago turned to them, in his astute way, but instead of speaking in their tongue, he fell to the ground like a weighted sack, and shook violently in building convulsions.

The Prince gasped, struggling to his feet. Maleek once again drew his blade and stood in front of his weakened father, closing in on Jago's throat.

CHAPTER ELEVEN

Maleek bared his teeth, spitting out venomous warnings against Jago's seizure. To my mind it meant only one thing. They had never seen this malady before and assumed it was sent by dark spirits of the underworld, a part of the curse. I have never jumped up from the ground so quickly in my life. Pushing myself between Maleek and Jago, I hoped to the gods that he would stay his hand and not strike me down. Jago foamed with spittle and looked to be choking. I knelt by his side, twisting his slender body by the shoulder and cradling his head until the drool fell to the floor clearing his airways.

The Phoenicians all backed away from us, each holding spears and daggers for protection against the perceived threat.

Tallack returned from the dunes and saw me and the trembling slave in the sand. He trudged past his girlfriend and growled at her. "You couldn't make yourself useful and help her I suppose?"

Brea examined her nails and snarled her retort. "Why should I? He's just a slave. Kill him, don't kill him, what do I care?"

She cared alright. She wanted Jago dead and burned to keep him quiet, and then she'd only have me to deal with. I shot her a glare but it went unnoticed. Tallack spoke soft words to calm the visitors down. None of them had any clue what they meant, but Maleek seemed to trust him. He put away his curved sword and instructed his men to do the same.

I stayed with the boy, wiping his mouth and preventing him from wriggling into the hot embers surrounding the clay statue. When he finally came to his senses, he tried to stand but lost his balance and fell once again. With a little wine to revive him, and some cool water splashed on his face, he was able to speak.

"You must tell them that you were not taken over by a demon to attack them. Be honest. Explain why these fits come from time to time." Slowly and with faltering words, Jago told the Prince about his head injury, and that our tribe now believe that he can communicate with our gods. I watched their expressions as they took in this information and assimilated what that might mean. Suliaman was the only one to reply. When he was finished, Jago flushed with embarrassment and hung his head low.

"What did he say?"

"The Prince was kind about my situation. He said that you must be very fond of me to treat me with such care."

Brea was not amused. "Oh, for the sake of Cernonnus, save me this gushing kawgh." For a mountain tribe girl, she certainly uses plenty of our expletives. She stood up and tipped her head at Tallack, indicating for them to be alone. I suspect that she realised her grip on him was loosening and that she needed to apply more physical methods to bend him to her will again. It was a pivotal moment. If he went with her into the sand dunes, I knew that she would persuade him to return home, leaving Jago and I alone on this quest.

He scratched at his chin and watched her repeat her signal. Cade saw it too, for it was hard to miss. He giggled at her brazen attempt and helped himself to more wine. Tallack closed his eyes, taking in a deep breath. He snatched the cup from his cousin and emptied Cade's wine down his throat. Brea had failed. Inwardly, I rejoiced at my minor victory. All was not lost.

Brea huffed her disgust and slipped away into the dunes alone. The night drew on and the clouds cleared, rendering the air frigid. She would have to return to the fire to bunk down for the night or freeze among the foxes and weasels. I gave her little thought. As long as Jago and I stayed close to the Prince, we were safe from her potential attack.

Cade returned to the subject of our ships out beyond the tidal pull to the beach. Tallack had set up a rotating guard, allowing the men to come to shore for food, water and rest before returning for their watch. The delay in making a decision made them restless. The collective wealth on the vessels made them vulnerable too. In returning home to the other end of the long Channel, they would have to navigate strong currents and pass less amicable tribal lands. Without Tallack and old Renowden to guide them, they would be leaderless and prone to infighting.

Tallack spoke quietly to his cousin. He was keen to keep his concerns to themselves.

All I heard was Cade's response. "Then it's settled. You will come and be our guests in camp and speak with my father. Send your ships home with the morning tide and if you choose to return after them, we can provide you with horses and provisions."

I said nothing, but saw my nephew nod his head. We are at least one step closer to completing this enormous task, but the rewards of such a far-reaching alliance could be good for the Cantii as well as our own people. Before bedding down for the night, I mixed more burdock tea and peeled a fresh section of root for the Prince to treat himself. He seemed especially dazed that evening, as though he'd taken enough resin to numb his mind from the cold. His healer stood over him, watching the guards make up a bed of dune grasses and furs by the fire.

Jago slept by my side, afraid that Brea might stab him while he slept. The thought had crossed my mind too, and without Jago to translate for us, she would cast the blame on our visitors, who would be unable to defend themselves in our language.

The morning was another damp and hazy one. The fire had burned down, but was not so low that it couldn't be revived. How I longed for fresh goat's milk warmed through with a handful of grains. It would be a long time before I could make porridge on my own hut fire again. Propping myself up on my elbows, I saw that Brea had returned to our camp and slipped beneath Tallack's furs. He snored a short distance from the fireside, unaware of his bed mate.

The Prince sat in his tall chair, looking surprisingly refreshed. He took a burdock root from a pocket in his robes and held it aloft. "Good." He said with a faint smile. "Thank." He placed his palms together in front of his chest, trapping the root between them. Closing his eyes, he bowed to me. It was such a touching moment. I returned the sentiment. We were forging our own bond of trust.

I made my way over to the dunes, thinking about how we could convey this weak man to the main settlement of the Canti Tribe. It was not far, but walking any distance seemed to tire him no end, and his gait was unsteady over rough ground, rendering him liable to further injury.

Cade's horse appeared to be our only hope. With a germ of an idea forming, I headed back towards the fire.

Renowden stood over our sleeping Metern and jogged him with his foot. "Hey, mighty Chieftain. I bring fresh food." Slung over his shoulder was a number of fat pollack hanging from a length of rope threaded through their gills. Such happy tidings for the early morn. Renowden and Tallack set about cleaning and gutting the fish, while Suliaman's men pushed the statue out of the fire using sturdy poles and banked it up with more wood.

Cade took his horse to fresh water and returned for his share of the white fish flakes, served hot on a flat rock. He peered up at the grinning sculpture with the extra-long arms. "What's all this about?" He curled his lip at the sinister object and then looked at me for an answer. I had no explanation for this peculiar item. The guards brushed it down and left it to cool. Its face was almost enough to put me off my food. The position of its right hand appeared to be important.

The Prince caught me examining the statue between mouthfuls. Initially he just smiled. He'd already ascertained how curious I was. After a little while, he pointed to the icon and then mimicked its long-tangled arms with his own, before resting his right hand on the sore on his neck.

Was he trying to tell me that this creepy effigy was supposed to represent him? He pointed again at the statue and then himself. It started to make sense. In his homeland, they believed that they can pass their illnesses and curses onto clay figures of themselves. I grinned at him, nodding my head.

It was a far stretch to think that a man can be made from clay and then be used to cast out demons. My understanding of the object was later confirmed, when a guard came back from the dunes wrestling a large gull. It struggled and pecked at the man, but he would not let it go. With one arm clamped about its body and his hand squeezing tightly around its neck, he handed the creature over to Maleek.

The old man lifted himself from his chair and staggered over to the statue. Helping himself to Maleek's curved blade, he uttered a series of words in a single tone, closing his eyes as he chanted. We stood in silence, recognising another's religious rites mid ceremony. His guards and healer clustered around, listening to the incantation in their mother tongue.

I leaned over to Jago. "What are they saying?"

He whispered back. "It's old magic, Fur Benyn. Better you do not know."

Maleek raised the flapping creature over the grinning icon, exposing the throat of the white bird to his father. The blade made a squelching noise as it pierced the gullet, spilling blood, raw fish and bile all over the statue. The stench sent me reeling. In the sizzling blood, Suliaman used the tip of the blade to paint a symbol onto its forehead. The heat from the baked clay cooked the gull's blood, sending it dark brown and crispy. While those of us from Inglond's shore looked on, the foreigners all knelt in the sand muttering their prayers.

The thing that shocked me the most was Jago's reaction. He too fell to his knees, holding his eyelids shut with a screwed-up expression across his face. I have seen that look before. The boy was petrified. What had Suliaman brought to life in this eerie statue?

When the Prince had completed his ritual, he ordered his men to their feet and issued new instructions. Two of the guards ran over the dunes and out of sight. Others began packing away all their bedding and provisions. We were getting ready to move. Cade caught up with events and ran off to collect his horse.

Tallack gave his men orders to return to our tribe with the traded copper. "Brea, you will sail with them. Tell Blydh what I have planned to do and that I know he will protect our lands in my absence. This trade alliance is too good an opportunity to miss."

Brea jutted out a hip and rested her knuckles to her waist. "I'll do no such thing, and you can't make me."

"Brea, we've had this argument before. I am the Chieftain now. You will return to Dumnoni lands." He grabbed her arm and pulled her out of earshot from the others. I could still catch their words. I may be old but I am not deaf.

"You could be gone for many moons, maybe a whole cycle. Do you expect me to wait for you in the mining settlement?"

"No, of course not…"

"Your mother once told me that they have a holy man in the Canti compound."

"So?"

"Bind with me tonight, or by the gods I'll leave you."

"Kyjya, Brea!" Tallack growled. They stared at each other with the kind of intensity that only lovers can achieve. Hers was tinged with a longing to harness his status and power. His was pure frustration. She was not going to back down. Tallack shook his head. "Do what you want. You will anyway." He marched away, leaving her with the impression that he'd conceded to her desires. I wasn't so sure. The first thing he did was to seek out Maleek and offer his help in clearing away their belongings.

She waited for a moment, adjusting her hair and clothing, before picking up her bundle and sitting in the sand to wait for us. Suliaman's men returned from the direction of the dunes carrying four long, thick hazel poles from the trees further inland. Suliaman sat back in his tall chair. The poles were slid beneath the legs, allowing his guards to hoist him in the air. Using a similar arrangement, the bloodied idol was lifted onto a length of thick fabric and attached to the other two poles. With his remaining guards each carrying their supplies and treasures, they nodded to Cade to lead the way.

Brea appealed to Cade for his pony, claiming that she was our new tribal Ruvane, and as such, deserved the horse more than any other. His answer was in the form of an action. He gathered up the reins and led his horse over to me.

"Ho there, Fur Benyn. Come on, I'll give you a bunk up." Cade interlocked his fingers and bent low so that I could tread in his hands while he lifted me onto his horse.

"That's really good of you, Cade. Thanks." I couldn't contain my grin. Brea seethed, but there was little that she could do or say. Later I saw her ranting at Tallack, but he shrugged her off. With my heavier items slung across the horse and Jago stumbling along beside me, we followed Cade and Tallack in a long procession across the dunes and flat homesteaders' lands, past woods and copses to a large settlement inhabited by the new Chieftain and his family.

The Cantii have several favoured settlement sites, all within easy distance of the sea. Some are heavily fortified against incursions at the border with the Regnenses Tribe to their west. They, like us, have a similar relationship with periods of tolerance followed by more volatile times. Our abiding friendship was forged during my father's reign. Since then, our families have maintained firm ties via wedlock. Cryda's brother is their Chieftain now, following her father's death.

Cade informed us that the Chieftain's family were encamped at a large settlement on the Great Stour River. Its winding meanders made it awkward to navigate, thus rendering it useless to hasten travel. There was no other way but to walk to the site, carrying all our belongings without ponies, that is, except for me.

With a few rest stops, we made it to camp just after sunset. The compound walls were high and had an extra barrier of spiked ramparts and ditches. The river flowed beneath their walls and through the centre before dipping under the opposite side. Both causeways were protected with the trunks of young trees stabbed into the riverbed to bar anyone from swimming into the camp.

Their gate watchmen signalled our arrival by blowing a horn from a goat. The gates opened, allowing us entry into a wide grassy space next to a Long Hut. It looked almost the same as ours had, before it was ransacked and burned to the ground. There were raised boardwalks crossing one long thoroughfare that were far wider than ours. In short, they had spent a great deal more time improving their camp conditions than we had. I hoped that it gave Tallack a few ideas for when we returned home to the River Exe.

Cade's family were there to greet us. The new chieftain, Arundel, stepped forwards to Tallack and touched their foreheads together.

"Uncle. Thank you for receiving us. I was sorry to hear about grandfather. He sits with Cernonnus in the Summerlands, along with my father." Tallack moved along the row of well-wishers, and stopped at a frail woman, whom I barely recognised, her hair now white, her eyes rheumy and pale. Tallack reached down to her and scooped her up in his arms, squeezing her tightly. "Grandmother." He kissed the top of her head and lowered her back to her feet.

She gave him a playful smack across his shoulders. "Put me down, you'll break me." She meant not a word of her admonishment. Smiling she lay her hand on his chest. No one could dispute his likeness with her departed husband. It both pained and comforted her in equal measure.

I clambered down from Cade's horse and let Jago unload my things. Clicking the joints in my hips and back, I took a moment to right myself. Brea saw this as her opportunity to make herself heard. She pushed past me and walked straight up to Arundel, reaching out for his arm in greeting. Tallack looked on in horror at her lack of propriety, but there was little he could do to stop her. These formalities may seem unnecessary, but they have helped to maintain order and social structure in tribes for generations.

Arundel was left in an awkward position. He should have welcomed me as the next with Metern blood after Tallack. Being the gracious host, he tamed his look of shock and received her intruding arm against his own with gritted teeth. He said nothing, waiting for her to work her way down the line before me.

Brea moved on to Tallack's grandmother, Hylda. She puffed out her little chest and frowned at the interloper. She may be frail in body, but she was no weakling.

"I know you. I've seen you before at the summer gatherings. You're that mountain trollop of Aebba's." Hylda withdrew her arms and folded them across her chest.

"I am no trollop. I am to be the next Ruvane of the Dumnonii." Brea practically shouted her retort, ensuring the entire tribe heard her.

"Over my dead body." Hylda exclaimed, snorting her derision. She turned around on the board walk, and stomped her noble feet across the planks into the Long Hut.

Brea was left high and dry, looking the shameless fool that she is. Tallack grinned at her misstep, and made no attempt to rescue her. I greeted the Chieftain according to time honoured traditions, with a humble smile on my face and bearing a gift of furs and tin, but inside my heart was pounding with fear. Hylda may have predicted her own near future. I know full well what Brea does when she is upset with her social standing.

CHAPTER TWELVE

You can always rely on Tallack to sooth emotions and calm frayed tempers. Aebba did well choosing him to lead his trading voyages. The lad can negotiate just about anything with just about anyone. I watched him from the corner of my eye as he made the proper introductions with all the tribal elders. He paid special attention to Arundel's new young wife, complimenting her tunic and sewn embellishments.

Tallack's shrewd ways were not lost on the Chieftain. He sent his son, Cade into the Long Hut to divulge all that he'd learned about our foreign travelling companions to Hylda, while he offered the Prince his hospitality. Jago ran from one group to the next and back again, doing all he could to translate messages of greeting and welcome.

After such a bumpy ride I was keen to stretch my legs, but I knew that the duties of being a guest would entail a long night of feasting and talking. Brea stood idle at the end of the line of elders. Her young years had not prepared her in the ways of a Ruvano. She had no idea what her place was or how to conduct herself. Tallack completed his ceremonial offerings with jewels and a fine beaver pelt for the Chieftain's wife, before taking Brea by the arm and dragging her to a quiet spot at the side of the Long Hut. I lingered in the doorway, keen to hear what he had to say.

"You have utterly disgraced yourself, Brea. I told you to go home." He rasped at her, trying to keep the anger from exploding out.

"And I told you that we are to be bound together, regardless of what that nasty old crone says."

Surely, she had surmised his altered feelings for her? Had her desperation mired her sight to that extent?

"That old crone, is my grandmother. She is from the longest line of Chieftains in the land. You'll go in and apologise, then pay tribute to her. That bracelet the Prince gave you should suffice."

Brea looked aghast. She covered the golden bangle with her hand, shielding it from him. "No, I will not. She insulted me. She should be giving me apologies and gifts. Now go and find the holy man, I don't want to wait for us to wed."

"You can forget that. I'm more likely to bind myself to that kyjyan statue than you. It'll never happen. If you're going to stay, make amends. If not, go, and never return here."

It was a dangerous ultimatum to give to someone as murderous as Brea. Whatever she decided would not result in a happy outcome for Tallack. I was still in the doorway and at risk of discovery. There were only so many times that I could pretend to adjust my shoe before the Canti elders insisted that the door panel be wedged in the opening to shut out the draught.

It looked to me that Brea had turned on the tears to engender pity, but Tallack would not soften. Perhaps she'd used the ploy too often in the past, for she spun about, flicking her hair into his face and stomped down the boardwalks towards Cade's pony. "I'll go, and then you'll be sorry." She bawled over her shoulder. Still he was unmoved. "I'm leaving." As the door panel rose and blocked out my view, I saw him roll his eyes at her. A moment later, the thundering hooves of a single pony quietened the room. Brea had stolen Cade's horse.

Flushed and panting, Tallack pushed through the gap in the doorway and approached me. "Good riddance." He muttered. I could understand his relief even if it meant coughing up enough tin to pay for her theft, but she was dangerous before he slighted her. Only Jago and I knew her true capabilities, and that would always end in sadness or worse.

Cade beckoned me over to sit at his side. It was a great honour for me, since he was the next in line to become Chieftain as the eldest son of Arundel. Their tables and seating arrangements were much the same as ours, but they allowed their guests to outrank those close family members, who were only too happy to move further from the top table for a short duration. To the left of Arundel, sat the Prince and his son, with Jago standing behind them all, doing his best to keep up with the conversation.

As I predicted, the Cantii used this opportunity to extend the alliance we had brokered to include themselves. Arundel spent most of the evening discussing potential goods trades and frequency of trips with the Prince. The details and complexities were left to lowlier members of the tribe.

Hylda tapped Cade on the shoulder and asked him to swap seats, so that she could speak quietly with me. I had a feeling that she would cut to the core of the matter, but I thought she might prefer Tallack's sweet words over mine.

"Meliora. I am pleased to see you here. Was the journey tolerable?"

A polite start to my grilling, but I played along. "A storm on the crossing to Frynk, but a better return, thank you. You look well. Are you in good health?"

"Must we waste time with petty ailments and wearisome banter?" One brow lifted high on her forehead. She was no older than I, but her bearing and manner seemed more aged than the hills. In truth, she intimidated me a little. Brea was stupid indeed to take on such a formidable woman. This must be from where Cryda gets her stubbornness. I shook my head.

"Good. My grandson tells me that you have brought a cursed foreigner into our camp. Is he likely to harm any of us? Do we need to double the guards?" Hylda said, ever the practical one.

"As far as I can tell, it's not that kind of curse. He is not violent or demented, he does not lash out or channel demons. This is a curse of illness. He weakens daily and suffers great pain. He's no threat to us. In fact, I believe that his homeland is beyond our imagining of wealth. Forging an alliance with these men could bring prosperity to both our tribes."

She listened to my account and nodded. "Yes, that's what my son thinks too. Look at him simpering at the purple Prince. You'd think that dying fabric an unusual colour makes the man a god."

I snorted loud enough to garner attention. She always was a hoot at summer gatherings in the past.

"How fares my daughter? I hear I have another grandchild now."

For a moment, I wondered whether I should direct her to Jago, who knew more about the babe than ever I did since he was there at the birth, but I held my tongue. The Cantii are not so easy minded with their slaves as us Dumnonii. If he spoke out of turn in this Long Hut, he was likely to receive a beating for his efforts. Instead, I took my time in explaining how bonny the new child was and that Cryda had still not settled on a name for her.

"Shame about Aebba." She said, leaning back on her bench. She lifted the ale jug and poured more into my cup. "He was a fair man and a fierce warrior."

"He was." My reply was more tearful than I expected it to be. I croaked through my grief. "He will rest in the Summerlands with Hale. Did you have his burial rites in his ancestors' barrow, or succumb to these new burning rituals?"

"We buried him. You said, he *will* rest. Does that mean that Aebba is still above ground?" Not much gets past her quick mind.

I thought carefully about my response. "His skull is interred in the Great Barrows at Stonehenge. Cryda keeps his long bones with her until she is satisfied that a monumental quoit can be built on Higher Tor for him."

"Hmm. She was a sentimental child. Sounds like she hasn't altered much." Hylda murmured. I had no answer for her. Cryda and I had become close over the last few moons in the mining settlement near to Land's End. It was hard for me to hear of her spoken of in such scornful tones. I had the notion that she'd never quite approved of Cryda binding to Aebba. For why, I could not say, since Aebba and the Dumnonii were known to be the wealthiest of all the tribes in the land. What mother wouldn't want a secure place for her daughter? But then, he was not named Aebba the Wild for nothing. Perhaps she knew of his younger more wilful days while I was back in camp and away from the tall tales of his ill-advised gambles. I let the matter drop, choosing to steer the topic back to our quest.

Hylda had much to say about that too. "Cade tells me that you plan to ride all the way to the stones at the top of the world. You should have told the foreigner that the stones of the Seven Sister's in your region had the same healing effects, or even the Men an Tol. At least then you could have shoved him through the round stone and be done with all the travelling. Not to mention that biting cold up there. You must be out of your mind."

"It didn't occur to me at the time, and I had no way of knowing that he would ask us to take him there." It mattered little how I said it, Hylda made everyone seem idiotic. She had that interminable smugness old women get sometimes. It made me realise how I must sound to others when I am annoyed. I was starting to wish I was back on the beach with Renowden's fresh catch of pollack.

Tallack rose from his bench and wandered over to us. "Catching up on old times, grandmother?"

She melted as he approached. Gone was the sour tongue and pinched face. "Dear boy. How proud we are of you and Blydh, working out your differences and sharing the role of Chieftain."

His face dropped from the jovial clown to that of a concerned Metern. "It came at a steep price."

I knew precisely what he meant. Hylda looked puzzled. It was then I realised that she had not heard about her granddaughter's bid for supremacy. How Wenna directed her husband and warriors of the Durotriges Tribe to attack our settlements while we were all away at the midsummer gathering, or how she lost her life in the process. The whole event was still raw to me. I couldn't face hearing it again, and so excused myself and went outside.

The night air was chilly, but a welcome relief from the warm smells around the Long Hut fire. When I turned the corner onto the planking, I spotted Jago outside too.

He hurried over to me. "Fur Benyn, is everything alright?"

"Yes, I'm fine. I just needed a breather from the Cantii intensity."

"They were unkind to you?" Bless him, he didn't understand my meaning. I smirked and he let the comment go.

"The big Chief here is trying to take over your quest."

"How do you mean?"

"I was helping the Prince and his son to understand Chief Arundel's speech. After a while, he said that he'd like Cade to go with you on the trip."

"He probably means as a guide, to help broker a deal with the tribe north of here."

"Hmm, no I don't think so. He offered a lot of warriors and horses to go along too, so that you and Metern Tallack can return home."

"Is that so? Was Tallack listening to this at the time, or was this a private conversation between Arundel and Suliaman?"

"It was private."

That backstabbing brute. I thought that he would be an ally in this venture, not cut us out entirely. This situation needed careful handling if we were to retain control and garner Arundel's support with horses and supplies. I returned to the Long Hut, positioning Jago behind the top table as my spy. No one thought it odd that he was there, since the Prince had grown used to his skill with languages.

When I thought that the Cantii were all busy eating, drinking and chatting amongst themselves, I pulled my nephew aside and told him about the plot.

"Are you sure Jago understood Arundel's meaning? I can't see him being so underhanded."

"Can you not? The last time you saw him, he was an amiable uncle biding his time until his father gave up the Chieftain's seat. You only ever saw the best side of him.

Hylda tells me that petty jealousies and squabbling began the moment old Hale died. It sounds like it was worse than your Metern trial against your brothers. Arundel and your Uncle Lewin fought in single combat."

"I wondered why I had not seen him about."

"No, and I wouldn't stir things up by mentioning the outcome either. Your younger uncle died in disgrace. They buried him in an unmarked pit next to the midden pile." There was more than a hint of similarity between his own brother, Paega's behaviour. I didn't need to point it out to him. The difference being that Paega lived in exile. Who knows if the boy will find a way to wreak his revenge?

Tallack pulled a face. "Even still, I can't let them take this opportunity away from us. I have to say something."

I agreed. There was a need to clear the air and stand firm on our agreement. If the Prince abandoned us now, it would speak volumes about his character as a trade partner.

Hylda was at the top table whispering into her son's ear. Every little while, she looked up at Tallack or me as she spoke. Her expressive brows were enough for me to realise that she was encouraging Arundel to force the Prince's hand.

I turned to Tallack. "The sooner you raise the subject the better."

He nodded to me and stood up with his cup raised. "Let us drink to our hosts in appreciation. True friends, true family and strong allies." A roar of cheering followed and then a supping silence as everyone around drank their ale.

Tallack was not done. "To Arundel the Angry, may our continued alliance be an honest and fruitful one." There was more cheering and supping. Hylda shot me a glare in warning. I had undermined her attempts to carry off the Prince. Arundel himself, wore a look of annoyance at having his plans ruined. He gazed at Jago, knowing full well that he'd been the source of our information.

"Tell me, Uncle…" Tallack yelled above the clamour. "Do you wish that you were embarking on a trip such as ours yourself? Do you yearn for your early days of hunting and raiding?" We all knew that he was goading a response, but would his reaction be in anger, or diffused in mirth?

Maleek sat by his father's side, analysing the stiffness of Arundel's posture. If I had to guess, I'd say that the young foreigner was picking up our words quicker than Jago could translate them. He whispered into the Prince's ear, who kept his sight fixed on the two Chieftain's before him.

For a moment, I thought I saw a flash of temper cross Arundel's face. If it was there, he did well to temper it, for he plastered a fake smile on his lips and stood up to match Tallack's forthrightness.

"I am not that old, Nephew. I am still a warrior and more than capable of whipping your arse should the need arise." He grinned to his elders and their families. They in turn rapped the tables and stamped their feet in support. "In truth, I do miss the travels and adventures. Now it is the duty of my sons to patrol the borders and forge new trade links. If it pleases you, Cade will act as your guide through the next territory. We have strong ties with the Catuve-Llauni north of here. Now that our mines are in working order again, we can supply a copper trove in tribute to them."

Tallack listened to the carefully worded response. The Chieftain made certain to mention the plentiful metals that would lessen the Dumnoni reliance on the mountain tribe source of copper and remove the need for the agreement with the Prince. I watched my nephew mull over the information. It would not do to antagonise our hosts by accusing them of a plot against us. I hoped that he would steer the course carefully.

"Uncle Arundel, it gladdens my heart to hear that your copper deposits are worked efficiently once again. Our great families can provide the whole world with the means to forge bronze. We should sit down and plan out our long term aims for such a profitable alliance." Tallack stopped speaking, waiting for a sign that the Cantii favoured an accord rather than hostility.

The pause was heavy with possibility. Tallack held his nerve and his cup high in expectation. When all was said and done, the Cantii still needed our tin. We held the upper hand.

"Fill my nephew's cup. We have a lot to celebrate." Arundel leaned across the table with his ale held out for Tallack to knock against his own. It was the closest thing to victory. I breathed deeply, in realisation that I'd been holding in stale air the whole time.

Hylda huffed her disgust. She was more ambitious than I'd credited her with. While the elders and our few men drank and cheered and filled their cups alongside the foreigners, she glowered just a short distance from my table.

When at last the noise died down, the old woman rose to her feet and pointed a bony finger directly at the Prince. "You'll bring pain to my family and to those we call our friends. You mark my words; this curse will be the death of us all."

CHAPTER THIRTEEN

The feast did not continue for long after the shocking outburst of their wise woman of the tribe. Her words carried weight, especially with the elders, who made their excuses and left the Long Hut through fear and a growing sense of foreboding. Arundel made no attempt to gain say his mother, choosing to ignore her warning and covering his anxiety with more ale and raucous songs.

Tallack was quiet for the rest of the night. He brooded over the accusation and forbade Jago from translating to the Prince. When even the hardiest of revellers had supped their fill, furs and blankets were brought into the Long Hut and the tables and benches were stacked to one side. Jago busied himself, filling sacks with grasses and straw to lay on the rushes next to the fire.

I could tell that he was avoiding both Tallack and the Prince, choosing to see to my comfort before all else. His furtive glances towards Maleek and the Prince troubled me. His reactions in their presence were strained and twitchy. Catching him before he left the hut for more bedding, I asked why he was uneasy.

"It's nothing, great lady. I will bring your kit to rest by your furs."

"Out with it, boy. I know when you're dodging me."

"The Prince has asked for another animal to sacrifice. Something bigger than a seagull, since his last offering did not stop the sore on his neck from spreading."

I peered over at the Prince. Maleek was stirring more poppy resin into the liquid in his father's cup. Suliaman's robes were pulled up over his shoulders, covering his throat. Either his vanity prevented him from revealing the extent of his curse or he feared that the Cantii would send him packing with such visible signs of suffering.

"Here, pass me my bag. I'll give you some tin grains. Go and see if you can find someone to trade for a chicken." Jago lifted my kit bag onto my lap. Digging in among the beakers and jars sealed with wax, I searched for what was left of my tin. The pouch had gone. I frowned up at Jago. "Have you moved my tin purse?"

"No, Fur Benyn. I haven't touched your kit since we left the beach."

Fearing the worst, I pulled out my knife wrap and unwound the leather folds. Each of my fine bronze knives appeared from the smallest chisel to almost my largest blade. The biggest of all was missing.

Jago held up his hands in supplication. "I haven't taken it I promise. Please believe me, Fur Benyn. I would never steal from you."

"Calm yourself, boy. I know that." I sighed a long, exasperated breath. "You know who has got it though, don't you?"

Jago nodded slowly. "The Lady Brea."

I wondered how she intended to cross so many tribal lands on Cade's horse without any metal, barring the gold bracelet, to her name. It's a dangerous and long ride back to our homelands. She would have need of both my blade and my tin. If she does make it back to the River Exe in one piece, I had no doubt of her plans for Tallack's twin,

Blydh. We had set loose a desperate woman with no qualms about killing to achieve her aims.

I sent a brief message to the gods to keep him safe from her in our absence. The one thing Blydh had in his favour was a general lack of trust for anyone who was not Tallack or his mother. Perhaps that will be enough to preserve him.

I sought out my nephew and told him of Brea's sticky fingers and the need to barter for a sacrificial bird. He shook his head in despair at her boldness and threw a pouch of his own tin over to me in recompense. With Jago on the lookout for a chicken in the dead of night, I watched the foreigners carry in the long armed, grinning statue and place it next to the fire in pride of place. The blood from the gull still stained its ghoulish face.

Suliaman's warriors and servants knelt in front of the object and lowered their outstretched arms and heads to the rushes on the ground. A resonant metal drum was struck. The echo was hypnotic. The gong sounded a second time and Suliaman lifted himself from his tall chair and began to intone a prayer in his mother tongue. It lasted for such a long time. The drone lulled me into a trance like state.

Jago appeared shortly after, clutching a live cockerel by the feet and fending off its sharp beak with his fist. When he heard the incantation, Jago fell to his knees trembling. The chicken escaped his clutches, flapping about the stacked tables to roost. Maleek crouched low and dragged it by the neck to the statue. The curved blade was unsheathed again and the squawking bird was no more.

I'd dearly love to know what the Prince chanted, since the effect on Jago was profound. No amount of coaxing would induce him to tell me. Jago remained rooted to the floor long after the Prince had completed his ritual.

Maleek approached me and bowed his head a little to speak with me.

"My father, please." He gestured to his neck and then pointed to my kit bag. I knew what he was asking of me. Suliaman required more soothing burdock root.

Nodding, I grabbed my kit and gave Jago a shove. "Get up, lad. It's all done with. Stop hiding and sort out the bedding."

Repeating the respectful head bow, I stood in front of the Prince and mimed the action of removing the material covering his neck. This he did with a little help from Maleek. The sore was weeping and much larger. With such an open wound, I feared that the burdock root might make things worse. Picking up the bundle, I pushed it away with my other hand and shook my head, dropping the burdock to the ground. The Prince frowned at me. From inside my bag, I took out a pot sealed with wax. It contained plantain and honey paste, mixed with goose grease. I chipped off the seal with my thumb and smeared a little onto the back of my hand, before pointing at his neck.

Suliaman's healer stepped forwards. I could tell by his gruff manner that he was warning the Prince against using my ointments. It was understandable. I am a foreigner to them, although if we were to wish him harm, we would have attacked while Tallack's men were still on the beach and outnumbered their warriors. It mattered little though, since Suliaman waved his healer away and nodded at my little jar of balm.

Shuffling closer, I gently applied some of the grease to the sore on his neck. I admit, the recipe is one of my mother's and she would always complain about the stink. Maleek held his nose and pretended to cough. We all chuckled at his antics, especially Tallack. The closer I got to the Prince, the more I noticed peculiar symptoms. The lids of his eyes were pale and thin on the outside and yet, red raw on the inside. It was the same around the holes of his nose. This curse appears to attack a body from the inside out. What witchcraft could summon such powers?

When I'd finished treating him, I turned to Maleek and gave him the entire pot. By this time, our gestures and mimes were becoming a language all of their own. I clasped my hands together at the side of my face, closed my eyes and pretended to sleep. When I opened them, I stretched and yawned and then pointed to the balm before wiping my finger against my neck. He understood. The plantain paste would need reapplication morning and night.

I say he understood, but Maleek wasn't paying me much attention. Tallack had caught his eye from across the Long Hut. They exchanged knowing glances that went undetected by almost everyone. I know these flights of fancy well. My nephew has a liking for pretty young women, and pretty young men. That, I have no problems with, but this is not your everyday pretty man. Maleek is the heir to the Prince's kingdom. They are powerful and extremely wealthy. An entanglement of a frivolous nature could reap tragedy later.

Scowling at my nephew did nothing to curb his behaviour. In fact, he barely noticed my loud tutting or my severe frown. Maleek paid me no heed either. He passed the small jar to the Prince's warrior servant, and smiling, he moved the door panel and stepped out into the night. Without a backward look, Tallack dropped his cup on an upturned table and followed him. That boy has no shame. What if the coupling of men is an offence in the Prince's homeland? What if their union damned the pair of them for all time?

I fretted and drank warm ale. Sitting wrapped in my furs opposite that repellent statue, I feared the end of the world. It was only after three more cups and some stale bread and cheese that they returned, flushed in the face and giggling like children. Twisting myself around to see the Prince's reaction, I found him fast asleep. His guards did not move a muscle. I couldn't fathom whether it was sheer luck that the Prince had taken too much resin water to notice or whether it was deemed acceptable practice. Either way, my nephew needs to be more discreet in future.

The night wore on and I eventually slept. Jago jogged me awake after dawn when almost all of our things were packed and loaded onto horses on the grassy area outside the Long Hut. It would seem that while I dreamed of curses and demons and grinning statues, Tallack was up early negotiating a compromise with Chief Arundel.

"The deal is simple." Tallack muttered to me as I mounted a white horse stacked with bags of food and my belongings. "I have agreed to extend any trading voyages to include a stop at their primary port, before sailing for Frynk. That way, I can carry Uncle Arundel's goods as well as our own."

"And in return we get a Chief's son to guide us plus a few horses. That doesn't seem like a fair deal to me." I grumbled in an equally low tone.

"It isn't, but I shall arrange for the trip to go ahead as agreed and delay the delivery of any return goods. By the time he gets his hands on the Prince's exotic provisions, the fresh stuff will have gone bad. If we continue to drag out the process, he'll decide that the effort is not worth the long wait for a return on investment."

"You know you're craftier than you look."

He grinned and treated me to a knowing wink. "Right now, that deal has ensured that we retain control of this trip and become Inglond's first trade partner with the

Prince's people." Tallack threw his leg up onto the horse behind me. Jago held the pony still by its reins.

"Don't get too full of yourself. We still have to cross more than five tribal territories before we can deliver our promise, and that's a lot of tributes and raiding parties to avoid."

Our procession was surprisingly large when all of Suliaman's warriors and treasures were loaded onto a cart or the ponies. Tallack rode alongside the wagon that carried the Prince and attached a long hazel pole with a white square of fabric tied at the top. It was the agreed symbol for all tribes in Inglond. It showed scouts and border guards that we were on a peaceful pilgrimage and intended no trouble or harm.

Of course, the banner was often misused, making scouts mistrust the symbol prompting their Chiefs to investigate. Others had successfully crossed tribal lands under the white flag only to cast it aside and launch an attack on fortified compounds when it suited them. In short, the banner was no longer trusted. Cernonnus only knew what those barbarians up in Skotek do to those passing through, whether they bore the flag of truce or not.

Arundel made sure that his eldest son was journeying with us. In the unfortunate event that either Tallack or I fell foul to marauders, Cade would be there to step into the breach and take over the entire trading partnership on behalf of the Cantii. For the whole morning's ride, I churned over Cade's character and the likelihood that he might serve us up to the Catuve-Llauni Tribe at the earliest opportunity.

Maleek and Tallack rode along the track together behind the wagon. Their smiles and jostles were clear to everyone in our party. They were more than firm friends. It is probably just as well that Brea fled. I could easily see her slipping hemlock into Maleek's ale to keep Tallack to herself.

I kicked my heels into my pony, catching up with Cade at the front of our group. "How far is it to the big river on your Northern Border?" I asked.

"At this speed, more than two days. We might be lucky, but it's likely we'll have to go around some of the boggier areas."

I didn't like the sound of that. I'd heard from my father once, that the Cantii were great fishermen. Their rivers wound in loops and bends, and often overflowed into the meadow lands and forests. The region was bordered to the west by their enemies, the Regnenses Tribe who coveted the great river and fought to restrict the Cantii from its banks.

"Can we still cross on your territory?" It was a rude question, one that accused them of losing land to a more ruthless tribe. Cade was sent to ease our way. If the Great River was too wide for our ponies, then we had two options left to us. Either we paid the boatmen to take us across a few at a time, leaving the horses and cart on the southern bank, or we ventured into the Regnenses land to find a narrower crossing.

Cade sucked his teeth, pulling an odd face as he considered his answer. "My scouts tell me that the Regnenses are all overwintering near to the south coast. We'll be fine inside their borders. They won't even know that we've passed through."

I could see that whatever I asked him, he would give me a dulled version of the truth, but that was a problem for later. Pulling up on the reins, I slowed my white steed until I drew level with the Prince's cart. Jago sat next to the giant warrior servant steering the horses. His eyes were fixed on the trail ahead, his posture taut and anxious.

"How's the Prince doing?" I asked Jago. At first, he pretended not to hear me, cupping his hand to his ear and threatening to jump down from the front of the wagon. I yelled it a second time, adding for him to stay in his seat.

"It's no trouble for me to walk, Fur Benyn. I do not deserve such fine treatment."

"You know full well that your lame foot would slow us down. You'll stay on that cart or we'd be forced to leave you behind." I looked at his downcast face. I thought he'd like the chance to speak to others from his region of the world, but he seemed intent on avoiding them. "The Prince?"

"Ah yes. He tries to sleep, but the track is bumpy and his stomach does not settle."

Was it the bumps that made the old man queasy or the over dosing of poppy resin? I'd heard that habitual use can make a man fall for its lure. They can't think of anything except for when they will next obtain more. For a man as wealthy as Suliaman, the supply was limitless. Too much of the stuff addles more than your brain. If he was taking as much as I predicted, there was every chance that the resin would do him in quicker than the curse. I needed to find a soothing mixture of herbs that would take away the sickness as well as calm his wits. Why the old man even bothered to bring a healer as useless as his is beyond me. The man did nothing but bleed out the Prince's humours or warm his feet in hot water.

My kit bag of Frynkish medicines ran low of hops. I needed more supplies but none of the things I required grew at this wretched time of the year. Riding back to Cade, I asked him where I might replenish my stocks.

He didn't answer me straight away. It was as though he was weighing up how desperate my need was for healing herbs. "Can't you wait till spring comes and collect your own?"

"The Prince needs our help now, and anyway, what if you or Tallack need an ointment or two? Do you know of a healer in your lands who might trade with us?"

He rubbed his chin and bit at his bottom lip. "There are tales of a woman on the eastern fringes of the marshes, between two tributaries of the Swale, but no one ever goes there. Rumour has it that she keeps a pack of wolves to chase off intruders and eats babes in payment for her services."

I stifled a laugh. "She sounds as though she is fed up with people taking advantage of her kindness. I wonder if the same is said about me across Dumnoni lands? Lead the way, Cade. We won't get far if the Prince is too sick to travel."

He grumbled and muttered under his breath.

"You're surely not frightened of the old healer, are you?" I couldn't believe what I was seeing. A grown man, proven warrior and heir to the Cantii, was too scared to approach an old medicine woman in the marshes.

"No, for kyjyan sake. It'll take us way off course that's all, and I was hoping to make camp further along our route tonight."

It was a lame excuse. I yelled over to Tallack, explaining the reason for our diversion. He hardly acknowledged me at all. He and Maleek were busy learning a new and mysterious language of their own, not all of which was spoken.

After a brief stop at the end of a large forest, I grabbed a few evergreen items I thought might come in handy and mounted my horse. Heading north-east, we veered away from the trodden path towards the marsh lands. It was mid-afternoon, and the light was dimming fast. On we trudged, through boggy fields until we reached a riverbank that ended with a large pond.

Cade dismounted. “We stop here for the night. Can’t take the horses and cart any closer.”

“How far away is the medicine woman? I’d like to treat the Prince tonight if I can.” I stayed on my horse, hoping to change his mind.

“I told you. She lives in the marshes. Just you and I go from here by boat.”

I could see him sulking even in the poor light. Sliding down from my horse, I walked across the path to where Jago sat on the wagon, and handed him the reins. “Make sure he’s fed and watered, would you? I’ll go with Cade to get the medicine.”

“Are you sure that you should go, Fur Benyn? I heard the warnings he gave about the strange lady.” Jago looked worn out and in need of a good night’s sleep.

“You think I’m frightened by tall tales? I bet she’s exactly like me.” As the words left my mouth, a deep incessant howl rose from the marshes.

CHAPTER FOURTEEN

Jago's eyes almost popped out of his skull. The lengthy howl lessened in noise and then stopped.

"By all the gods," I tutted. "It's just a wolf. She's probably got one tamed from birth as a pet. That'll be where the rumours come from." I took the tin pouch that Tallack had given me from my bag and tucked it into a pocket in my cloak. Another howl started. This time, it was joined by several other wild hounds. Each tone blended into one chilling noise and the inescapable fact that the medicine woman did keep a pack of wolves.

"See." Cade said, taking his short sword and wooden shield from his horse. "I'll go and find a boat."

Tallack glanced over at his cousin. Their unspoken exchange prompted him to slide from his horse's back. "I'm coming with you. There are enough guards to keep the Prince safe.

I didn't argue with him. After all my brash disregard of their rumours, I was ashamed how scared I felt. The Prince's guards made camp and started a number of fires. I left Jago with my medicine kit and instructions to help Suliaman's servants with our meal preparation and followed Cade and Tallack to the riverbank. The pair of us waited while Cade wandered upstream to a hut on stilts. By the light of our torches, we could see a dugout boat moored alongside. With a considerable amount of copper exchanged from Cade's purse, its owner permitted our use. Paddling downstream towards us, Cade threw out a rope for Tallack to catch. We boarded and sat in the water collected in the hull.

"Better put your muscles to work boys or we'll sink before we get there." It was my attempt at lightening the tension, but their lack of response told me that it fell on deaf ears. Each of them was concentrating too hard on navigating the tributary downstream, avoiding the rotting masses of bull rushes and weeds collecting in the river. Every so often, the wolf pack would start up their howling. Their echoing cries grew louder the further we paddled.

Holding the lit torch high above my head, I muttered course corrections over my shoulder to guide them as they steered with the oars. As the river widened, the weeds lessened in density, allowing us to speed along with the current towards the ocean. On our left, the boggy land gave way in places to more streams and channels. Without Cade to guide us, I was sure we'd be lost within the marshes. The howling stopped as we rounded a sweeping bend in the river, but the plants on our port side rustled with the movement of animals. The wolves were keeping pace alongside us.

I leaned out to the left with the torch held at arm's length. That was when I first caught a glimpse of their eyes shining back at me. Gasping with the sheer number, I held my composure. I didn't want to alert Tallack and Cade to my fear. Beyond another, tighter bend I could see a fire outside a hut. That had to be our destination, for there were no other dwellings visible in the darkness and the tidal waters were receding. This was the most remote homestead I'd ever seen. Long poles stuck out of the water supporting various animal skulls. Carcasses of crows and rabbits lay in bloodied messes across the grasses - interrupted wolf snacks.

"Where do we land?" I asked, trying to keep the tremor from my voice.

"We don't. The moment we set foot on dry ground; her wolves will rip us to shreds." Cade grumbled. Before I could protest, he called out towards the hut. "Ho there! We come to trade."

We all looked towards the hut, expecting the medicine woman to appear in the doorway. Instead, a croaky voice echoed across the water from behind us on the bank. "Be gone from here. You bring a deathly curse to these marshes."

I snapped my head back to see her silhouetted against the light of the fire. Her shape was not as wizened or frail as I expected. She appeared to be hearty and filled with vigour. A massive black wolf stood at her side, snarling and baring its teeth. I was so entranced by her sight that I had not paid attention to her words.

Tallack had though. "How could she have known about the Prince and his curse? She must truly be a mystical seer."

Cade nodded his agreement. "I told you so. This was a bad idea all around. We should leave before she gives us a curse of her own making."

"I need those supplies. There's bound to be a reasonable explanation for this. She probably has scouts watching our every move and reporting back to her." I said, determined not to be bested by one of my own kind. I shouted above Tallack's head. "Ho there. We are in need of medicine and ingredients. We have metal to trade. Can you help us?"

The snarling and snapping increased. The old woman chuckled at its posturing, patting the evil creature between its ears. "You have made a foolish mistake." We waited for more, but she seemed to have finished her reproach.

"In coming here, you mean?" Cade yelled back.

We'd drifted so close that I could feel the spittle flying from the wolf's maw as it snapped and growled. Her arm shot out in front of her, pointing directly at me. "The dark one you lead will be your undoing. He will take that which you love the most, turning your heart to stone."

"What nonsense." I scoffed. "You saw us coming from quite a distance, didn't you?"

"Don't be so quick to judge, Meliora. Folks around here say she's a powerful seer." Cade rasped and wheezed at me, as though he could stop the old crone from hearing him. It was the first time he'd used my proper name. It pulled me up sharp.

"I need valerian and hops, plus mallow seeds and roots. If you can spare any soured apple juice and dried thistle tops, I'd appreciate a trade for those too." I shouted up to her, ignoring her show of doom.

"You're a healer then?" She said, silencing the wolf with a single hand gesture.

"I am medicine woman to the Chieftains of the Dumnonii, friend to the Cantii. We travel with a foreigner to the Callanish stones at the top of the world." The explanation seemed to alter her defensive stance.

"I've got all that you seek, barring the juice. I can't spare that. Took more than three cycles to make, but I can give you a little of the murky cloud from within it and you can sour your own." She did not move, despite the willingness to trade.

"Appreciate that. We have tin or copper in exchange. Call off your creatures and we'll settle up on the bank there." I said, thrusting my torch towards the drooling wolf.

"No. You stay right there or no deal shall be made. I can bundle your goods and fling them to you. Throw the tin up here and I shall take what is fair."

Tallack grumbled and moaned, tipping out the majority of his tin nuggets into his lap and leaving what he deemed to be a fair quantity. "How can we trust that you'll give us the herbs?"

She shrugged. "Do you want the stuff or not?" Holding out her hand she waited for him to toss over the tin pouch. She was surprisingly nimble as she stepped closer to the edge to catch the metal. With a curt word to the wolf to stay, she turned and walked towards her hut.

"That's the last we'll see of her." Cade muttered.

I snorted at him in annoyance, but I admit, the thought crossed my mind too. We waited for what seemed like forever, hoping that she was true to her word. When Tallack and Cade had all but given up on her ever returning, she appeared in the doorway clutching a number of herb bundles and a wooden lidded beaker sealed with birch sap.

"Hold out your oar." She called out to Tallack. "There ain't no more if you drop it." She warned, balancing one item at a time on the flat of the rowing pole. My nephew gradually pulled the oar in, holding it as steady as he could. Three times this was repeated, until I had all that I needed in my possession.

"Farewell and good trading." I yelled at her as the men made ready to row us back upstream. Before we reached the first bend, she called out to me using our Dumnonii tongue.

"Heed my warning, Fur Benyn. He'll take that which you love most. Don't let him turn your heart to stone."

Her words chilled me to the core. How could she know my Dumnonii nick name? I could barely catch my breath on our way back to camp. I shivered in the front of the boat, trying to hide my discomfort from the men behind me. Was she really a gifted seer, or a malevolent old woman with plenty of spies surrounding us? The men exchanged more than a few glances when they thought I was not watching. Their sly looks and repeated throat clearings put me more on edge than the old woman's caution.

"Out with it." I barked at them, twisting around to sit facing their backs in the boat.

"It's just, how could she possibly know your name, even if she did have scouts watching us?" Tallack said, his voice soft like when he was a little boy and he wanted his own way over something.

"She had to be talking about Suliaman, right? I mean, he seems an alright kind of man even if he has odd customs that we're not used to." Cade said, lifting his oars from the water to let us glide for a while.

When I said nothing, Tallack tried a different approach. "You've spent the most time with him. Do you think he means to harm us when we get further along our journey? His guards outnumber us three to one. We wouldn't stand a chance." None of us moved in the boat. The chilly breeze stilled, allowing us to hear the rush of tidal waters lapping the mud banks on the opposite side. I had spent time with the Prince, and yet learned nothing about him that would suggest he would do us harm. Perhaps there was more to his story about how the curse came about. Maybe he was a tyrant in his homeland or offended his own gods in some way. Shame kept me quiet. I should have learned more about the man before encouraging Tallack to agree to his offer.

Both men looked to me to provide a voice of wisdom and reason. I had no answers to their questions, but their insistent stares forced my hand. “I don’t know. He is generous to a fault and is reliant on our abilities to trade with locals and discuss tributes for passage across tribal lands. I can’t imagine why he would want to hurt any of us.”

“Jago speaks their tongue. He must know more than he is letting on. What has he told you about their ways?” Tallack asked me, twisting around in the boat to reach for my arm.

“That’s just it, Jago won’t speak to me about them at all. He avoids their company when he can and tells me that it is better that we do not know.” I lowered my head. I was ashamed for bringing my family into such potential dangers, no matter the promised rewards.

Cade leaned back and blew out his cheeks. “That doesn’t sound good to me.”

“No, but we made a deal, and we only have a crazed old wolf woman’s word for it that the Prince is bad news. I trust Maleek. He would never do us harm.” Tallack returned his hands to his oars and dipped them back into the water.

Cade shook his head. “Hmm. I think it’d be safer if we had more men to watch our back.”

“Bit late for that. We’ll have to put Jago in the watch rotation at night. That’d be alright wouldn’t it, Aunt Mel?” Tallack asked.

“It would. Put me in the mix too and make sure that you don’t wander off.” I shot him a reproachful glare.

“What do you mean?” He whimpered, although I could tell that he knew precisely what I meant.

“If you can’t keep it in your leggings, I’ll fry up some mallow seeds in a bit of pig fat. That’ll cool your ardour for a while. You might trust Maleek, but I don’t.”

Cade almost choked he snorted so loudly. At least it wasn't only me that had noticed his partiality for the man. Cade seemed fully aware of my nephew's preferences. I was relieved that there was no need to hide it from his cousin. The same could not be said for Suliaman though. None of us knew whether there would be repercussions should their dalliance become common knowledge.

When we reached our setting off point, we clambered up onto the bank and left Cade to return the boat to its owner. Tallack helped me to carry my new stock to the camp site.

Rich smells of spiced meats wafted from the cooking pots. Jago stood next to the horses with my medicine kit slung over his shoulder. His skinny little body shook from the cold.

"What are you doing so far from the fire?" I asked him, puzzled by his behaviour. He didn't respond. His eyes were fixed on the long-armed statue sitting in a central spot.

A young badger cub lay at its base, its throat sliced open to its belly, blood trickled down the face of the idol. Maleek appeared from the rushes behind with wet hair and arms. He stood next to the fire and flicked his head from side to side until droplets of river water flew from him and sizzled in the flames. His fine tunic was covered in red splashes. Another sacrifice was offered to their gods.

I paced closer and pointed to a spot on my neck and then at the Prince sitting in his high chair. Maleek knew what I was asking. I wanted to know if his father's neck sores were worse. The young man shook his head and pinched the fingers on his left hand with the thumb and forefinger of his right. I wasn't sure what he was trying to tell me so looked to Jago for a clue.

"He means that the Prince is suffering from something else. The numbness is spreading from his fingers." Jago said inching backwards with every word. It was something I'd only ever seen with injuries. A warrior with a healed arm might lose his sense of touch lower down.

"Jago, ask the Prince if he has any wounds on his arms."

Suliaman sat in his tall chair with his eyelids drooping. I could tell that he'd taken a considerable amount of poppy resin. Perhaps his fingers were fine after all. The effect would wear off as soon as the resin had stopped working.

Jago shouted my question from the shadows by the horses, refusing to step closer into the fire light. "He says he has no cuts other than the sore on his neck which is not so bad after using your balm. The Prince expresses his gratitude and asks if you have anything to bring his fingers back to him."

I didn't want to upset the foreigner, especially after the wolf woman's warning. Despite the trade with her, my medical supplies were not sufficient to treat him. If we were travelling in midsummer, or we were in my homelands where I know the best spots to harvest plants, I could have helped him. All I could do was to collect some trailing ivy by torchlight and entwine it about Suliaman's highchair and arms.

"Tell him that my gods will protect him this night from evil spirits. This ivy forms a protective barrier from further harm." The Prince allowed me to wind the scratchy vines about him. He seemed to trust my judgement more than that of his own healer.

Tallack drew a blade from a sheath on his hip and stooped to pick up the dead badger. "Not my favourite supper by any stretch, but it'll do in a pinch."

Every single one of Suliaman's guards took out their curved swords, stepping forward in a collective lunge towards him. Their blade stopped just a hair's breadth from his neck.

"What? What did I do?" Tallack shrieked. Cade and I ran towards them, begging them not to harm my nephew.

The tremor in Jago's voice said it all. "No one can touch the offering under penalty of death."

CHAPTER FIFTEEN

Tallack stood stock still. The whites of his eyes almost glowed in the firelight. “What do I do?” He yelled, unable to defend himself against such a force.

“You need to drop the animal, Chief Tallack.” Jago insisted, moving closer for the first time since we got back from the marshes.

Tallack did just that. He opened both hands and the badger along with his knife fell to the ground. The guards did not retract their threat. More than a dozen blades rested next to my nephew’s head.

“Do something!” Tallack screamed at Cade and me.

Jago stepped up to the Prince. He knelt down in front of his chair and spoke quietly to Suliaman in a humble and apologetic tone. Despite the use of resin, the old man heard Jago’s plea. With a small hand gesture, he commanded his guards to put down their weapons. Panting and staggering from shock, Tallack snatched up his knife and scurried away. Cade and I hurried over to see if they had broken his skin, but he was unharmed.

“I think we can safely say that we are travelling with extremely dangerous men.” He sat against a felled tree trunk. I fetched him a cup of ale to settle his nerves. When

I looked back towards the fire, Jago was still on his knees at the Prince's feet. He muttered a continuous sound in a low tone.

"Jago!" I called over to him. "Come here, boy." He did not move. I shouted again and noticed a slight movement to Suliaman's hand. Jago got to his feet and walked over to me. "Didn't you hear me? What did you say to the Prince?"

"I said a prayer to the god, Melkarth." Jago clutched his arms about his middle as if the experience pained him.

"I didn't know that you had a faith. Is he a benevolent god?" We moved behind the empty cart of the Prince to speak privately.

Jago shook his head. "Not at all, Fur Benyn. He is like your Cernonnus, but angrier and harder to please. He rules over all their gods. I am not of their faith, but it is better for everyone if their rituals are respected. To touch a sacrificial offering is the highest blasphemy. It is not unusual for Princes to slaughter the entire family of one who insults the gods, even if they were starving."

"So, these people are not the generous traders we assumed?"

"The Prince thought that the similarities between your name and that of their highest god, Melkarth, was a sign for them to follow you. It may give you a little protection, but not the rest of us."

I poked my head around the edge of the wagon. The badger was returned to the base of the idol and laid out with care. Cade, Tallack and Renowden busied themselves building a second fire away from the Prince and his men to cook the latest catch from the skilled fisherman. My head swam with thoughts of fleeing. We were still on Canti land and relatively safe. There was still time to turn back and put the entire fiasco behind us.

Jago scrutinised my vacant expression. "If you are thinking of going back on your word, Fur Benyn, the consequences could be worse than insulting a god. They may look like simple traders, but they are also fierce warriors. In the warm ocean near my homeland, they have battleships bigger than Chief Tallack's boat. They say that they capture a demon from the underworld and trap it within the bow of the ships. Only its eye can be seen staring out at their enemies. Some vessels have bronze posts attached to the front to ram into attackers' vessels. Do not rile these people, great lady, or we will all suffer."

That put paid to all my thoughts of escape. How could I have been so blind to their real characters. There was sure to be more testing times ahead of us. How would they react under harsher conditions when the Prince was sicker with his curse? I patted Jago's shoulder and gave him a reassuring smile, but it failed to convince him that I was not concerned.

We joined Tallack around his fire and the huge pike Renowden had speared in our absence. Gutted and de-scaled the fish rested high over the flames, its flesh shrinking until the skin peeled and eyes clouded over. That was precisely how I felt, skewered. We could not go back and we were foolish going on. All the time we'd been heading north, our tribe back home was preparing for the battle of a lifetime against our warring neighbours. I looked to Tallack who seemed a little twitchy after his near fatal brush with the Prince's men.

My only consolation was that if anyone could repel the Duros, it would be Blydh. He inspired confidence and courage in his men and abject fear in his enemies. Cernonnus only knows what became of Tallack's half-brother, Paega, sent to roam the moors with the Priest Sect.

My recollections made me homesick, where before I sought only adventure. Now that our fates were sealed, I longed to return to our land all the more. There was little conversation around our fire or that of the Prince's. We ate the muddy tasting flesh from the fish and rolled ourselves in warm furs next to the fire for the night.

Jago and I were on first watch. He picked at the springy bones from the pike carcass and tried to buoy my mood. "We can make the best of this situation. It doesn't have to be bad for us. We will deliver the Prince to those healing stones and Chief Tallack will get his trade deals." Neither of us believed a word of his little talk. It was more likely that the Prince would die before we reached the top of the world and there was no way to know how Maleek would react.

Eventually, Cade took over our watch, leaving Jago and I to sleep in peace knowing that he or Tallack had us protected. Come morning, Suliaman was lifted into the wagon on his chair along with the provisions and leftovers from their meal.

Jago looked at me with those huge doe eyes of his, imploring me not to force him to sit at the front of their cart. I could now see why he feared them. With a flick of my head, he swung a leg up over my horse and rode behind me. Neither of us were much more than skin and bone so it had little impact on the beast. We trotted alongside the wagon having little to say.

When the sun was at its highest point, we stopped to water the ponies and consider our route. Jago was summoned to the cart. The Prince had questions for us, realising that we were heading full west along rough tracks and trails. Cade and Tallack discussed the course and options before us. I was sent to inform the Prince of our decisions.

"We head west, Prince Suliaman, because there are a lot of wide rivers to cross in this part of the world. Further east they are too wide and deep for our horses. Our problem is that if we venture too far west, we might stray into another tribal region, one where tributes and pilgrim flags hold no sway."

Jago did his best to translate, but the general response was a rash one. Suliaman wanted us to pick the fastest route, no matter the cost, whether that was in gold and jewels or our heads. I relayed the message back to Cade and Tallack. They sighed at his belligerence.

"He clearly has no idea of how big the Regnenses Tribe is. They have scores of clans and all are skilled in horseback warfare." Cade warned.

"So, what is our best plan? We can cross this smaller river without entering their territory, but the big one on your northern border is vast." Neither one of them had an answer. It was left hanging in the air like a bad smell as we set off once more for the crossing at Snodland. Cade wanted to make camp as soon as darkness fell, but Maleek insisted that we pressed onto the crossing in the dark.

Our torches picked us out for miles around. If there were any scouts on the western borders, they would surely report us to their clan leaders. Renowden kept us fed and watered, his age and experience with hunting small game had him darting off the track in pursuit of some tasty morsel every other moment. I was glad to have him with us, for he kept our spirits high with his ocean voyage tales and sightings of women with fins like fishes and siren calls taking them perilously close to coastal rocks. By the time we set up camp, he had five plump rabbits swinging from his horse and two ducks.

For the second night in a row, we made separate fires and ate separate meals from our foreign counterparts. Maleek looked over towards Tallack. His forehead was ridged with concern. I thought I saw something in Tallack's features too, a sort of wistfulness as if neither could resist the temptation to be together. Perhaps it was the notion of forbidden fruit, or the danger of being caught together that spurred them on. Either way, Maleek weakened first.

Carrying a bowl of food from their pot, Maleek wandered over to our fire and held it in front of Tallack. "For you. You like, very tasty."

His grasp of our language had progressed so quickly, it took us all by surprise, so much so, that I began to suspect some ruse on his part.

Tallack gently took the bowl from him and looked at the swollen grains littered with chunks of meat and flecks of strong-smelling spice. One long sniff of the dish had Tallack coughing. A huge grin formed on Maleek's face. Chuckling, he reached into the bowl with his fingers cupped together and scooped out some of the food before smearing the lot into his mouth. Chewing and smiling, he made pleased moaning noises, while encouraging Tallack to try some. This was a noble gesture on Maleek's part. It would have taken a great deal of prior thought for someone of his standing to make the first move towards soothing the tensions between us. I held my breath, hoping that my nephew would see the action for what it represented.

Tallack peered into the bowl again, pinched a small amount of the sticky dish onto his fingertips and popped it into his mouth. Swallowing quickly, his eyes started to water, his tongue shot out and he sucked in air. "By Cernonnus, what is it? It burns my tongue." Far from being annoyed, Tallack was amused. He sloshed a great gulp of ale down to cool his mouth and dug his hand into the grains for a second bite.

Maleek could not have looked happier. "It is good, yes? You like?"

I thought for a moment that the Prince's son would sit with us and cement the cordial atmosphere between us, but he heard his father grumbling something in their language and hurried back to their fire side. Clearly, Suliaman was not pleased that his son was fraternising with someone who insults their gods.

The attempt at reconciliation did not allay all my fears. Neither were Tallack nor Cade fooled into thinking that we were now safe from the Prince's warriors and Suliaman's swiftly changing moods. We kept the same watches running throughout the night, to ensure a quick response should anything go awry while we slept.

At Dawn, we ate a little watery porridge, and saddled our horses before following Cade to the shallow crossing point at the furthest reaches of the Canti border. The horses struggled to pull Suliaman's wagon through the silty riverbed even at the shallowest point.

Hitching our horses on the far side, we all mucked in to empty the load of supplies and jewels, metals and the Prince's tall chair, giving the ponies a fighting chance of dragging the cart to the other side. At the time, I thought little of how we all must have looked. Since then, I wondered if our every move was watched by scouts of the ferocious Regnenses Tribe. Now they would know for sure that we were more than poor pilgrims travelling under the white banner. We had treasures to raid and noble heads to take as trophies.

There was a continuous flutter of panic nestling in my chest for the entire day. During the morning we passed through sheltered woodland, where Renowden was able to stock up on enough game for a few suppers to come and I could stretch my legs and gather more winter stocks of bark, roots and evergreen shoots. I couldn't help but notice how few homesteaders there were in this part of the Canti lands. It reminded me of the region east of the River Exe where our border lands were continuously raided by the Durotriges. It looked to me that the Cantii neighbours were as unforgiving as ours.

We passed from the relative warmth of the forest to the wide expanses of the lowlands beyond. Here the wind almost cut us in two, it was so cold. Maleek wrapped himself in more layers of soft materials, while Renowden and Cade used their bedding furs to keep out the cold. Jago clung to me tightly, sharing body heat with the pony and gritting our teeth against the biting breeze.

Cade stopped at a thicket of brushwood and low shrubs and tethered his pony. At first, we all thought he meant to relieve himself in the sheltered dell, but he called to Tallack to lend him a hand. I turned my horse around to see what the fuss was about. As we drew closer, I could see Cade scraping at the dirt with a sturdy stick. "What are you doing, lad?" I grinned. "You been supping ale as you ride?"

He laughed at my assumption. "You're not the only shrewd gatherer, Fur Benyn. I know for a fact that there are wild parsnips at this site. I saw them growing with my own eyes. If we're lucky, there'll still be a few that are waiting to sprout come spring."

At this minor revelation, I jumped down from my horse and knelt in the filth to help him. With a sharp rock to protect my fingers, I dug and shovelled and scraped alongside Cade and Tallack, until the long white tubers came into view. Such a fine thing to see in such a bleak place. My mouth was watering at the thought of eating the sweet roots roasted and sprinkled with a little wild thyme.

I stashed a number of the parsnips in my kit bag and we set off again for the wide river at the northern border.

Eager to make camp, we picked up the pace and encouraged our foreign travelling companions to hurry along after us. This would be a feast to remember. Roasted rabbit and ducks with sweet parsnips, what could be better?

It was dark when we reached the shore of the big river. Cade chose the spot, making certain that we were well within the Canti borderlands.

"You know those parsnips would be even better roasted with some of the Prince's honey." He said, jutting his chin over towards the Suliaman's men building their fire. He knew that my small jar that Suliaman had gifted to me on the boat was all gone.

"You think we should share our find with them? Make peace like Maleek tried to do?" Tallack said with a hopeful frown distorting his forehead.

"It can't hurt to make amends, and we have plenty of food." I said, caving in to his pitiful look. He really did care for the man. That was when I realised that this was so much more than a fling with an alluring foreigner. Both men shared something beyond mere physical pleasure. Despite my misgivings, I suggested that they should invite the Prince and Maleek to share in our bounty.

"Actually, Aunt Mel, I think it would sound better coming from you. Particularly if what Jago said is true and he believes that your name links you in some way to their god."

I could see his reasoning and it made sense, but I was reluctant to go and negotiate with the Prince. His display of force had shaken me. It replayed in my mind every time I tried to sleep. Even though I guessed that he required my healing skills, I had withheld my services out of fear. Now I had to swallow my fright and pride to make peace.

Jago scuttled along behind me as we approached their fire. Maleek jumped up from his seat and allowed me to sit in his place next to his father. It was obvious that he favoured a resolution between us and was prepared to do anything to make that happen.

Jago stood at my side, his head bowed to the floor ready to speak my words to Suliaman.

"May I start by apologising for any offence my nephew may have given over your religious ceremony. It was never intended as such." I paused, giving my slave time to convert my words into their tongue. When he was finished speaking, the old man nodded curtly with closed eyes. I took this to mean that he'd accepted the apology.

I continued, even though my guts were churning inside. "Our different customs have brought about this misunderstanding. We will not touch the idol or any offerings made to it. Of that you have my word."

Another bout of translation and another nod followed, but still Suliaman's face did not alter from stern. I tried to gauge his mood but was left wanting. In a last ditch attempt I ended with an invitation.

"We would like to share our supper of roasted rabbit with sweet parsnip roots, if you would like to join us…" I found my shoulders rising into a shrug as I realised that I was wasting my time. Suliaman was no longer conscious.

CHAPTER SIXTEEN

I leaned closer to the Prince, using the fire light to see his features. The blackest circles inside his eyes were tiny. His skin looked like glistening wax. It was almost as though he had left his body behind. I stood up and put my ear to his mouth. Maleek stopped the guards from slicing off my head at this intrusion. I was relieved to feel a slight breath on my cheek.

"What are you doing?" Maleek asked me, standing up with his hand resting on the hilt of his blade. He didn't even need Jago's help to reprimand me.

"Your father's life is in peril." I snapped, examining his blue lips and fingers. This was not new to me. I had seen the priests of our tribe in a similar state. "When did you last give him poppy resin?"

Maleek was thrown. He paced and muttered to himself, but he understood what I had told him.

"When?" I shouted at him, but as I said it, the Prince slid down his tall chair and crumpled to the ground. Jago and I grabbed hold of his limbs, pulling him back into a sitting position and holding him there.

Maleek ranted slipping back into his mother tongue. How could he comprehend me in one moment and then not able to speak our words in the next? This realisation made me exceedingly uncomfortable, but I had to deal with the Prince before all else.

Jago put me straight. "He says that his father complained about a deep pain radiating throughout his body. He demanded resin to dull his nerves."

"You gave him too much. He is close to death right now. I'm surprised that he can still breathe." I tried not to let the panic in my voice turn into a screech but so much rested on the old man surviving. It would be just our luck for him to die at the hands of his own son's incompetence.

Maleek's arms flew about him as he trotted out a series of instructions to the guards and servants. They in turn batted me out of the way, thinking they were helping their Prince by picking him up and laying him on a bed of rushes.

"No… that's not a good idea. He can hardly breathe. Sit him upright… make sure that he can get the air down him." I tried to fight them, but they would not allow me to help. They sent me back to my side of the camp with Jago in tow.

Tallack greeted me with calm indignation, having watched the entire performance with Cade and Renowden. "That went well, Aunt." One brow rose in time with the sneer spreading across his face.

"How was I to know that those idiotic kyjyans had given him enough resin to fell an auroch bull?" I launched myself down onto my furs and sulked until the rabbits had finished roasting.

Over the course of the evening, we all sat and waited for news about the Prince and whether he had recovered his wits or fallen foul of his son's kindness. I mused over the event, wondering if these foreigners knew more about our ways than they were letting on, and if so, why keep it a secret?

With a chill wind blowing in off the great river, none of us slept well. In the early hours, long before dawn, I heard a mournful cry. At first, I thought that it was Maleek in despair having lost his father. We jumped up and out of our furs and raced over to their side of the camp. It was the Prince. He'd made it through the worst of the poppy fugue and the pain had returned to overwhelm his senses.

Whoever thought up this curse is wicked indeed. When the old man saw me lurking near to his bedside, he called out to me for assistance. How could I help when I knew so little of the progression of his ailments? Poppy poisoning aside, his symptoms puzzled me to distraction. He had pale sores along his arms, but those he could not feel. As for the skin surrounding them, Suliaman complained of a burning sensation.

I sent Jago for my medicine kit and asked Maleek to bring me cool water. When my slave returned, I told him to instruct the warriors to carry the Prince to the back of the wagon and make up a bed for him above ground. It may be away from the fire, but the damp earth was enough to set off the nerves of a strong man. I climbed up into the cart beside him.

Jago found my softest woollen cloth and dipped it into the cold water. This alone wiped gently over the Prince's face seem to soothe him. With my smallest blade from my knife roll, I stripped a fresh piece of willow and mimed chewing so that Suliaman would understand my meaning. There I stayed until mid-morning, humming a quiet tune and bathing his face until he stopped thrashing about and found sanctuary in sleep.

Jago ran backwards and forwards between Maleek, Tallack and me, updating everyone on the state of the Prince's health. It was apparent to all that we were stuck at the river side until the Prince was well enough to travel.

Cade rode off upstream to the boundary markers between the land of his people and that of their most feared rivals. No decision had been made as to whether we would abandon our horses and the wagon in favour of boats across the river, or whether to venture into the Regnenses land to find a crossing that could bear such a load. Either way, our position so close to the border made us vulnerable. Tallack explained this to Maleek, who in turn stationed his warriors as look outs at high spots further outside our camp. At least we would have warning if we were under attack.

Renowden kept busy hunting, gathering and salting meat in preparation for leaner times ahead. Tallack and Maleek sat and enjoyed far too much ale and the dwindling stocks of Frynkish wine. I only left the Prince's side to empty my bladder or stretch my legs. He seemed to whimper when he could not sense me close by, or if I stopped humming a tune to let him know that I was there to help him.

All the rancour and disharmony of the last couple of days vanished. We were one travelling party once more, with a restored level of trust. At least on their part, for I could not wipe the sight of Suliaman's warriors poised to chop off my nephew's head for touching a sacrificed badger. As far as I was concerned, they would never have my trust again.

At length, the Prince recovered from his brush with death. He found some relief in the willow bark, which was tough on his stomach but less dangerous than the resin. When he was able to sit up and talk, he reached down to pull the covers off his legs. Twisting his knees, he showed me the soles of his bare feet. Each one was covered in large weeping ulcers that ate into his flesh. Was it any wonder why he begged for the resin? One of those deep wounds looked to have started to rot.

With a wretched look plastered across his face, he gestured towards his feet asking me for help. I called to Jago. This would need cautious handling.

"Tell him that I will need to cut, or burn out the rotting flesh before applying my plantain paste to the affected areas. Tell him that it will hurt like every god in the world were aiming their vengeance at him all at once."

My slave did his best to translate my warning to the old man. To my astonishment he nodded and signalled for me to begin. I offered him more willow to chew, but he declined. I wiped my sharpest blades with a little of Maleek's wine, since I had no sour apple juice with which to clean them. "Tell him to brace himself." I growled to Jago. Holding his foot steady, expecting him to recoil, I started slicing away the black rot.

Shockingly, the Prince neither moved nor wailed in agony. I stopped, glancing up at him to confirm that he had not passed out with the pain. He sat fully upright, watching me conduct my work. He must have seen the look on my face for he told Jago to tell me, that he no longer felt anything in his feet. This was the main reason why his warriors carried him everywhere. He could stand for a short time, but he was too unsteady to walk any distance.

The spreading numbness allowed me to cut out all of the dead flesh, but it bled a vast amount. Since he felt no pain, I could staunch the leakage by singeing the vessels closed after heating my knives in the fire embers. It was just as well that I only had Jago inside the cart to assist me. I'd hate to think what his warriors would have done, seeing me taking a hot knife to their master.

The Prince took a little ale and some rabbit broth around mid-afternoon. Cade returned soon after that with news about the crossing. His elation stemmed from a speedy canter along the riverbank for most of the morning. He said that there were no signs of any Regnenses clans at all, not even old campsites or homesteads. His decision was based on the assumption that they often overwintered on the south coast, where fish were plentiful and the weather was kind.

I was less certain of his assessment. Tribes as large as the Regnenses had clans scattered right across the region. They were well known for their nomadic life and for ridiculing those who liked to settle. Midsummer gatherings at Stonehenge allowed me to capture a taste of each culture, and those from the Regnenses were not to my liking. Their tolerance of us Dumnonii, was on account of our tin supplies. We forged an uneasy trade alliance with them, but they despised all Cantii and our association with them.

Tallack seemed to be enthralled with the idea of keeping our horses instead of having to trade a significant amount of our tin and copper for new ones on the other side of the great river.

"I think we should tell the Prince that we need some of his tribute metals to pay for new horses and commission a couple of boats across the river from here." I ventured, knowing full well that my opinion counted little with Cade.

"We can make a saving by going around. One or two days at best." Cade insisted.

"The shorter the distance the Prince travels the better. He is still very weak, and a couple of extra days might finish him off. Tallack, say you agree with me." I peered up at my nephew with my most imploring look, but it failed. He sided with Cade, choosing to save as much of the trade goods as possible. His argument was valid in a frugal sense, since we had no idea how many tributes would be needed to pass through the remaining tribal regions.

With a heavy heart, I packed up my things from the cart and let Jago explain the plan to Maleek and the Prince. Night was almost upon us once again, leaving us at the mercy of damp riverbanks and a surging mist rolling up the estuary to blanket us in cold vapours.

Another supper of fish served both us and the Prince's men that evening, although our supplies of fire wood ran low and it was too foggy to search for more. To keep warm, we all huddled together around the low embers, taking it in turns to sleep. I got little rest that night. The idea that we would take a slow ride for as many as two full days to a crossing which may or may not exist through enemy territory kept me awake.

Maleek continued to sacrifice creatures to the grinning statue on his father's instructions to make up for the lost night of his poppy overdose. When I did finally get to sleep, that contorted idol haunted my dreams. Perhaps the Prince's curse had spread to the rest of us for helping him.

In the morning, we were all exhausted and chilled to the bone. Our fire had turned into cold ashes with no hope of revival. The Prince was carried down to the river to wash, while we chewed on salted meat and sipped our ale. There was no point complaining. The whole enterprise was my idea from the start. I had no option but to grin like that statue and bear whatever the gods threw at us in return.

We set off at a brisk pace, along a well-trodden track at the side of the river heading west. Maleek and Tallack rode alongside each other, oblivious to all else around them. Under any other circumstances, I would be happy for him, but I needed the ruthless Metern of the Dumnonii to be on his mettle. With him in a love sick haze, we were more vulnerable than ever.

I kicked my horse's flanks to speed up to Cade at the front of the group. "I thought you said that there were no signs of life this far north on Regnenses lands."

"I did. Can you see any campsites or homesteads? Have you seen hoof marks in the mud?"

I hadn't, but the track we rode along was bare of grasses and plants. If it was as truly deserted as he claimed, why hadn't the grass grown back?

The mist receded around noon, giving us a clear view across the width of the river, its choppy waves washed into the shallow banks with the tide. Cade underestimated the conditions of the track. His light-footed pony might be able to dodge the worst of the boggy ground but not a whole group of us. With a cart full of provisions, treasures and the Prince, plus the heavy steeds to pull it, we were barely covering any ground at all.

"How far is this crossing you speak of? Have you used it before?" I asked Cade, whose initial hope had begun to wane.

"Our friends on the other side of the river told me about it. Their region is vast and they patrol the northern bank daily. It should be no more than a day's ride, but at this pace it'll be more like two." His furtive glances made me wonder if he was making the whole thing up, but then I couldn't see what he would have to gain by lying to us.

Maleek sent a few of his guards ahead to scout the fastest route and choose the best spots to make camp. He too looked anxious about our trespass on rival tribal lands. The rest of his men surrounded the Prince as he lay inside the wagon with a plentiful supply of willow bark and salted meats.

Few of us had much to say. The danger hung in the air like the stink of offal. When at last we caught up with the scouts, I was exhausted from the worry. Cade insisted that we had no fires, despite the freezing conditions and the need for a hot meal.

Some of the foreign warriors were suffering from chilblains. Without hot water, there was little I could do to help them, but I steeped some crushed mistletoe leaves in a beaker with a little spring water I collected on our way. It really needed a couple of days to stew, but I figured that it wouldn't require dilution as I would normally do for such a potent plant. I made enough to treat four warriors plus some for the Prince's ulcerated foot.

Suliaman's healer was travelling inside the cart with him, having kept a low profile for a number of days. I suspect that it was his mixing of the poppy resin that overdosed the Prince, rather than Maleek's order to administer the medicine. I fixed him my most lethal stare as I climbed into the rear of the wagon, but he did not seem to notice.

Lifting the furs up from the Prince's legs, I saw that his healer had wrapped his feet in a thick linen. Since it showed no signs of staining, I assumed that he'd washed off my plantain paste before binding. Against my better judgement, I kept my mouth shut. Suliaman's eyes rolled to the back of his head, a sure sign that he'd taken more resin. I left the mistletoe tea with the healer, but as soon as I had climbed down from the wagon, he threw it out on the ground.

I have done all that I can to assist him. His health is up to them now. Jago stood and shivered behind Tallack as Maleek prepared another sacrifice to the ugly idol. Animals and birds were thin on the ground as it was, without wasting good food on a clay statue. Tallack handed me some salted pork from his saddlebag. Slim pickings were all we could hope for on the southern bank.

We were encamped in a gully between two rolling hills, within sight of the river. The deep blue of the night sky arched over our heads, showing us all the points of light from the Summerlands. Gazing up, all I could think about was how Aebba would call us foolish for agreeing to this journey. My nephew broke my reflections, covering my back with a fur of his own and standing up to stretch his long legs. I assumed that he was wandering off to make water, but he frowned, peering into the distance.

"Cade, how far are we now from the crossing would you say?" Tallack said, his voice low and shaky.

"Half a day, maybe a little more. Why?" Cade stood too, turning to see what had caught Tallack's eye.

"There's smoke in the distance. A clan is encamped nearby."

CHAPTER SEVENTEEN

I scrambled to my feet to confirm my nephew's words. There on the crest of another hill in the distance, was a thick line of smoke rising into the sky. My first instinct was panic; theirs' was to freeze on the spot. In absence of any other elder to guide them, I had to swallow down my fear and speak up.

"Could it be where the river winds and that smoke is from across the water?" I asked Cade, who should have had a better knowledge of these lands than any of us.

"I suppose it could be but I doubt it, which means that they aren't a friendly clan." He muttered, his eyes fixed on the smoke.

"Do you think that they are camped at the crossing?" Tallack asked.

Cade just shrugged. "I have only been in this territory once before and I was just a small child. I honestly don't know if that hill is where the bridge is or not."

"We can't afford to risk it without further investigation. We won't be able to escape them if the Prince is with us." Tallack warned, looking down at his stocky older cousin.

My mouth opened before I could engage my brain. "Then Jago and I will go on ahead. If we meet any rival clans, we have nothing to offer them and no reason to fight. We are no threat, nor any use as slaves."

The men looked at each other in surprise, but as the reasoning filtered through their minds, they could see that it was a good plan.

"And what if they kill you both and take your horse?" Tallack said.

"Why would they when there are herds of wild horses further inland?" I could see that he liked the idea but didn't want me to risk my life. "We'll be fine. As soon as I find the crossing and can see that it is safe for you to approach, I'll light a big fire and send black smoke into the air." I touched his arm with affection. "It'll be okay, you'll see."

There were few options open to us that didn't involve bloodshed and he couldn't exactly forbid me from going. I removed all but one small knife from my kit and gave them to Tallack, along with most of my tin. "Keep those safe for me. They'll never believe that I'm a poor healer with that much metal on me." I chuckled nervously. What had I let myself in for?

Jago seemed pleased to be away from camp and that grinning statue. He packed some of Renowden's salted meat and our furs, and climbed on the back of my horse. We rode through the night together in silence, stopping only to rest and water the horse. Before dawn, we neared the source of the smoke.

As Tallack predicted, they were not from the other side of the river. Their horses were painted with clay and woad, with feathers of crow and raven plaited into their manes. These were warriors patrolling the northern borders of the Regnenses tribe. Rather than meet them in the darkness, Jago and I double backed a short distance, ate a little of our rations and tethered the horse beneath a wooded area near the water's edge.

It gave us a short time to rest in the shelter of the trees, before we could investigate the crossing. We made no fires nor any sounds, barring the occasional whinny and footfalls from the horse. My stomach knotted with hunger and nerves, but I had to succeed in my mission. All our hopes rested on my ability to act like a helpless old healer woman.

From the edge of the woodland we watched for signs that their fires might be stamped out, suggesting their move from camp. There were none. If anything, the smoke grew thicker, increasing my fear that Tallack might mistake it as a signal from me that all was clear to cross. It was time for decisive action. I gave Jago my knife and told him to cut some beech bark and willow to fill my medicine bag to its fullest. By mid-morning, the fire still burned just as strongly. The warriors had no intention of moving on.

Loading my bag, along with a few bundles of the twigs and branches to the back of my horse, we walked towards the warrior camp. My knife and what little tin I had was hidden about my person. I exaggerated my bent back and we moved closer. Jago had no need to emphasise his limp. The poor lad had healed as much as he was ever going to after the incident on Tallack's ship which broke his ankle.

The morning was damp making the grass underfoot slippery. Jago led the pony, while I had a thumb stick to lean on as we approached the riverbank.

Ahead of us was twenty or more warriors with their painted horses tethered to hitching posts. Over their fire roasted a couple of fat ducks and a few rabbits. It smelled divine. As we broke cover, one of their watchmen saw us.

"Ho there. State your business in these parts. From which clan do you hail?" His accent was thick, but not so much that I couldn't understand him. He moved to intercept us, blocking our path to the bridge.

"Just an old healer and my slave, come to pick some willow for the sick children across the river." I croaked, barely looking up from the trail.

"There's plenty of willow on the northern shore. Why come here? You are very old for a scout." He glanced over at my horse, stacked with thin branches and twigs. When I failed to answer him, he pushed Jago out of his way and rummaged in my medicine bag, finding little of value and plenty of plantain paste and mistletoe. "Hmm. This crossing belongs to the Regnenses. There is a toll for its use."

"As you see, I have nothing of value. I can spare a little ointment or a tincture or two, but it would be stealing from those sick children…" By this time more of the warriors crowded around us curious about Jago's dark face. They prodded him and pulled at his hair. I flashed him a warning look not to react to their provocation.

"There is one potion that might interest you." I said, drawing them in close. From my pocket I pulled out a small pot of white clay and goose grease. "This was traded in a Frynkish port for more tin than you've ever seen in your life. They say you only need a tiny amount to keep your pintel stiff for days, so use it sparingly, and don't blame me if you punch a hole in your leggings."

"Where would an old hag like you get hold of that much tin?" The astute warrior scoffed.

"I didn't. I cured the sickness of a wealthy trader with my healing skills and he gave me that in payment. What say you? Is it enough to let us cross in peace?"

Before he could make a decision, another man snatched it from him and opened the pot, sniffing at the white grease. A second man took it from him, digging his little finger into the mix until a host of men were crowded about the thing. I bit my lip to stop a chortle from exploding from me. They were so engrossed in the thought of what pleasures they might have with the worthless paste, they did not see me and Jago heading for the bridge.

It was a strong structure, with entire tree trunks embedded into the river bed to hold up the platform. It didn't wobble one bit as I led the horse across the planks to the sandy shore on the northern side. Jago breathed a massive sigh of relief the moment we entered into the Catuve-Llauni lands, although our mission was not yet over.

As soon as we could, we sought out another thicket of trees and shrubs close to the river and within sight of the warrior camp. We may have passed without trouble, but their presence prevented the rest of our group from using the bridge. Having any association with the Cantii would be fatal, let alone having the heir to the tribe among them.

Jago kept a look out while I searched for food and wood to build a fire. By his accounts, the warriors bickered and fought over my little pot of grease for some time. Then after they had wound themselves up to a frenzy, Jago called out to me that they had mounted their horses and ridden off in a southerly direction. My ruse had worked. I suspected that they were keen to try out my magical potion on any young women on which they could lay their hands.

As soon as they were out of sight, we stacked up wood and gathered as much green plant matter as we could find, ready to light the fire. When we thought they had ridden far enough away, I struck my flints together and lit a handful of bull rush kindling, blowing the sparks into a decent flame. Jago cheered when the rest of the small sticks caught, until the flames licked the sky. The warmth it kicked out was incredible. As the weak sun reached its peak, and the thicker branches were turning to embers, we piled on the green stems and leaves.

Thick smoke filled the air, rising in tendrils above our heads. Jago unpacked our furs and wrapped one around me while I stewed some of the salted meat with the last of the parsnips. That day without others from our group was one of my best memories. Every so often, I'd chuckle at the thought of those gullible warriors smearing their pintels with chalky grease thinking it would make them last like a stallion.

It was long after dark when I first heard the rattle of the Prince's wagon approaching the bridge. I sent Jago down to the water's edge to see if he could bag a few more ducks for the pot. I hadn't thought to expect them so soon. They must have set off early in the morning after Jago and I had left them, instead of staying put and waiting for my signal. That was a risky decision, particularly if the Regnenses warriors had ridden east instead of south.

Tallack was first to dismount and greet me. He threw his arms about my middle and heaved me into the air. "I wasn't sure I'd see you again, Aunt. I was convinced that they'd run you through with a blade after all that Cade had said about them. You're a sly one that's for sure."

As soon as I could convince him to put me down, he insisted on a blow by blow account of our little adventure. It didn't have much impact when it was spoken out loud, but he was glad that I was safe and unharmed. The guards and servants unpacked the idol and unloaded the Prince on his chair to conduct his own sacrifice to Melkarth. It was good to see that he'd recovered enough to be out of his furs, although he did seem to be more than a little addled. His healer's preference for poppy over willow is a dangerous one. A part of me wonders whether the shifty little kyjyan isn't trying to slowly kill Suliaman, although I couldn't guess what reasons he might have.

Tallack prodded the roasting ducks. "Hmm." He licked his finger. "Almost done." He poured me some ale and settled himself next to me. "Do you believe that statue has the power to take the Prince's ailments away?"

"If it can, it's making a poor show of it. They've killed a dozen creatures in its honour and Suliaman gets worse daily. If it genuinely is a clay version of their gods, then they are pure evil and not worth the tributes." I muttered it quietly so that none of the Prince's men could hear.

"Do you think Father really believed in our gods?"

It was a strange thing to ask me. I'd seen Aebba the Wild pay tribute and observe the correct rituals and rites that our old faith entailed, but I always got the impression that he was doing what he thought people expected of him. I could never be sure that he believed. "I don't know, Tallack. He never said one way or the other but it pleases me to think of him sitting at Cernonnus' side in the Summerlands with my brother and father and all the greatest warriors before him."

Cade joined us. The rich aromas attracted him and made his stomach growl. "If I had an aunt like you, Fur Benyn, I'd be as fat as Tallack." He lifted one of the roasting spits from the fire and pulled off a duck leg. The juices ran down his arm scalding his wrist. He didn't drop the meat though. He could fling insults at his cousin all day long and none would stick. They were as different as could be, Tallack's slender grace was quite the opposite of Cade's bullishness.

We were a merry crowd that night. Suliaman was in relatively good health, we had escaped the detection of a rival tribe, we had food enough to feed us all to bursting and a big fire to toast our feet. Life was good. Tallack and Cade clowned about play fighting and teasing each other to the extent that all language barriers were overcome. I could almost forget the threats made on my nephew's life, almost.

When the silly antics subsided and the elation and relief had sent most of the foreigners to their bedding, we discussed the next leg of our journey.

"If we keep this fire burning for long enough, one of the Catuve-Llauni will find us. They are an amicable lot and have trade alliances with almost all the tribes in central Inglond. With a small tribute paid, they'll allow us to roam freely." Cade explained.

"Is it worth offering them more to secure one of their scouts as a guide through the territory?" Tallack asked.

Cade shook his head. "I know the land well enough. Better to keep how much metal we have to ourselves. The more tribes that know of Suliaman's treasure, the greater our risk."

We both knew of what he was referring. Tribal elders make lofty deals for the foot soldiers to carry out. Even if the elders are trusted to keep their word, not all warriors are able to keep a secret, or quell the temptation to raid the trove for themselves.

"Agreed. We keep it in the family." Tallack held his arm out for his cousin to grasp. To them, it was a reinforcement of their commitment to the Prince. To me, it looked as though my nephew wanted reassurance that Cade would not turn on us given the opportunity and make off with all Suliaman's wealth. Tallack knew Cade far better than I, but this small gesture told me about his confidence in his cousin's promise.

I slept better on the north side of the great river. It is amazing the difference it made. Our whole party rose from slumber refreshed and ready to continue the journey. Cade instructed us to put out the fire and for us all to head north. When I asked him about waiting for the Catuve tribal elders, he waved his hand, dismissing my suggestion.

"They'll see our tracks and catch up with us. It's no big deal. We can pay them then." His carefree attitude to customs and rituals was the first in a long list of troublesome decisions on his part. I favoured waiting and requesting permission to pass through Catuve lands but was outvoted by almost everyone.

In an attempt to avoid Cade and his poor judgement, I chose to ride at the rear of our procession, behind Suliaman's wagon and the guards. It also kept me well away from Maleek and Tallack, who had resumed the same closeness as before the business with the dead badger.

Lagging behind, I used the opportunity to gather all that I could from the dense woodland north of the river. Yew needles and bark, more willow and ivy, plus a few plants that were sheltered from the worst of the frosts by the trees. Jago collected a huge amount of moss, packing it into a cloth bag and hanging it from my horse. With any luck, it will dry out before we make camp again and I can use it to cushion my head. It has so many uses, it is worth the effort to collect the stuff.

We spent the next night looking up between the trees at the thick clouds above our heads. Cade built another big fire, with hardly any regard for its potential to spread to the fir trees at the edge of our camp. Both he and Tallack appeared to have forgotten that we shared the same floor space as foreign warriors whom a couple of nights before threatened one of our lives. I whispered to my nephew about maintaining a watch at night, but he shrugged it off with a smile. No wonder he didn't want any of us monitoring the comings and goings about camp. Soon after we had eaten, he disappeared into the woods. Shortly afterwards, Maleek followed. They couldn't be more blatant if they tried.

I kept my eye on Suliaman's reactions to his son wandering off to be with my nephew, but I judged him to be half-addled with poppy again. As we were laying out our furs and my sack of dry moss, Jago froze with fear.

"What is it, boy?" I demanded.

"You did not see that, Fur Benyn?" His eyes were wider than I'd ever seen.

"For the sake of Cernonnus, boy, what's the matter with you?"

"The sky is falling in."

CHAPTER EIGHTEEN

For a moment, I couldn't think what he might mean, until a soft clump of snow landed on his head. He almost leapt over the fire in panic.

"Calm yourself, Jago. It's just snow. Surely, you've seen that before. They have snowfall in Frynk."

He shrank back behind me, trying to hide from the increasing number of flakes tumbling out of the sky. Suliaman's warriors jumped to their feet from the fire side, waving their spears in the air to stop the flakes from landing.

"Tell them it is cold water, Jago. Look..." I held out my tongue until a few flakes dissolved into the wetness. Still they glowered. "Snow." I said loudly, looking up until I had collected enough on my face to make blinking difficult. Jago raised his palm in the air. The flakes melted against his warm skin. One of the guards responded to the Prince, who heard the ruckus from inside the cart.

While I rejoiced in seeing the white stuff, the foreigners viewed it with great caution. Suliaman ordered his men to lift him outside. The wind picked up a little, drifting the flakes in swirls about his head. It was almost mystical.

The Prince smiled for the first time in days. He spoke to Jago, asking him to relay a message.

"He says that he had heard about this white magic from travellers to his homeland. It is more beautiful than he imagined." Jago said, pulling his tunic up about his neck.

"He won't be saying that in a few days when we're trekking through heaps of the icy stuff." I laughed. In truth, it had been many years since I'd seen actual snow. Seasons had been a continuous source of rain and mud for at least ten or more cycles. My last recollection of significant snow was from my childhood. Jago's courage grew. He caught flakes on his hand, his nose and finally his tongue before tiring of his game.

I stacked the fire with logs and went in search of more. If we were to avoid freezing to death, we would need to build a shelter for the night. With a flaming torch in one hand, I called out for Tallack all the while building a small wood pile for him to carry back to the camp fire for me. I shouted his name several times before he answered me, lumbering over the brambles and shrubs to lend a hand. When he did come into view, his hair stuck up in all directions and his clothes were untied and hanging off him.

There was no need to guess what he and Maleek had been doing in the shelter of the trees. "We can't sleep out in this all night. We'll need to build shelters. Suliaman's warriors won't have a clue how to make them snow proof." I tried to keep the annoyance from my tone but it seeped out anyway.

Tallack blushed. "Leave it with me. I'll get them chopping hazel poles and fir branches while Cade and I start weaving them together. There are enough men to make light work of it." He ran off before I could begin nagging him over his choice of lover.

Jago helped me with the logs in the end. I held up the torch for us both to see while he carried them back to the fire. Renowden appeared from out of nowhere with a half dozen rabbits hanging from a long stick by their sliced ankle skin. I was glad to see him. All the cold and extra work had us all ravenous. The Prince sat in his high chair by the fire transfixed by the snow. It settled on his head and shoulders and glued his lashes together, but he made no attempt to move.

"I suppose it is far too hot for it in your land?" I ventured, filling the awkward silence with polite chatter, and waiting for my slave to translate.

"He says that's true. He never thought he would live long enough to see and feel such marvels. It is colder than his poor bones can cope with here, but delights such as this make it worthwhile."

For a brief time, I looked at my homeland through his eyes. Tall trees, lush vegetation and freshwater at every other turn. A dry and sunny day was a rarity for us. Suliaman lived with droughts and curses and precious stones that glinted with coloured light. It must have seemed like another world entirely to him.

"I should like to visit your homeland one day." I said it before I'd thought it all through. I was too old to embark on such a trip despite the desire to go. "What is it like to live there?" Jago fed my question to the old man and told me his reply.

"It would amaze and astound you. The houses are stacked on top of each other, high into the air. As many as six families can live in one building. Across the warm seas, some of their huts are shaped like the cone of his hat. For hundreds of cycles they were called mounds, with thick walls to protect them from the sun. The Prince lived in a palace, a house of great magnificence. Their settlements are huge, with more people than all your tribes put together living in the same place. In the cities, they build temples to the gods. The sun bakes them all day long before it dips below the ground. Only then, is it cool enough to sleep."

"It sounds incredible. Why did you go to Frynk if your homeland is so well developed?" I asked, thinking it would be a simple enough question for him to answer. He took his time, thinking how to phrase his response. I guessed that he was wondering how to make a bad situation sound better.

"He says he was banished from the city by the elders in his family, until he found a way to lift the curse. Before leaving, Maleek refused to let him go alone, pledging that he would do whatever it took to return his father to the throne." Jago explained.

"What's a throne?"

"Oh um…" Jago considered. "The Chieftain seat for the whole city."

"So, they are without a ruler right now?" My persistent questions seemed to irk the Prince. His voice turned sharp and snappy. I should have minded my own business.

"Prince Suliaman's brother now holds the title, but he has no heirs. Maleek will rule when his uncle dies. The Prince was once the King, until the curse was laid at his feet."

Now I understood why his manner and that of his son's was so arrogant. Suliaman lost everything but his son since the curse took hold. I wanted to ask more questions, to delve deeper into the actual event leading to his misfortune, but the Prince summoned his men to carry him back into the wagon. He had lost interest in both me and our unusual weather.

The white flakes settled on the ground fast. Tallack and Cade worked like demons to make a temporary shelter large enough to accommodate us all. Some of Suliaman's men shuttered off the space beneath the cart, while others made a lean-to roof against its sides. With all our body heat collected inside the temporary hurdles, and our furs distributed between us, we made it through the night unscathed and remarkably chipper.

The fire succumbed to the white stuff not long after we all turned in for the night. By dawn, I heartily wished that we'd continued our shift of watches, if only to keep the fire ablaze for our morning porridge.

The snow crunched beneath my feet as I pushed my way through the undergrowth. Everything was still, not a hint of breeze to dislodge snow which had settled on the evergreens. Crouching down and lifting my tunic, I heard the rustle of branches. It was a small herd of red deer less than a boat length from my spot. I stood up slowly, so as not to spook them and a buck raised its magnificent antlers up to stare me directly in the eye. We regarded one another for some time before my innards began to tremble. The spirit of Cernonnus, God of the Wild Forest and Death, sought me out with a message of danger. I was frozen in time, as was he. With a steamy snort to add to my fears, the stag leapt away, taking his hinds with him.

As my senses returned to me, I realised that spears and arrows were flying past my ear in search of the animal's flanks. Suliaman's warriors were hunting them. What could I do but to return to the camp with my message from our god and hope that the men had not killed him?

"Tallack?" I flitted about seeking my nephew. "Have you seen him, Jago? I must speak with him right now." My wits were all over the place in panic.

He came out from the bushes on the other side of the clearing. "What's got you in a spin. Can't even take a leak without you getting in a state."

"Cernonnus appeared to me in the form of a giant stag. It's a warning of death. We must leave this place at once."

"Or it was just a stag, Aunt. Not every buck with big antlers is a god. This is a good place to be right now, with the snow like it is. We have shelter, plenty of food, and a tasty spring over yonder…I'd be happy to stay until summer."

"He looked me right in the eye. I tell you he was warning me."

"Even if it was Cernonnus, death will come whether it's here and now or two moons away when we're at the top of the world. You can't know for sure." He tied his leggings up around his waist and kicked the snow from the remaining logs in the fire pit. "Relax, Fur Benyn, you know I'm right." He gave me such a sneer I walked up behind him and clipped his ear with the back of my hand. He jogged away from me laughing. He was right. I couldn't be sure. Perhaps it was just a feeling that something was not right within our group of travellers. The cordiality seemed forced. They tolerated our needs and customs as we did theirs.

My heart took a little while to quieten. I removed a small stash of dry sticks and branches from beneath the wagon and threw them down at Tallack's feet. "Make yourself useful and build a fire. We'll all need something warm to eat if we are to trek in this weather."

"You do remember that I'm your Chieftain now don't you, Aunt?" He grinned, ducking for cover as I slung a stick at his head.

Tallack and Blydh were the fourth and fifth Chieftains during my lifetime, and none of them expected me to observe the hierarchy as another tribal member would. I was daughter, sister, aunt and great aunt to each of them, allowing me a unique favour from all. On this day, I needed that privilege more than ever.

Renowden went in search of more food for our supper, while Cade and Jago strapped the new hurdles onto the sides and roof of the wagon. We would need those at our next stop to stave off the bitter cold winds.

I went to check on the Prince's health. Clambering up the back of the cart, I was met with a string of garbled words and his healer blocking my way. I tried to ask after Suliaman's wellbeing, but he would not allow me to see or speak with him. I dare say he'd doped him up on too much resin again and was keen to hide his actions.

Cade and Jago cut enough poles and withies to construct another two panels, and then stowed the additional kindling under the cart. Suliaman's warriors returned with three red deer, tied at the ankles to poles and hoisted up on their shoulders. These beautiful creatures will feed us all for days. I gave a silent prayer to the Summerlands, that the stag was not among the kill.

No one seemed in any particular hurry to leave. Each of the men helped with the butchery, or wove new shelter panels or sharpened axes and spears. I was left with a growing restlessness, knowing that Tallack and Maleek were missing once again, and the available light was fading behind the trees. I tried to busy myself, looking for useful plants to harvest, but I found none and fretted all the more. Keeping within a short distance of our clearing, I was able to see when Tallack arrived back in camp. The moment he did, I pounced on him.

"If we don't leave now, we'll have to stay here for another night." I chided, trying to keep the whining tone from my voice and failing.

"So? I like it here. What's the harm in restocking our supplies and resting the horses for a bit? We've pushed them hard in the last few days." He didn't wait for my answer, wandering off towards his new love. His statement summed up his decision all at once.

"Hmm, no wonder you like it here." I muttered beneath my breath. "Plenty of cover for you and Maleek. I hope to Cernonnus that the Prince does not find out." There was nothing I could do. Cade and Jago took the hurdles down from the cart and bound them together in a sturdier shelter for the night. Suliaman's men carved great chunks of meat from a deer carcass and rubbed a reddish-brown powder into the flesh, mixed with a little oil.

Our fire was even bigger than the night before, sizzling with the fatty splashes of grilling meat and smoking with cooked spices from the other end of the world. The men drank their ale and laughed with bawdy jokes and had such a feast worthy of any Chief's Long Hut. I remained quiet and observant. Tallack seemed to have forgotten the incident where his lover's men almost severed his head but I hadn't. There was little they could do now to earn my trust, even if food and bedding and the warmth from the fire was shared equally.

The Prince was well enough to perform his own sacrificial offering to the grinning idol, who now had its own shelter for the night. I was glad that it didn't have to squeeze in among the rest of us to give me the creeps while I tried to sleep.

The skies cleared in the early morning, plunging the temperature and freezing a thick crust on the top of the snow. Now when we walked, it made a cracking noise with each footfall. Tallack had no excuse for lingering at this place. Between him and Maleek, the camp was packed away and our ponies made ready for the next leg of our journey north.

In bright spirits and renewed vigour, we followed the trail through the remaining part of the forest. As the spaces between the trees grew wider, I saw the diminished herd of deer running from our path. Twisting around on my horse, I watched them leaping and bounding over bushes and fallen trees into the dense undergrowth. When they were almost out of sight, the stag stopped and faced me once more. His breath billowed from his nostrils in great plumes of steam. Kicking out at the snow, he stared me down. I knew then that I was communing with the God of Death. In that moment we shared the same thought. One of us will die.

Filled with remorse and regret, I watched Cernonnus fly after his herd and disappear. For a few moments afterwards, I was caught in a trance. My stomach danced inside me. I rattled through all the potential ways for us to leave the quest, but came up with nought. We had to see this through to its lethal end, or suffer Suliaman's wrath for breaking our word. Desolate and fearful, I slumped over the horse's mane, cuffing the tears as they spilled from my eyes.

"Great lady, are you unwell?" Jago enquired, resting his gentle hand on my back as we rode together on my white steed.

"I am sick in thought and deeds, Jago." He didn't understand me, bless him. He offered to make a tonic for me, or to stop and light a fire to warm my heart. His kindness is all the warmth I need. There was no point in informing Tallack of my latest sighting. He would have dismissed it as the ravings of a silly old woman. I rode on behind Cade and Renowden, and before the Prince's wagon.

"There's just one more long bend in the track, if memory serves me, and then it's flat fields and lowlands for a couple of days." Cade announced to no one in particular.

He was right about the final bend in the forest. What he did not foresee, was the enormous gathering of tribesmen awaiting us as we cleared the tree line.

CHAPTER NINETEEN

The sight was as incredible as it was frightening. The number of warriors standing in our way was in the tens of hundreds. A massive camp lay in the distance, sporting coloured flags and a great many fires. At the head of our welcoming party was an older man astride a huge black stallion. He wore the skull and tusks of a boar on his head and his face was streaked with red clay.

I watched as Cade rode closer to him with his arms held up in a signal of submission. Every one of the warriors at the man's side, wore a stern frown and held a glinting spear. This tribe meant to harm us. Tallack cantered to the head of the line, passing me in all haste.

"I thought you said that the Catuve were allies?" Tallack yelled as they drew near. "They look pretty angry to me."

Cade bowed his head and stopped his pony a short distance from their leader. "May we approach?" He shouted. The man at the heart of the tribe nodded. Cade kicked his horse and trotted towards the party. Tallack followed keeping his head bowed and his swords sheathed as he drew closer. I crept my pony up to their backs, hoping to hear what was spoken. This was the leader of the Catuve-Llaunii. He stared Cade down without uttering a word.

In respect to his seniority and position, Cade dismounted his horse. “Chief Osbert, I hope that we find you and your family well on this cold winter morning.”

“You did not find us at all, Cade of the Cantii. You took it upon yourself to march right through our lands without tribute or permission.” Despite his small frame, the chief had a booming and authoritative voice. I jumped when he began to speak, making my horse fuss and fidget.

“You know that I would have waited at the crossing for your blessings if I could, but we are on an urgent errand. It will not happen again. Of that you have my word.” Cade placed his hand on his chest and smiled a big toothy grin. I winced at his insincerity. If I could detect it from behind, I was sure that the Chief had.

The older man sneered. “Your word means nothing, or you would have respected our ways and paid tribute under the arrangements with your father.”

“As I said, this was an exceptional case, and will never be repeated. We bring your wives gifts of gold and spices from exotic lands.” Cade stepped aside and pointed to the wagon as though it were filled to the roof with jewels instead of a sick old Phoenician man.

“What use are spices and gold when our allies go back on their promises? You have insulted my tribe, and I grieve for the loss of goodwill between us.” The Chief picked up the reins of his stallion and pulled them to one side, turning the enormous beast around. Those surrounding him followed suit, leaving just the warriors with their spears at the ready and blocking Cade from following.

“Please, Chief Osbert, I beg you. My father would string me up for insulting your honour and that of your tribe. How may I make amends?" Cade shouted above the crunching hooves in the snow. "Please?"

This was precisely what the Chief wanted, a complete capitulation. He had Cade on the back foot, willing to do whatever it took to heal the rift before his father learned of the insult. From where I sat on my horse, I could see the Chief halt. The tusks of the boar skull came into view as he turned his head a fraction and nodded.

Each of the warriors pulled back their spears and allowed Cade through on foot. The moment he cleared their line, they raised the defences against us.

Tallack moved his horse abreast of mine. "What do you suppose he'll make Cade do?" He asked me, as though I had all the knowledge in the world up my sleeve.

"If he has any sense, it'll be a hefty penance. Old Osbert will use this as a warning against other tribes trying the same thing." I said.

"You think he'll kill him?" Tallack shrieked.

"What, and start a war with the Cantii? Don't be daft. Anyway, the Catuve need to trade for copper. I dare say Osbert wants to teach the young upstart a lesson that's all. Who knows what he'll come up with?" I almost laughed. If he'd taken my advice at the bridge, this entire delay could have been avoided. "Jago, hop down and tell the Prince and Maleek what is happening, or they're likely to force their few warriors to put up a fight they cannot win."

While Jago did my bidding, I scanned the horizon, counting all the tents and shelters and estimating the number of warriors Osbert had at his command.

Tallack must have been doing the same thing. "I didn't realise that the Catuve were such a large tribe. Considering their peaceable reputation, they are extremely battle ready, wouldn't you say?" Tallack whispered to me. I think he was in shock to think that his cousin would be idiotic enough to upset such a mighty force.

After a while, we realised that this was not going to be a quick apology to make things right. Cade was ushered into the largest shelter, where we assumed the Chief had quartered. I got down from my horse and led it to where the Catuve warriors had cleared the snow. If we had to suffer the cold together, the least we could do was make sure that our horses were not ankle deep in half-thawed slush.

We were surrounded by tribal warriors, each with a spear and shield, and enough furs to keep their teeth from chattering. I wore every layer I had and wished that I'd brought more. Jago looked to be suffering the most. His skinny little body was unused to the cold at the best of times. I instructed him to unpack our bedding and wrap it around himself, while I wandered to the wagon.

Maleek stopped me, trying to use our words unaided. "Why are we here?" He pointed north with an outstretched arm. "Need to move."

"Yes, I realise that, but unless you want to end your days on one of those spears, we must do as they say." I gave him a thin-lipped smile, and wondered how much he'd understood. Something about their furtive discussions and the way in which Maleek and Suliaman concentrated on our private talks did not add up. I must have stared too long in my ponderings as he frowned at me. "Your Father?

Maleek assumed I wanted to see him, rather than enquiring after his health. He waved in the general direction of the cart and wandered off to stand alongside Tallack.

With nothing better to do, I climbed up the wagon to see the Prince. For once, he was attentive and sitting upright in his tall chair. His warriors had lashed it to the sides of the cart to prevent the Prince from sliding around in the back. When he saw me peeking through the gap in the greased fabric, he beckoned inside.

It was surprisingly warm within the covered area. Suliaman had furs around his shoulders and another across his lap. He offered one to me, but I could already feel the difference from the chilly track. He seemed keen to engage me in conversation.

"Tell me about your boy." He said, with a tilt of the head that made me think he was being polite. There was not a hint of confusion over the use of our tongue. It was fluent and well thought out. I tried to hide my shock, but it left me reeling. Was not knowing our language all a pretence?

"Oh, well, he's my nephew, one of twins. You know two boys born at the same time to the same mother?" I held two fingers aloft to emphasise the situation.

Suliaman shook his head. "Not he, your Jago. Tell me of him."

Baffled by his sudden interest, and still dazed by his deception, I took a moment to calm myself. Why on earth would he ask about a little slave boy, stolen from his homeland and sold to a Frynkish flesh trader? It was a miracle the boy survived after all he'd endured. I frowned at his curiosity. "He's just a slave. Tallack's father gifted him to me to help me gather herbs for healing. Why do you ask?"

"I heard one of your tribe call him the Chosen One." A sly grin spread across his face. The wily old man observed more than he let on. He must have heard Renowden or Tallack call him that. I can't imagine how Cade would know that name.

"It's true that he has fits, as you have witnessed yourself. That made my people believe him to be special, that he could talk with the gods." I said with caution, wondering where he was going with this line of enquiry.

"What makes you think he cannot speak with the gods? Perhaps that is what gives him seizures. It would be a great strain on a mere mortal channelling your Cernonnus, would it not?"

His ability with our tongue was too good to have only learnt it in the last few days. This man knew what we were saying all along. I shuffled back on my knees in the confined space, dumb-founded. Why would he pretend if not to trick us? I creaked and moaned getting to my feet to leave.

"Come, Fur Benyn, don't be cross with me. That is what they call you, isn't it? Wise woman?" There was something sinister about his tone, as though he relished getting the better of me. "I am truly grateful for your healing balms and tonics. You have greater skills than that useless man I brought with me."

I was at the entry way readying myself to climb down, but something made me turn back. "Why did you insist on having Jago translate for you if you understood every word we said?"

"I did not know whether your kin could be trusted. They spoke freely in my presence thinking I did not understand."

"And what did you learn?"

"That you love your tribe more than anything in the world and would see them prosper even at your own expense."

That wasn't the answer for which I was looking. If they meant to dupe us, why didn't they do this in Frynk? He was certainly not faking his ailment. Ulcers such as the ones on his feet would be cruelly painful to anyone with normal sensations. I held up the entrance flap and stopped. "What did you really do to be cursed in such a way?"

His grin vanished and with it the space seemed cold and unwelcoming. "A story for another day." He signalled his warrior servant to help me down the back of the wagon.

I was reeling with this revelation. Seeking out my nephew, I whispered this new information about Suliman's deceit to him. He listened to all I had to convey and simply nodded. He made no fuss. There was no outburst of fury, or confrontations with his lover.

As he began to walk away from me, I grabbed his sleeve. "Did you not hear me? They have lied to us for all this time."

The look he gave me was grave, but he said nothing. His gaze flitted towards Maleek and then over to their guards, as if to say, *we are in enough trouble right now – don't make a scene.* Did Tallack know about their abilities with language? How did Suliaman and Maleek learn our tongue?

These and many other questions sent me giddy with doubt. What had they in store for us when the quest was over? I hurried towards the line of Catuve warriors blocking our path, craning my neck to see if Cade was out of the Chieftain's talks. He wasn't. The sooner this trip was over, the better.

Renowden skinned his latest catch while Maleek and Tallack sat giggling together mounted on their horses. How could my nephew forgive such falsehoods and carry on as if nothing had happened?

Jago sensed my confusion. "Shall I build a fire right here, Fur Benyn? You look cold."

He stopped short of adding, *and agitated.* There were no indications for how long the discussions might take. I was starting to wish that we had stayed in the forest. Just as I was about to agree with Jago over the fire, I caught sight of Cade. At last we would discover what his penance would be.

"Well? Tallack asked.

Cade scratched his chin and winced. "I'm to be bound to his eldest daughter this very day, or lose the favour of the whole tribe along with our trading agreement."

"Kyjya! The old man doesn't mess about, does he? What's she like?" Tallack cackled.

"No idea. Never met her. I had to agree to take no other too, so that our sons inherit the Cantii leadership."

"Cunning old kyjyan. Your kin will command the largest tribe in all of Inglond."

"That's his game I reckon, yes." Cade looked utterly despondent. Virtually all Chieftains in the land were afforded as many wives as they liked. This agreement shackled him to one. He could have as many slaves to couple with as he fancied, but no other offspring could bear his title. With strong blood ties in neighbouring lands, the Regnenses would be outnumbered and running scared. It was a sensible move for Chief Osbert, especially if his first son was a little on the weak side, as rumour suggested.

Maleek assumed that we could be on our way, leaving Cade to his nuptials, but our host was insistent that we all remained to bless the binding. Cade was also keen to continue the arrangement, giving him more opportunities to make off with the prize of a profitable trading partnership with Suliaman.

At length, our horses and the wagon were led to a space between their shelters. Osbert's massive tent was decked out with boughs of holly and ivy, while livestock were butchered for the feast. I got the distinct impression that preparations were made before our arrival at the forest. No doubt Osbert's scouts were tracking our whereabout before we even crossed the river.

The ale was warm and plentiful, our hosts gracious and kind. I was not sorry to be stopping in such fine shelters or eating such delicious foods. Formal introductions were made between Osbert and his kin and our foreign visitors. They were given pride of place, next to the wedded couple and the Chief. Jago, the warriors, and servants of Suliaman, were given victuals and ale in a separate tent since all the Catuve elders were invited to the ceremony. In lieu of a wooden henge of life, the ceremony took place at the foot of a massive oak tree.

Cade stood next to Tallack holding a ribbon of fine woven cloth. Osbert stood before them and called his daughter to the front. She held in her hands a posy of ivy heads surrounded with trailing stems. Cade looked pleased with his match since she was a pretty little thing. She looked less satisfied with the union. It took several low growls from her father to force her to Cade's side.

Two young maidens skipped up to the couple each holding the end of a springy length of willow, decorated with entwined leaves and berries. They arched the bough over their heads and waited for Osbert to say the oath. I have attended more binding ceremonies than I can remember. Each tribe has their own way of doing things, little quirks and customs, but none so strange as the Catuve Tribe.

Beneath the oak tree the snow was cleared and a thick layer of rushes were laid. Idina, the bride, took Cade by the arm and encouraged him to lay down. She gave her posy of magical ivy to one of the girls holding the bough over their heads. Much to everyone's surprise, Idina began stripping him of clothes. Cade shrieked and wailed but held his tongue when Osbert afforded him a silencing glare. When Cade was completely naked and surrounded by snow, Idina took out a bronze blade and started shaving his body. Not just his chest and his legs, but every single part, from his scalp to his toes.

Tallack and Renowden laughed until they choked. Maleek and Suliaman's brows were sky high and stayed there. Only the Catuves did not find the spectacle amusing. Idina took her time, softening his bristly hair with a warm cloth and scraping the blade over his skin. When at last she was done, and the men of our tribe had finished ridiculing him, she collected up the hair, wrapped them in ivy leaves from her posy and buried it beneath the tree.

Cade shot up from the rushes and dragged his clothes back on in double quick time. It was his turn to shave his wife. This time, she sat on a stool facing the trunk of the tree and offered him the same knife. Cade stood and looked at Osbert, puzzled.

"Shave just her head, but leave a small tail with which to drag her to your bed." His voice so solemn, it could hardly be mistaken for a joke and yet Cade stood and laughed.

"You're kidding right? Her hair is beautiful, *she* is beautiful. Why would I shave it all off?" He argued.

"That's our way. You will learn to love her without her hair. It will stop others from your tribe being attracted to her, and eventually it'll grow back."

With a shrug and a defeated shake of the head, he began the task of lopping off her incredible black hair. The maids gave him warm water to pour over Idina's locks. With two fingers to the side of her face, he tipped her head away and held the blade level with her scalp. Pausing, he lowered his arm to think again, before moving her in the opposite direction. When the pressure of us all staring got to him, he lunged with the knife, angling it towards her skin and pushing down on the blade. Idina jumped a little on her seat, biting her lip but making no sound. Cade drew back the knife and noticed the streak of blood trickling down his bride's face.

CHAPTER TWENTY

A solitary tear mixed with the blood on her cheeks. Cade stepped back. Everyone could see the knife dripping with Idina's blood. At first, we all thought he'd killed her, until she swivelled around on the stool. His bungled efforts had almost scalped the girl. Osbert threw his arms in the air and ranted at Cade's incompetence. I fetched my kit bag. I've never been called to heal a bride at her binding before.

To speed the process along, Osbert entwined their hands and wrapped the ribbon of fabric about their wrists, before pronouncing them wedded. A feeble cheer came from the crowds as the Catuves realised that they were now allied by blood to the stupidest heir in the land.

By the time I got to washing her skin and hair of matted blood, Idina was inconsolable. Nothing I could say or do would stop her pitiful cries. Cade made matters worse by telling her that after I had stitched up the wound, she could keep her hair. Between the snot-filled sobs, she said that a shaved head was the mark of a newly married woman and without it, they were not bound in the eyes of Cernonnus.

"If I don't stitch you up, you'll never have hair again." I grumbled, trying to hold her still and thread my bone needle with fibres of rabbit back strap. "Maybe Cade can have another go at it when it's healed." That just made her cry louder and more hysterical. I was starting to think that Osbert chose this daughter to punish him.

When I'd finished treating what I could of her hairline, they walked into the Chief's tent with their hands still bound together. Osbert's slaves had the feast ready and it was time for the bridal tributes. Idina's friends and female relatives gave her fabrics, furs, bracelets of woven horsehair and copper beads, and more carved spoons than could be used in a lifetime. These she laid in a basket by her side.

Tallack gave her tin ingots. I had a set of tin ear studs to place in her basket. Maleek gifted her a golden bangle that shone from every tiny facet beaten into its surface. At long last, it was time for the Prince's tribute. His warrior servant helped him to his feet and held his arm as he staggered from his chair at the top table to the centre where the bride sat.

"For one so beautiful and noble, something with which to defend yourself, if ever you should need it." Suliaman announced, his slow blink calming her tears and fuelling her curiosity. From his sleeve, the Prince pulled out a curved dagger of the finest bronze. Its hilt was made of gold and embedded with jewels of red and blue. As he unsheathed the knife, Idina gasped at its shine. He edged forwards and laid it into her open palms.

"Be careful, it is sharper than a lynx tooth." Backing away, he left Idina to marvel at its lustre.

"Thank you." She gushed, not taking her eyes from it for a moment. At the time I thought it was a generous token indeed, until I saw the glint in Idina's eyes. What thoughts of mischief brewed inside her mind? Did

Suliaman gift her a dagger to use upon her new husband when she tired of his advances? From her reaction, I am sure that it crossed her mine too. The Prince seems to be fond of stirring the pot. She should have traded for the knife with those carved wooden spoons.

Instead of stepping back to his seat, his warrior servant handed him a flat section of wood with distinctive markings on its surface. Taking it close to the bride, Suliaman leaned in and whispered something to her. Idina blushed, clasping her hand over her mouth. Everyone in the tent, including me, was desperate to know what the object was and what he said to her. Idina took the wooden item, turned the marked side to her face and smiled. With a tiny bow, the Prince retreated back to his seat.

These foreigners fascinated, and at the same time, terrified me. Why would he give her a piece of wood? I couldn't make out a use for it nor a reason for marking its surface and clearly his explanation was meant only for Idina.

Tallack crouched low so as not to be noticed as he sidled over to my side. "Any chance of cutting and running before the day is out?" He said it quietly so that only Jago and I could hear.

"Not likely, unless you want Osbert to cast his anger on us too. He might have other daughters if you're interested." I smirked. Idina was pulled to her feet by her hand maidens and urged into a traditional dance. Cade looked more interested in our discussion. I could see him straining to hear what was said.

Tallack wrinkled up his nose. "I'll see if we can leave first thing in the morning without Cade. I expect that he'll have to stay and do his duty by his wife."

Before I could reply, Cade hurried over to us. "You can't leave without me. I know your game. My father instructed me to accompany you and the Prince all the way to the top of the world. I'll tell Idina and Osbert we'll stop on the way back to pick her up."

"I can't see that going down well. Mind you don't make matters worse. Osbert is tricky. One false move and you'll lose your manhood as well as your trade alliance." I warned, but it made no difference to the headstrong youngster. He rushed off to speak with the Chief.

The dance was long and tiresome, involving all the women of their tribe. Idina led the way, while her hand maids held onto what should have been a tiny tail of her hair. Osbert's first wife held the hair of one maid, and so the train of ladies grew. More wives holding on and dancing their way around the gathering until all the women were collected. Despite the weather, Idina led them outside to gather more tribeswoman to the dance. Some of the men followed them, stamping their feet and cheering, while watching the younger and older women flit about.

Cade sat next to a scowling Osbert, speaking in a low and respectful manner. I guessed that when he pointed towards Suliaman, he was explaining the reason for our urgent quest.

That was when Osbert's eyes widened, his nostrils flared and he rose from his bench with a puffed-out chest. "You brought a cursed foreigner onto our land?" This he bellowed until all the drummers and pipers stopped playing and the elder men turned around.

"It's not that kind of curse, Osbert, more of a targeted illness. Only he was affected." Cade reasoned, following the Chief across the tent towards the Prince. They stared each other down for an uncomfortable time before Osbert deigned to speak.

"I have nothing against you personally, you understand, but you cannot stay here. I have my entire tribe to protect, and your curse could devastate what I have spent years building. You may take fresh horses and grain from us, but be gone by nightfall."

That was our cue to leave, before the Chief decided that it was better to be safe than sorry, and lop off all our heads. I grabbed my things and called to Jago. Tallack signalled Maleek and got everyone from our group moving.

Only Cade was left standing in the centre of the tent. "Osbert, with the curse in mind, it is safer that Idina stays here until I can return for her. You wouldn't want her wrapped up with this foreign witchcraft, would you?"

Osbert narrowed his eyes. He was still panting with indignation, but we could all see the logic in Cade's suggestion. I felt sure the old man would agree to the condition, but he snarled at his new son, baring his few remaining teeth.

"If this is your idea of wriggling out of the binding, just because you botched the ceremony, think again. Idina comes with you, along with her household and dowry treasures. Bring her back to me when you can boast a son of your own to rule when you're dead." A vessel in his forehead pulsed, his face was darker red than oxblood such was his temper. And these were peaceable people? I dreaded to think about those we might meet further north.

Although the day length had begun to draw out, nightfall was not far away. Our troop now consisted of one sick old Phoenician and his son, two green warriors, a new bride and her handmaids, plus an old woman and her lame slave. I shook my head at us all. We couldn't have looked more like victims if we tried. Suliaman's men did their best to appear fierce and surround us, but their numbers were limited. Renowden complained to Tallack that he couldn't possibly catch enough food for all the mouths we now had to feed. Cade sulked at his tearful wife, and rode on ahead to find a suitable campsite.

At least while we trod Catuve lands, we were relatively safe from raiders. All in the tribe knew Idina by sight. She was the key to our fortunes through this massive region. We pitched the tents that Osbert had provided and staked out the hurdles for windbreaks against the barren land. The wind whistled through the gaps and fanned the flames of the large central fire.

The idol was lifted from the wagon and set down before the flames.

Idina curled up her lip in confusion. "What is it?" She called to me, thinking that I was in the best position to answer.

"It is the vessel of Melkarth, God of all our gods. We summon him to keep the Curse of Byblos at bay and to take the pain in my stead." It was Suliaman who answered. Idina, I could see, was brimming with more questions but too intimidated to ask them. Pity, for I would have relished the chance to learn more and Suliaman seemed most open to explaining to her. It helped that she was young and beautiful and highly impressionable. Old men like him always grant the young pretty ones their favour. Stupid dolts.

I glanced over at the grinning, long-armed idol. He was one ugly god. It made me uneasy to think that Suliaman had the power to bring the spirit of his most revered god into a clay figure. Did he also have some kind of evil magic lurking within him. I was used to the tricks and games of our own Priest Sect. They could be explained away easily enough, when you saw behind the showmanship and staged antics. Their fondness for hemp and poppy resin baked their brains until any observant person could see through their rituals.

Suliaman had no such tricks that I could see. I burned out his foot rot without him uttering a whimper. Either he was in league with his gods, or he had more powerful magic than we could begin to imagine. The question remained, were his gods benevolent or wicked?

I moved myself from the fire and retired to the shelter. I'd seen and heard enough sacrifices and chanting over that idol to last me a good long while. Jago came with me, but sat bolt upright in the doorway trembling as Suliaman started the ritual. Whatever he was saying in his language, it terrified my slave.

By morning, the snow had started to melt. We packed up the camp and set off for the lowland plains of the Catuves. We'd trotted along for nigh on a quarter moon, camping in sheltered dells, wooded valleys and near clean waters and still we had not left Idina's borders. She had taken to riding alongside me on the trails. Jago had a horse of his own and garnered much attention from her handmaids. He seemed to like it so I left him to their giggles and questions. The new bride was not as cheery as they.

"I heard you crying in your shelter last night, Idina. Does Cade hurt you? I have plenty of willow…"

"No, it's not that. I mean, he is a great lump and I don't much like him, but no, he doesn't hurt me." She toyed with the hair of her horse's mane, distracted.

I had nothing better to do and so pressed further. "Why the tears? Do you miss your family that much?"

She stared into the distance and heaved a massive sigh. "Not my family…just…"

I comprehended it all. The tears, the sad pout and wistful stares, she was in love, and not with Cade. I stifled a cackle and fetched some mallow seed disks from my kit. "Here, chew on a few of these. That'll cure the melancholy for a time."

At length we came upon a large area of scant soils and rocky outcrops. The horses struggled to pull the wagon along the track, making us alter our course to accommodate them. It took us through rugged valley floors and scrambling over jagged stones until a couple of our ponies went lame. Jago was back sharing my horse and we had enough meat to last us for a moon or more.

"We are passing into the Coritani lands now. You should swap the flag of pilgrims for my banners or they might attack." Idina said, gesturing to a maid to pass her blue swatch to Cade. It hadn't occurred to me that she would prove an asset. Until then, she and her maids were more reasons to slow us down.

She kicked out at her horse and cantered to the front of the line. Whatever she told her husband, we veered from the path and took a north-westerly route instead.

The following day, Cade led us all north once more. The hills grew steeper and did nothing but hinder our progress. Suliaman was suffering from another one of his poorly spells. A quick visit to the rear of the cart told me that his healer had dosed him once again.

Maleek intercepted me this time. "He grows weak, Meliora. He won't take food, his sores fester, his ulcers worsen. Resin is all he will accept."

I'd tried every remedy I could think of and more besides. Nothing seemed to turn the symptoms around. Perhaps the sacrifices to the idol were working at the start of our journey, but they did nothing for him now. "It must be a fearsome powerful witch who laid this at his feet." I said, trying to judge Maleek's receptiveness. "What brought this whole situation about?" I was careful how I approached him, avoiding words that would lay blame on his father.

Maleek thought for a while looking to Jago for his services in translating, but the subterfuge no longer held power. We all knew that both he and his father spoke our language well, and I held a grudge over the lie. It didn't stop me from pressing them both for answers to my questions.

Maleek cleared his throat and began. "We Phoenicians are a proud people who work hard and travel incredible distances to trade. That is what we are known for and so learning languages is of critical importance. My peoples' wealth grew from a skill in making fabric dyes, trading cedar wood and creating fine glassware. From those things, we learned how to work metals, increasing their value to trade partners." Maleek paused and took a gulp of fresh water from a bladder hooked to his horse before continuing.

"There is no land called Phoenicia. We are one people, of course, but we have cities in many hot places next to the sea. My father ruled one such city which shared the same stretch of water as two others further north. For many years, my family grew fat on the trades of our Tyrian violet dye, made from the crushed shells of the rock sea snail. Our divers went out daily, whether seas were rough or calm, to harvest more for the fine linen rolls which were sold to the richest people in the land. That same violet purple is what you see my father wearing. It is the colour of …" Maleek stumbled over the word. "It is the colour of the leader of a vast tribe."

I listened patiently, wondering how the curse came about, but still intrigued by the descriptions of his homeland.

"One day, there was a bad storm. The waves crashed against the beaches and flooded parts of the city. Homes were battered and lives lost, ships wrecked and the seabed churned. When the collectors went out after the storm, the snails were gone, washed out to sea."

I could see where this was heading and I wondered just what Suliaman did to secure a new harvest.

"The Tyrians ventured further along the coast, checking lagoons and rocky outcrops for a new supply, but they met with resistance from those collectors belonging to the City of Sidon. As the number of snails declined, fighting broke out between people from each settlement. Many died in the conflict, until the ruler of Sidon called a truce so that they could arrange talks between the cities' rulers. My father agreed to be the host, decorating the terraces and verandas with linens and olive trees for shade, having their favourite dishes made from Sidon and Byblos, and even commissioning statues in honour of their god and goddess, Baal and Astarte. The ruler of Sidon brought his sons, daughters and his wife, the High Priestess of Byblos. He had forged an alliance with the ruler of his neighbouring city by binding with the man's daughter. Together they argued with my father over the shoreline and the right to harvest the snails."

I could hardly bear the tension. Maleek took another sip of water. It was thirsty work recounting the hardships of his family. He volunteered the rest without the need for prompting.

"The row broke out when we were all on our most beautiful terrace with a glorious view over the ocean. The son of Sidon squabbled with my father, calling him many unkind and untruthful names and accusing him of stealing the shells from their collectors. My father struck him and the man toppled over the edge of the balustrade, smashing his skull open on the rocks beneath."

CHAPTER TWENTY-ONE

There was no need for him to complete his story. I'd already guessed how it ended. Nevertheless, Maleek concluded the tale.

"At first, everyone present could not speak, the shock was too great. The Prince and heir to Sidon was dead and by my father's hand. That was when the High Priestess of Byblos swiped her pointed nails across his face and spat into the wounds she had inflicted. She summoned a curse so potent that there was no doubt in our minds that he would suffer the worst kind of fate. She said that the misery would linger and wipe out our entire family unless he made amends."

"And did he?" I asked unashamedly, enthralled by the tale.

"He tried. We gave up the best snail grounds and paid tribute to their deities by building a temple to Baal. Initially, we thought he had escaped the priestess' wrath, but then he grew sick."

"And he was forced to give up leadership and seek healers to fix him?"

I watched the glimmer of hope fade from his dark eyes. His nod seemed so final, so dejected, so lost. A part of me felt relieved knowing the full story. I had built it up in my mind as the workings of evil demons after a wicked act. Suliaman was no more a demon than I, and probably a lot less violent than our own Chieftains. It made me wonder what the priestess did to him when she scratched his face. Had she laced her nails with a poison so that it worked its way slowly through his body?

For the rest of that day, I pondered this and rejected it as false. My own experience of poison tells me that if you survive the first quarter moon, you're likely to recover fully. Unless, of course, you're in constant contact with the stuff like those down at the mines near to Land's End.

When we made camp, Idina stood between Cade and Tallack as they indulged in ale and banter.

"Move aside woman, we were talking." Cade fumed, catching her by the hipbone and shoving her out of his view.

"You are taking us fully north, when you should be heading west." She said, straining against his arm.

"What would you know about it? We have to go north to the stones." Cade laughed, treating her like she was addled. He pulled a face to Tallack who smiled his response.

"Go north and you stray into Brigantes territory, then may the gods help us. Your Prince will not last the time it takes to avoid them. Your horses are too weak to pull him over the mountains and trust me when I say that those hills are not a patch on the massive peaks at the top of the world."

Cade tittered, until he saw the look on Tallack's face. Her reasoning was sound, even if Cade did not understand.

My nephew called to his shipmate, Renowden. "You've sailed all the way around this great land haven't you, Ren?"

The old sea dog ambled over and stood with a rabbit pelt swinging from one hand and a filthy blade in the other. “Aye. Right round and jumped islands too.”

“Are the mountains as big as those from the Ordoviches Tribe in Kembra?” Tallack looked pensive, awaiting the answer.

“Bigger, I’d say. It’s tough up there, that’s for sure.” Renowden threw his knife into the soggy mud and sat on a rock.

Tallack glanced at Idina. “If we go west, isn’t there just as much chance of meeting another unfriendly tribe?”

“There is, yes, but they are fewer in number and the terrain easier to walk. If we get to the coast, there are many fishermen with reasonable sized boats. You can sail the rest of the way for a little gold or tin in exchange.” Idina smiled at Tallack, looking him up and down. He was a fine young man by any standards. He attracted just about any woman, or man in his vicinity. Compared to the squat Cade, he must have seemed a much better proposition for the daughter of a great Chieftain. I sighed, anticipating more drama further ahead.

It was our best option by far, and yet Cade seemed determined to derail her. “The Prince gets seasick. It may well kill him to go by sea.”

Tallack leapt to Idina’s defence. “He’ll have to cross the ocean to get to the stones on the island off the Skotek coast anyway. He won’t make it if it takes us another two moons to trek over the mountains. Aunt Mel can give him plenty of herbs to stave off the sickness.”

Cade growled and cursed under his breath, knowing full well that his voice was not that of the leader. Tallack had made up his mind. He went in search of Maleek, to communicate the altered plans.

The relief of shortening our journey had a profound effect on our travelling party. Warriors laughed and talked together around a fire of their own, Maleek and Tallack drank and caroused, while Idina and I settled to stitching furs together from Renowden's treated collection of pelts.

When the Prince was well enough to receive the news, he seemed to visibly brighten. He took a little food and ale and strengthened to the point where he asked to be lifted in his chair to the fireside. Idina leaned on the carved wooden board that the Prince had gifted to her as she stitched. I could not help but admire the markings on its surface. When she lifted a pelt next, I slipped it from her knees. Tracing my fingers over the evenly spaced markings, I tried to make sense of the peculiar scratches.

The Prince caught me entranced. "You like the votive panel, Fur Benyn?"

"I do. It's fine work. I like the swirls and tracery around the edges, but I don't understand why there are so many different scratches made in rows." They were uniform in depth and some were repeated with gaps in between.

"This is how we mark our speech in our homeland. Those scratches form words so that we can record our history, our trades and send messages great distances." The Prince said with a self-satisfied smile. "Do you not record your language here?"

I shook my head, marvelling at the ingenuity. "We tell our stories to the younger people in the tribe. Sometimes they are sung. We have no need to mark bits of wood. We speak to messengers who then ride to another clan."

"What about your ancestors? How will people remember them?" He asked, perplexed by our ways.

"We honour them at the midsummer gatherings where their songs are sung and tales told. They are great celebrations of life and death, most often between clans from the same tribe but every few cycles all the tribes are represented at Stonehenge on the borders of the Durotriges land."

Suliaman gave me a slow respectful nod. I could see that he thought this an inefficient use of time and efforts, but to learn all those scratches would take even longer in my view. Yet another difference between our cultures. At least he did not claim his way was better than ours.

Later in the evening, Suliaman performed his own sacrifice over the grinning idol. His health came in fits and starts, some days faltering, other days he was buoyant, but the sacred statue had its fill of blood daily, even when food was scarce.

Taking a westerly route through the rolling foothills of the Coritani lands, we passed across their border into the western tribe of the Cornovii. Idina advised Tallack to send a scout ahead in search of settlers and tribal campsites, allowing our party to avoid any potential rancour. She instructed Jago to hoist the white flag of pilgrimage over the wagon. I thought this odd, since we'd displayed her own colours throughout the neighbouring lands.

"My father has no alliance with this tribe. They would see my banner as a declaration of war, since they do not know me. It's far safer to show white." Idina explained when I queried her actions.

Tallack seemed inordinately taken with Idina. He trotted alongside her horse whenever he was not flirting with Maleek. He was like a dog with two tails. I really must have a word about his inconsistencies. This is not the behaviour of a respected Metern of the Dumnonii. As I thought this, my mind wandered back to our homeland, pondering on our tribe's state of readiness for attack.

The further along the track we rode, the more I pined for home. Blydh was too young and inexperienced to organise battle plans without our help. He did have the respect of a great many warriors, even if those from the Priest Sect were at odds with his decisions. It made me wonder what had become of their half-brother, Paega. Perhaps he too could forgive and forget the past in order to help Blydh secure the Dumnonii future.

We passed through a wide, shallow valley where the tufted grass grew sideways from the constant funnelling wind. After a brief stop to water the horses and refill our drinking supplies, we picked up the pace towards a large swathe of moorland. This place was much like our own, similar heathland plants, boggy central lowlands and craggy hilltops. By late afternoon, the mist descended, making our bones ache with the cold dampness.

Conversation dried up as we hurried in single file along a track which threatened to engulf the wheels of the wagon. This eerie place gave me the chills. Through the fog ahead of us, the sun sank behind a solitary low tree. I recognised it immediately - the lonely hawthorn. Tallack cantered ahead, riding in a circle about its base.

When we caught up, he dismounted and unsheathed his sword, stabbing it into the mossy ground at his feet.

"What are you doing? You must stop at once!" Idina cried out. "A hawthorn marks the site of a forgotten grave. You must not disturb the dead or the demons from the underworld will rise and smite us for its desecration." Idina led her horse as close as she dared, taking cautious steps towards him.

"Rubbish. That's what tribe's folk tell the young ones to stop them from stealing the troves of metals and jewels buried beneath." Tallack kept stabbing the ground at regular intervals in the hope of hitting a trunk under the soil.

"Seriously cousin, she's right. At the very least it's bad luck to disturb the roots. Foul things lie at the heart of a hawthorn. Why else would it stink of rotting corpses come spring?" Cade stood next to his wife, united in their panic.

"Is that right, Aunt Mel?" Tallack said as I reached level with our group and dismounted.

"Well, boy, it ain't our custom, but we're closer to their lands than ours. Best leave it alone to be on the safe side." I could see him trying to hide his pout. "A lonely tree in the middle of the moors should be honoured. Give it some of your ale as an offering, in case the gods are watching over it."

"Bless you, Meliora." Idina said. "I think that's best. I'll make my own offering too." She reached into the bags slung across her horse and pulled out a beautiful necklace of shells and hooked it on a branch close to the trunk. I watched her bow her head and utter a prayer to the gods for protection. Tallack had already wet its roots with his best ale before the Prince sent word demanding the reason for the delay.

Every part of me ached to leave this place. It was more than a hollow where stale mist whirled and disorientated us, it had an otherworld feeling like a mouth of a burial cist or one of the barrows at Stonehenge. Despite my misgivings, Tallack ordered us all to make camp for the night. He did not seem disturbed by the place one bit, dancing about the lonely tree as though it was his friend.

Idina suggested only one small fire in this desolate, frozen wasteland. She feared that too much light would be seen by roving tribe's folk of the Cornovii.

"Have you had much dealing with this tribe, Idina?" I asked, keen to keep the sounds of the night-time at bay with our chatter.

"Very little. What I know about them come from tales with our allies the Coritani. They are brutal people, by all accounts. They trade little and raid a lot. Their warriors make necklaces from the fingers of their enemies. They say that their old chieftain's necklace had three long loops of bones." The poor mite looked scared for her life. I dared not tell her that Tallack's brother preferred to hang the entire head of his foes from his horse.

"Every tribe tells frightening stories to protect their lands from invaders." I said, patting her shoulder to soothe her. "I expect they are nowhere near as scary in person."

She gave me a look that said, *you know nothing, old lady,* but she did not voice her thoughts.

That night, the idol was lifted down to the fireside and Suliaman along with it, but there was no fresh creature to offer in sacrifice. The Prince sent out his warriors in search of rodent, rabbit, deer or fowl, but all came back empty handed. Tallack suggested more ale poured over the statue, Idina offered her bowl of salted pork stew, but both were deemed insufficient. According to Jago's translations of the Prince's growl, nothing would suffice but warm blood.

Cade, Idina, Tallack and I all looked at each other in fear. In the absence of animal blood, would Suliaman resort to that of mankind? His warriors all fell to their knees in regret at their failure. Maleek stepped before them glaring at each one in turn. Was he deciding who should donate blood to their god? When he reached the second to last man, Maleek unsheathed his curved blade from its scabbard. I held my breath as he drew his arm back.

"Don't suppose this would do?" Renowden said, looming into view through the mists holding a bucking hare by the scruff. It's a bit scrawny, granted, but it's still kicking. My relief was overwhelming. All our shoulders slumped in collective relief. For a sailor, Renowden was the best hunter in all our lands, and his timing could not have been more perfect.

Maleek thanked him and offered him a small quantity of gold for his troubles. Renowden gestured that it was not necessary, but when Maleek's face turned from smiling to cold and angry, he took the metal and gave his thanks. That sacrifice seemed to mark a change in our foreign friends. Something had shifted in their manner, but I could not put my finger on precisely what was different.

The Prince completed the ritual and returned directly to the confines of his cart. Maleek sat with the healer and warriors, speaking quietly in their own tongue. Jago sat behind me out of sight, with our new furs wrapped about him. I tried several times to engage him in conversation but he remained silent and troubled. Tallack and Cade drank with Renowden, while Idina and her maids stitched by the firelight. Everything looked fine to anyone watching from the outside, but my stomach tied in knots from the bleak and unforgiving atmosphere among us.

I woke from an uneasy sleep before dawn and set about reviving the fire. By the time everyone else had surfaced, I had a tasteless porridge cooked and all our possessions packed and ready to leave. There was no way I was going to hang about in this place for another day. Jago dashed about between us all, chivvying people along and rinsing bowls almost before they had finished eating. He too was keen for us to leave. At my age, you got used to trusting your gut and mine told us to get moving as quickly as possible.

The mist still lingered as we left the moorland hollow and entered another much narrower valley. I could just make out the ridge tops silhouetted against a grey sky. A massive gathering of crows was disturbed by our noise, squawking and flapping over our heads in a black mass of feathers. Idina looked petrified as she clutched the reins of her horse to her chest in fear.

“Pay them no heed, my dear.” I shouted over to her. “They won’t come closer with all these spears to protect us.” It didn’t seem to quell her panic. She and her horse slowed down, leaving the rest of us to trot along without her. I couldn’t figure out why until we got close to the other end of the gorge. Her eyesight was far better than mine. Now I could see why the crows were gathered in such large numbers at this end of the valley.

Stretched across our pathway were twenty or more spikes driven into the ground. Each of them supported the rotting heads of men, women, children and their horses.

CHAPTER TWENTY-TWO

Tallack and Cade pulled their ponies to a stop and called after Idina. When she failed to respond to them, Cade rode back to where she sat still on her horse.

"Is this just a warning or does it mean something else? Do you think they are camped nearby? Idina!" Cade shouted. "Talk to us."

She blinked herself alert and tore her stare away from the severed heads. "It's a warning to go back. We shouldn't have come. I am so sorry to have led you all here." She twisted the reins to her left and kicked her horse, urging it to turn about.

"We can't go back. We have travelled too far into their territory to return and anyway, you said yourself, we'd never make it over the mountains to the north." Tallack yelled after her, stopping her from cantering away. "Listen, we've made it this far without trouble. How many days are we from the coast?"

Idina's fretting affected her horse. It fussed and skittered about, spinning in circles. "I don't know, two maybe three days."

"Dry, fast tracks or slow and awkward?" I asked, thinking that we could afford to push the horses for longer each day if they were to rest at the coast.

"Not sure… I haven't been this way since I was really young." Idina confessed.

Tallack took charge. "No fires, we take the trail as fast as it will allow and sleep under and around the cart. Four-hour watches, Suliaman's warriors scouting ahead and bringing up the rear. I don't want any surprises." He sounded a lot like his father, may Cernonnus take him into the Summerlands.

I rode ahead of the wagon with Idina at my side and Jago on the rear of my pony. Cade took the lead up front, while Tallack kept his eye out behind us. His mastery of his horse allowed him to ride sitting reversed on the animal's back. I felt a little safer for all these precautions, but we needed more than luck to see us to the coast unscathed. Idina could not stop talking about the decapitated heads. That surprised me, since living with the Catuve all her life, I expected her to have seen her fair share of bloodshed.

When we reached the furthest end of the valley beyond the spiked heads, visibility was down to a few horse lengths. Tallack insisted that we kept up the fast pace, despite the wheels on the cart creaking and groaning with every rock and stone they hit on the trail. Cade pushed us all on beyond nightfall, until the scouts returned to us with news that the path ahead was boggy, and that they would need to seek out a new route come daylight. As a result, we were forced to make camp in a wooded glade at the base of a wide moorland dell.

The river water was sweet and cold. Our horses took their fill and I bathed my feet. Sitting on the riverbank with my legs dangling in the water I relaxed for a few moments and washed myself. Suliaman sat in his tethered tall chair looking out from the wagon at me. I called to Jago for a cup and filled it with the fresh liquid from further upstream. With my wooden pattens covering my clean feet, I wandered over to the cart and held the cup aloft. Suliaman's healer took it from me and handed it to the Prince. He clamped the cup between both palms, his fingers curling into stiff and bony claws.

He drank the entire cup down in a few gulps and breathed out with its freshness. Two teeth were missing from his smile. "I have never tasted water so good before. In my land, if you can let the sediments fall to the base, it is still warm and tastes of sand."

"Well, water is something we never go short of here." I said, almost in complaint. I was about to turn away when I noticed a thick red liquid trickling down his top lip. "Your nose is bleeding."

The healer stepped up and held a cloth to his face. "I didn't notice." His eyelids twitched as though he no longer had control over their movement. These were new symptoms of his ailment, and I was at a loss as to how to help him. The sores on his arms had toughened into raised lumps and now appeared on his forehead. Even if his nerve pain had lessened, the other symptoms showed him declining at a frightening rate.

I took some willow bark from a pocket in my cloak and gave it to the healer. He sneered at me as he reached out, but at least it was not an outright refusal. Tallack was close by, feeding the horses with some of our grain to supplement the grass.

"The Prince is failing fast." I told him, muttering quietly so that no one else could hear.

"Then we must press on. We'll rest for a few hours and set off before dawn." He walked off to relay his instructions to Cade and the others. Jago and I watched Maleek directing the warriors, as they performed their nightly task of lifting the idol from the cart. I knew for what they were preparing. Their god demanded another sacrifice to hold the curse at bay for long enough to reach the stones. The problem was that we had not spotted nor heard a hint of any animal activity all day. Even if Maleek's warriors hunted all night, it was doubtful they would return with anything dead or alive.

I glanced over at Renowden in the hope that he could give us some good news. He shook his head, predicting my request. Maleek looked deeply troubled. What would happen if the great Phoenician god, Melkarth was not given warm blood? Did he have the power to strike us all down in a raging storm, with bolts of lightning filling the skies? I was starting to wish that I'd taken a sprig of sacred hawthorn when I had the chance to protect me from spiteful vengeance.

Tallack explained how precarious our position was and the need for his warriors to patrol a boundary further out from camp. With visibility so poor, a series of signalling whistles were laid down for the watchmen to use, before Maleek sent them out into the mist. Chilled, afraid and hungry, we huddled together eating dried salted pork and drinking cold ale.

Two warriors remained in camp, heaving Suliaman from the wagon, and setting him down next to the grinning idol. The Prince called to Maleek. They spoke quietly at first, with Maleek's tone pleading and apologetic. Suliaman on the other hand, grew in volume and temper. His anger flared up along with a resurgence of blood from his nose. His changeable temperament shocked us all. At one point in their heated debate, Maleek pointed to his horse, but Suliaman simply shook his head. The number of our ponies was too few as it was. Losing another would mean more of us doubling up and tiring the creatures quicker each day.

Jago looked panicked once again, crouching behind my back and whimpering. He was the only one of us who understood the row between them and it clearly disturbed him. This reaction was becoming so commonplace, I assumed that conflict of any sort brought back the sad memories from the past. Cernonnus knows, he had been through many of them.

With the fog increasing in density and dampening our clothes and furs, they argued in their own tongue until Maleek's shoulder's slumped in defeat. Suliaman began the incantation without an animal to offer to their statue. Stained in layer upon layer of fetid humours, the lurid grin and twisted arms were still visible in the diffused moonlight.

Suliaman's healer helped him to his feet to conduct the final part of the ritual. Maleek stepped forwards, rolling his tunic sleeve up over his elbow and thrusting his forearm above the idol's head. With his curved blade, the Prince's son slashed his own arm and allowed the red life force to trickle out of his body and over the clay god.

We could hardly believe what we were witnessing. Suliaman had demanded this of his son, despite the risk that the wound might fester and rot in the damp conditions. How could a man expect this of his own flesh and blood?

The Prince was vexing and puzzling in the extreme. One moment he rejoiced in the simple pleasures of cool fresh water and polite conversation and the next he expected his son to slice open his veins. He was gentle and generous in one moment and wrathful and wicked the next. I cannot begin to understand their culture or religion, but to expect your son and heir to weaken themselves as an offering is beyond my tolerance.

Moreover, if Maleek was now an offering, did that mean that none of us could touch him in order to dress his wound for fear of retribution? Did he mean so little to Suliaman that he was to lie down next to the statue and drain out before us like the badger and all the other creatures forsaken in this unholy mess?

Cade, Tallack and I all stood around wondering what to do. None of us wanted to make matters worse with so many of his warriors surrounding our camp. I wanted to ease Maleek's suffering. After all, he had done me a service when the thief tried to take my medicine kit in the Frynkish port, I felt that I owed him.

I took a deliberate step closer and stared at the Prince. In a way, he was indebted to me after all the tonics and healing balms I had made for him. I figured that he might spare me, if only for the similarities of my name to their God of Gods, Melkarth. "Prince Suliaman. Maleek must be treated at once if we are to prevent rot." I held his glare, each of us elders facing off in a mental dance of authority. He may have the warriors and the gold, but this is my homeland and leaving them here in the dead of night would secure their fate. My narrowed eyes conveyed as much. Their heads would refresh those on spikes at the other end of the valley before the next moon grew fat.

He attempted to move a leg forward, his muscles wasted and weak. At length he fell backwards into his tall chair. Neither his healer nor his warrior servant rushed to catch him. Perhaps they knew more about his quicksilver moods than we did. What other unpleasant ways was the old man hiding?

"You are brave, Meliora, but foolish. If you interfere with the offering to Melkarth, you invite his ire." Despite his weak body, his voice was strong and unsettling.

"He is your son and heir to a great city. Would you see him succumb to the green rot of the flesh, to writhe in agony as the bad humours send him mad with fever?" I saw a flicker of pain cross his face for a moment, before he recovered his composure. For a man so intent on regaining his title and position, he seemed to think little of the generation who would follow him.

Maleek stepped closer to me, covering the slash on his wrists with his free hand. His knife dripped from within the case strapped to his waist. He said nothing, but stared at his father with a poisonous glare.

"Surely you can break the rules in order to save your kin? He is your flesh and blood. Melkarth would not punish you for a little healing ointment and a few stitches." I held my gaze for longer than it was comfortable. Maleek alternated his stare between his father, me and Tallack.

Suliaman's eye's twitched again, showing how far the curse had spread through his bodily control. He tried to curl his lip in disgust, but it manifested as a strange grimace instead. "Do what you will, but when the Gods strike you down, don't be surprised."

It was neither permission nor censure. At first, I was unsure whether to proceed or whether the Prince would have me killed for touching Maleek's arm. Holding my hand aloft to stop Tallack from walking towards his lover, I stepped between them and led Maleek over to my medicine kit. Jago flitted about, fetching clean water, and handing me prepared muscle fibres, my bone needle, plantain paste and fresh leaves to cover the wound site.

When I was finished, Maleek tried to give me a golden fibula in payment. Expressing my thanks, I politely rejected his offer. I do not want to be beholden to him or his father any more than we already were. Maleek was greatly surprised at my refusal to take his gold. Material possessions are obviously very important in his city. They afford those who hold great wealth the power to choose who lives and who dies. In the Dumnoni lands, trust and honour are valued above all else and he and his father had failed to prove either.

Our supper was a far cry from luxury. Cold ale and a few strips of dried meat to lessen the hunger pangs. The Prince ate nothing, favouring more resin water instead. I was starting to see the benefits of having him dosed up on the stuff in preference to his wakeful savagery. Maleek disappeared into the mists to check on his warriors at the guarded perimeter. I supposed this to be either side of the cool river and beyond the confines of the wooded vale.

Tallack, Cade, Renowden, Idina and I stayed close to the cart, wishing that we could light a big fire to ward off the damp. The mist stuck to our clothes and our faces and soaked us all through.

"We should keep our own watches through the night, Cade. I have a bad feeling about this place." I said to the son of the Cantii.

"And miss out on the chance to get some rest. You heard Maleek. He's got all his foreign warriors surrounding us. We are safer in the centre here than out on the track." Cade unrolled his bedding and took a prime spot beneath the cart for himself and Idina. She stayed close to me. Idina had barely uttered a word since the discovery of the severed heads.

Tallack shrugged and packed away our dried rations. I watched him take an age to move each item and fold a waxen cloth about the meat. It was only when I spotted his smile as Maleek appeared from between the trees through the fog, that I realised he was dawdling on purpose. He intended to hide with his lover away from camp.

Maleek looked stern and drawn. I doubted that it was from blood loss, as I was quick to bind his wound. It seemed to me that his frown was a result of an internal struggle of some sort. Tallack watched him approach, beaming with promise of delightful times ahead, but Maleek strode right past him without uttering a word. New wrinkles and deep-set shadows mired his youthful complexion.

Tallack jumped to his feet and ran after him, catching him by the shoulder and spinning him about.

"Don't touch me, infidel!" Maleek bellowed.

Tallack staggered backwards, reeling from the rebuff. "What's got into you?"

"Don't you understand? I belong to Melkarth now. Other than healers like your aunt, No one can touch me ever again." Maleek panted, his shoulders heaving in rhythmic waves with his despair.

"But that's ridiculous." Tallack sneered reaching out for Maleek's arm. "You know that don't you? You can't go the rest of your life untouched, it's just not feasible."

The Prince's son snatched his limb away, turning from his lover with a pinched frown and tears pooling in his eyes.

"Aunt Mel, tell him that he is over-reacting." Tallack spun about to seek my help. What could I do? It was their faith, their beliefs, not ours. No one could gain say hundreds of cycles of worship and rituals. I looked to the ground and said nothing.

They spoke in hushed growls, Maleek laying out his bedding while Tallack crouched at his side trying to reason with him. Suliaman sat in a dazed stupor having drunk the poppy water mixed by his generous healer.

Jago and I moved further away, acutely aware of our intrusion into their private discussion. Cade and Renowden both snapped their heads back towards the trees, startled by the same sound. The noise of dry sticks snapping underfoot. Renowden scanned everyone in camp. It looked to me that he was counting us, figuring out who from our party was missing. There were none absent, we were all accounted for.

"Pssst!" Renowden signalled to Tallack. A few hand gestures later and he, Cade, and Tallack made ready their weapons.

Maleek caught up with events. He jumped to his feet and ordered the two remaining warriors to investigate the source of the noise. The burly men ran off in the direction of Tallack's outstretched arm. We all waited, fretting and poised. They did not return.

Renowden looked to Tallack for his Chieftain's orders. My nephew nodded. With spears, swords, daggers and axes, they formed a line next to Maleek and marched into the dense fog between oak and ash.

Just Jago, the healer and us women were left in camp to protect the Prince. I stood one side of the tall chair, Jago the other. Both of us held blades from my healing kit, and shook from fear. Idina slipped past me and ushered her handmaidens under the cart, before retrieving a longbow and quiver from her belongings. The Prince took a few deep inhalations, clearing his mind of resin fog. He was alert enough to understand that we were under attack.

He signalled to the healer with a jittery hand, and barked an order to him. The healer bowed, scurried over to the cart, fetched a long bronze sword with a golden hilt and stood behind the tall chair.

"In front of me you coward!" The Prince bellowed, but the healer looked to have pissed himself.

A blurred host of wild men came into view through the swirling mists, screaming, yelling and hurling axes and spears.

CHAPTER TWENTY-THREE

They came at us from all angles, their faces daubed in woad, chalk grease and the blood of their enemies. We were outnumbered and surrounded. The river lay at our backs hindering any possible escape. The mist concealed the scope of our opponents. We had no idea of the fate of our warriors or whether they were fighting at the boundaries of the wood. Jago trembled at my side. Idina shushed the terrified handmaidens. My stomach erupted into my mouth, but I swallowed the fear down. I'd had a good life. If this was to be my end, let it be, but I would go down fighting. I am Dumnonii after all.

The healer took one look at the marauders, dropped Suliaman's sword to the ground and fled. He threw himself into the frigid waters of the river and tried to wade through the strong current. His robes grew heavy, sucking up the moisture and slowing him down. He was less than a third of the way across when the first arrow hit him in the back. The second and third caught him in the ribs and neck, sending him tumbling face down into the stream.

The attackers were upon us. Arrows flew, hitting the Prince in the shoulder and sticking into the wood of his chair, pinning him down. I held up the material of my tunic and cloak, readying myself for the onslaught with the biggest knife I had left after Brea's theft. There was no time for nervous prattle or deliberations. We had to act, and fast.

Jago slipped behind the chair and picked up the sword. Grasping the hilt in both hands, he marched in front of the Prince and stood firm as the Cornovii raged towards us. I'm not so stupid as to think that I could over power them, but I am not a bad aim at close range. Ducking from the spears and arrows, I managed to dodge the worst of their weapons until I could see the anger in their faces. Drawing my arm back, I took aim and let my blade loose. My first throw found a home between the eyes of a massive warrior. He skidded to the ground at my feet as another jabbed a spear past me and towards Jago.

With surprisingly fleet footwork, Jago sidestepped the spear and thrust the blade home through the man's belly, ripping a gash wide enough for his guts to spill out at the feet of the Prince. A shorter clansman lunged next, slamming his dagger down onto Suliaman's wrist and grabbing at the metals strung about his neck. Jago spun around with a slicing swipe, nicking the stout man's throat with the tip. Blood gushed over the Prince, soaking all his fine robes and drenching his face in red humours.

I had all my blades lined up at my feet, stooping low and aiming high for their eyes. By my third knife, I'd taken down two more, before I realised that I was out of daggers. Jago stood in front of the Prince, his stance wide, his determination visible from his gritted teeth.

More Cornovii dashed from the trees into our small clearing. There were more than I could count at a glance. Outnumbered with only one sword in defence, I thought that we had reached the end of our quest. Idina let her arrows fly, taking out four more before they got within spitting distance of us. She threw her expensive dagger, hilt first across the ground to my feet, allowing me to dispatch another marauder.

Muttering a prayer to Cernonnus in the Summerlands, I asked for his assistance. It was as if he was watching over me, since Tallack and Renowden ran out of the trees from each side to help even up the numbers. Cade and Maleek came shortly after, wrestling, chopping, spearing and killing anything in their paths.

I used their presence to gather up my knives from the dead, allowing me to pick off a few more attackers from the side-lines. Even amid the fury and terror, I could see that Maleek was suffering from his wounds. The self-inflicted offering to his god had left him vulnerable. From that weakened stance, he had suffered new wounds from the Cornovii.

Tallack limped badly from a wound to his thigh, but still managed to out manoeuvre two Cornovi warriors. He dropped to his knees as each of them swung their axes. With their weapons tangled above his head, he grabbed a couple of daggers and stabbed both men in their crotches at the same time. I could tell from the amount of blood that his larger blood vessels were not ruptured. He would survive the scrape.

I was out of blades to throw. Shimmying on my knees, I ducked under the cart alongside Idina and her maidens. She had just three arrows left in her quiver. Mindful of her limited resources, she took her time to aim at those warriors who were inflicting the most damage. Every single one of her shots hit their precise target. She was a formidable woman.

Renowden bellowed over to Tallack and pointed at the cart. While we were defending our lives from the front, more warriors had pillaged the Prince's wealth from the rear. I turned about beneath the wagon to see them yanking the trunks of metals and jewels up the bank on the opposite side of the river. As a final act of defiance, one of the Cornovii kicked out at the healer's body, propelling it into the fastest part of the current to bloody the waters downstream. The few remaining stragglers retreated, leaving our party injured and without metal to aid our journey.

Idina and I dragged ourselves from beneath the cart and walked over to the carnage surrounding Suliaman. Jago still brandished the sword, swishing it about the air and twitching with edgy fury.

"You can put that down now, boy. They're all gone." I tapped his shoulder and had to jump out of his way as he swiped the blade in my direction. He was so revved up by the experience.

Tallack chuckled, leaning in to disarm my slave. "We should give you a new name. Jago the Underestimated… how about Jago the Giant, you know, cause you're so little?"

"He already has a name." I said, annoyed with my nephew for his ungallant behaviour. "He is the Chosen One."R I shot Tallack such a glare as to silence him on the matter. To Jago, I whispered, "Why would you risk your life for the Prince like that?" How had this slave boy overcome all his fears to brandish a sword so effectively?

Jago stammered. "He… he… All rulers are powerful priests, Fur Benyn. His dark magic could still reach me even after death. No one from my homeland would act differently."

I had no answer to that. Was this how the noblemen of Phoenician cities kept their people in line, by making them believe they wield the power of gods?

All around us were spilled guts, chopped flesh and leaking corpses. Heading towards the Prince's tall chair, I kicked a body over onto his back to remove one of my knives from his face. There was a severed hand next to the corpse, complete with jewelled rings and pale sores. Glancing up to the Prince, his fine robes ended with a bloody stump. His life force was trickling down the side of his chair, and yet no one noticed, not even the Prince.

For longer than I care to admit, I stood and pondered what might happen if I let him bleed out. If the Prince were to die, it would be from the attack. Tallack and I could not be held responsible. Would Maleek keep the old man's word over the trade agreements and payment if Suliaman perished? Would their homeland be better off in Maleek's hands rather than his changeable father? This was a man who valued wealth and power more than his own kin. I must have ruminated for too long, as Tallack saw Jago staring at the hand and raised the alarm.

The Prince began to panic. Until then, he was too occupied fighting the effects of the resin. His head must have been in a permanent haze. He was so busy watching our movements that he was unaware of his own body. Not only had he lost his hand, but he had not felt it happening. The curse was growing in strength every day.

Maleek dashed to his father's side. He too had injuries, but none were as urgent as Suliaman's. "Help him, please." He cried, falling to his knees at the side of the tall chair. I could hardly let him bleed out with everyone watching.

"Bind it tight. Strap a belt higher up his arm to slow the humours." I called to Tallack. "Jago, get wood and kindling. I need a fire."

"But, Aunt…" Tallack began.

I almost laughed. "I think it's a bit late for stealth, don't you? They won't be back this night. They have what they came for, and lost a great many warriors in the process."

No one disagreed. Renowden walked the perimeter, and came back with a collection of spears and a few arrows from the bodies of Maleek's men. "If I had to guess, Fur Benyn, I'd say that they were ambushed in the fog. All their metal stripped along with anything of value. I found these alongside the couple of Cornovii who were killed." The weapons were piled next to the fire. Other than what we carried on ourselves, it was all the wealth we had left between us.

Cade helped to drag the bodies from camp into a pile, while I heated my blade to seal Suliaman's wrist closed, just as I had done on his feet. He felt nothing. The man was still addled, allowing me to close the wound to his shoulder with ease. Tallack was my next priority. His leggings were slashed open, revealing a tear in his thigh muscle as long as my hand. I gave him a strap to bite down on and did my best to stitch the muscle fibres back together before closing the skin over the top. This patient felt every stitch and every movement. I could tell from his pinched face and sweaty brow, even though the ground around us was frozen hard.

By the time I had moved on to treat Maleek, Tallack was asking for willow bark and ale. Jago supplied both, but it did not ease the pain. By some miracle, neither Cade nor Renowden were injured. Whether they were better warriors, or just luckier in their opponents, I could not say, but both made themselves invaluable in sorting through the dead or dying, and calming the handmaidens of their hysteria.

It was Idina who surprised me the most. We had travelled through these lands at her insistence. I knew that she felt fully to blame for what had happened. She wore a permanent frown over her lovely face, and rushed about camp helping every one of us to the point of exhaustion. She may have suggested the route, but her warnings were clear enough. It was Cade and Tallack who had made the final decision to press on. And in truth, Idina had killed more than her fair share of marauders with her deadly aim. In my opinion, she had more than acquitted herself.

As soon as all the injured were healed, we all stood together next to the cart to make sense of the situation. By Renowden's reckoning, all but two of Maleek's warriors had given their lives protecting us. The Cornovii had lost more than a dozen in their raid. There was no time to waste. If the same raiding party returned for their dead, or worse, sought out reinforcements, the rest of us would perish too.

Suliaman and the remaining weapons were bundled onto the cart, along with Maleek. The rest of us mounted our horses and set off along the western trail before daybreak. The going was slow, with the wagon getting bogged down fairly often as the scouts had predicted. Idina took the lead up front, her knowledge of the area and superior eyesight giving us an advantage in the fog. She also refilled her quiver, with enough arrows collected from the dead, and rode with her bow resting on her leg. After all we had been through that night, no one would survive who crossed our path.

I did feel some pity for those poor warriors who were left as carrion for the crows. We dared not tarry to burn or bury the bodies, but I fully expected the Prince to demand an even greater sacrifice in their honour come nightfall. I looked at each of the people in our party. My anguish manifested as roiling bile in my chest. If his own son's blood was not sufficient to appease their wrathful god, then what would?

After a long morning of riding, Tallack complained that the willow was not sufficient to ease his pain. He rode alongside the cart and stepped onto the moving wagon, hitching his horse to the back. I suspected that he had used it as an excuse to ride with Maleek. He had suffered more devastating wounds in his time, and at a younger age with less fuss.

What disturbed me more, was that after I heard raised voices and shuffling footsteps inside the covered cart, Tallack reappeared with a small smear of resin on the sleeve of his leather coat. Maleek had banished Tallack from the wagon with some of Suliaman's poppy stash. What could I do, but turn a blind eye to the fall out and hope that they could make things right later on when things were calmer and nerves less frayed?

We stopped only briefly, to water and feed the horses before pushing on throughout the day at a steady pace. The closer we got to the coast, the more forgiving the trail, allowing us to travel swiftly to the large estuary on the western fringes. Here, Idina assured us, we could pay the fishermen to take us through the bay and north towards the isle where the stones lay.

We made camp at the water's edge. It was bleak and windswept. Renowden did his best to catch us some supper, but the fish were flat with strong tasting flesh and too many bones. Not that I was hungry. My innards were still in shock from the attack. I kept my mouth shut and my eyes peeled, watching my nephew making a fool of himself over the depressed Maleek. Time and time again, he tried to encourage discourse, only to be sent packing to our side of the large fire Cade had built for us.

Idina sat with her hand maidens, speaking in hushed tones. It looked to me as though they were plotting, but more than that I could not say. Jago did all he could to make me comfortable and then took care of my horse. There was plenty of firewood and lots of flat fish to eat, but we were a sombre crew that night. Only the Prince and Maleek chose to sleep in the wagon. The rest of us stayed close to the fire, keeping a careful shift system of watches throughout the evening. Cade even took to his horse to ride to the highest hill in order to scout for us, not that any attackers would give away their location by lighting fires as large as ours.

We had to take Idina's word for it that fishermen on the coast cared little for the raiding and pillaging that other clans took part in further inland. Theirs was an honourable lifestyle, fishing, gathering and digging for shellfish from the shores. They only cared if you strayed into their territory to plunder their catch before they could begin the day's harvesting. I took this to mean that the Cornovii were not as organised as other tribes. Each clan raided as and when they liked without a tribal leader to watch over them all.

Idina said as much when I asked her to confirm my suspicions. "That's more or less how it is, yes. There was a Chieftain of this region a few cycles ago, but he was slaughtered by his own men. They could not agree on a new leader, and so clan relations broke down."

Cade listened to his new young wife when he had returned from his scouting trip. He sat opposite her, smiling at her pretty face as she regaled us with tales of the treachery from this region. Once again, she apologised for taking us through a territory she truly believed to be safe. Her father had given accounts of the scattered clans, leading her to think that the northern trails would be abandoned.

All the while she spoke, Cade's eye lids drooped in an uncoordinated way. He was utterly besotted by her. She obviously had the measure of him, since she surrounded herself with her handmaidens, barring him all access to her body.

We were all starting to relax after such an ordeal, when the last two warriors lifted Suliaman from the wagon and then returned for the grinning statue. Each one of us shuddered at the thought of what would come next. Jago braced himself for another attack of tremors. Maleek remained in the cart, avoiding Tallack. Suliaman was still weakened from the blood loss, but with help, he managed to get to his feet and stand.

In the tongue of his homeland, he gave his warriors specific orders. They bowed and ran off towards the estuary in the darkness. We all sat their astounded to think that after all that had happened, this Phoenician tyrant still expected a ritual sacrifice for his god, despite the fact that it made absolutely no difference to the progression of the curse.

Suliaman chanted a few prayers at the idol, and then sat down in silent contemplation. The rest of us all exchanged glances, wondering if he was weighing up which of us should lay down our lives for Melkarth the grinning statue.

In the time it took to cook another flatfish, the warriors were back with arms full of clay. One stayed and began shaping the mud at the fireside. The second man returned to the bay for more. I took a long drink of my ale and peered down at the shape forming under the warrior's careful hand, the half-moon eyes and grotesque grin was disturbingly familiar.

Tallack looked to me with a pained expression and shook his head. Like the others around me, I thought he was fashioning a second grinning god, but the face was spread across a flattened slab of clay. When it was almost complete, the warrior took out a blade and carved two holes in the eyes, a long slit for the mouth and another two in its ears. Suliaman had ordered the creation of Melkarth face masks.

CHAPTER TWENTY-FOUR

When the warriors had finished their labours, two finely crafted grinning masks were laid into the embers and covered with hot ash. We looked to the Prince for an explanation but he was surprisingly tight-lipped on the matter. I jogged Jago with my elbow, hoping to illicit an answer from him, but he was dazed and trembling again. This can only spell more trouble. Suliaman was back in his tall chair and issuing more orders.

I grasped hold of my cloak and tightened my fist around a blade I had stashed among the folds. If the warriors came close to those I love, I would fight with every fibre of my being. Instead, the men stepped over our legs and bundles and walked over to the horses.

"The white one." Suliaman shouted to them, pointing at my pony with the grey dappled markings. The same horse who had seen me across hill and vale for days on end since our feast with the Cantii. Anticipating what the Prince had in mind, I opened my mouth to protest, but Tallack stopped me, grabbing my arm and fixing me a glare.

"Don't. Better a horse than one of us." My nephew muttered, although we all heard him.

I truly believe that my dear pony could sense what was going to happen. He fussed and whinnied and refused to walk closer to the fire. With a slap to his hind quarters, the warriors forced the beast closer to the Prince.

I couldn't look, my fondness for the creature balled up in my throat. Biting my knuckle to prevent myself from calling out, I turned my back to the ritual just as Suliaman raised the blade to the horse's neck. The noise was sickening. A metallic swipe, a visceral ripping, followed by a loud splatter of blood on dry stones and sizzling flames. My white beauty groaned and toppled, before crashing to the ground. So many creatures snuffed out and all for nothing. I couldn't stop the tears from falling.

Tallack patted my arm. "You didn't need him anymore. Aunt. It is probably better that he was dispatched by a skilled blades man rather than the butchers we would have traded him to come the morning. I knew he meant it as a comfort, but it was more like salt in my wounds. The rest of our horses and the cart would remain in this little cluster of fishermen huts and dwellings along the estuary, while we sailed onto our destination.

Jago stood at my side, frozen and staring at the masks cooking in the fire. It was as though he had not even noticed the sacrifice before his eyes. I gave him another bump, to make sure that he was not suffering from a form of his seizures, but it was just a fearful stupor.

We slept in shifts. Idina and her maidens were put into the watch rotation along with Jago and myself. With so few of us left, we had to be more vigilant than ever. The fire burned all through the night, cooking the clay into pot. Come morning, the warrior who had made the gruesome objects, pushed them from the embers and let them cool.

I made some porridge and served ale to those who were awake and making ready to leave. We all watched the foreigners with the expectation that they would kill another bird over the masks. They did not. Instead, they waited until they were cool to the touch and wrapped them in some of the Prince's spare robes, before tying them to their backs.

We took the wagon and remaining horses down to the riverbank and agreed to let Idina negotiate our passage. She assured us that they were more likely to trade with her, since she could almost understand their distinctive local dialect.

Tallack gave her some of his own tin with which to make the deal. I didn't envy her. The attack from the Cornovii had tainted my opinion of clans in this region. They fought with no honour, I suspected that they would trade in a similar vein.

Idina took Jago along with her after seeing his courageous defence of the Prince with the bronze long sword. I admit that it surprised me too. Jago was always such a soft-hearted lad, so compliant and hardworking. It was as though his previous masters had beaten any hope from his bones before Tallack brought him to our shores.

It gladdened my heart to think that his former personality might still lurk among his down-trodden ways, but I couldn't quite reconcile his actions during the raid. Ever since we met the Prince and Maleek, Jago had been petrified and respectful of them to the point of frozen fear, yet when the attackers approached the Prince, he stepped in front of danger to defend him. Even with the threat of dark magic, I'm not sure I would have done the same in his shoes.

I pushed the questions from my mind, concentrating on the next leg of our journey. Idina and Jago were gone for most of the morning in search of boats large enough, with fishermen willing to take us to the Skotek Isles. When at last she returned, Idina was full of apology.

"It took all of your tin to persuade them to take us. I gave them half up front, so we must hurry or they might cast off with your money and we'll never see them again. I left Jago to keep an eye on them, but they are wary of a boy with painted skin." She looked to Tallack for signs of forgiveness, although I thought how determined she was to prevail when others of our group might easily have faltered.

"Good on you, Idina." I said. "Let's wrap things up quickly and get going. Tallack has more than enough tin back home. Don't you go fretting about it now." I reassured her, patting her back as I hobbled past. Cade gave me a beaming smile. He was already bending to her charms after their brief marriage. Old Osbert knew what he was doing binding those two together. It won't be Cade leading the Cantii when his father perishes, but Idina and her clever mind.

Maleek stayed in the cart with the bloodied idol and his father until we reached the shore. The raiding party had shaken them both, not to mention the wounds that were inflicted. Tallack added the resin from his sleeve to water and drank it all down. It must have been a strong decoction, since I couldn't get any sense from him at all about the boats Idina had hired. He was half addled at a time when we needed his expertise.

In desperation, I turned to Renowden for advice. He peered over the water's edge to see the hulls of the crafts as they sat low in the water. They were all a good deal smaller than our own vessels, and a fraction of the size of Tallack's Phoenician trading ship.

Twisting his mouth to one side, he scratched his thumbnail against the hair on his chin. "Seen better, seen worse, Fur Benyn. They'd be alright on calm waters, but up between them Skotek islands…" He sucked air across his teeth and shook his head. That did not fill me with confidence. Jago saw us from further along the bank. He looked fresh faced and self-assured, rising from a cross-legged position on the grass to greet us.

It was only when the two warriors lifted the statue down from the cart that Jago resumed his terrified stance. What power does this clay figure have over his people?

With the boats moored in a long line, we all set to unloading the few remaining belongings, provisions and weapons down from horses and the wagon until all was safely stowed aboard. Cade insisted that Renowden took the lead boat, having the most knowledge of the coastline among us. Jago and I squatted in one of the central boats while the Prince, Maleek and his two warriors took the largest vessel at the back. Idina and her handmaidens travelled with Cade and Tallack in the second largest vessel behind Renowden.

As small as the boats were, I felt easier knowing that if one capsized, there would still be adequate room in the remaining vessels for us all to reach land. We set off almost immediately, leaving the cart and horses with the settlers as part payment for the journey ahead. My medicine kit stayed with me, although not wrapped about my person. I had learned the dangers of blades at sea during our last voyage.

The hops I bought from the wolf lady on the Cantii estuary were steeping in one of the fresh water bladders, providing the Prince with a plentiful supply of sickness tonic on his boat. With Maleek and his warriors to take care of him on a separate vessel from us, Jago and I relaxed and let the tidal waters carry us into the bay.

I reckoned that we were travelling at a faster speed than a cantering pony. The fishermen steered us into the choppy waters in the centre of the channel, which swept us all out to sea long before nightfall. I kept watch along the river banks for any signs of vicious raiders who might set loose a shower of arrows from the sides, but the place was deserted. A cold supper of dried meat kept us going, until later in the evening when Renowden's lead boat steered towards shore. The fishermen, it seemed, were not prepared to sail through the night.

The tide was out when we helped to pull the boats onto the sand banks near to the next river mouth. Grasses were scant and gave us little from which to build a fire. The Prince's warriors hit the beach running, ordered to search for another sacrifice suitable for the godly statue. I could not stop thinking about the grinning masks wrapped in fine fabrics and untainted by blood.

When we all congregated together, I noticed that Tallack had regained some, but not all of his senses after the resin dose. Maleek still avoided his gaze and loitered like a pouting child behind Suliaman's tall chair. Jago followed Idina and the girls into the dunes in search of useful material for a fire and anything to supplement our meagre rations. He seemed his most cheery in their company, and I was glad to have him away from the effects that the idol had on him.

The Prince slid down the back of his seat, crumpled into a wizened heap. The tonic of hops was not helping his sea sickness. I hovered close to him to try and catch sight of the state of his stump. The bindings were black with dried blood. It really needed a clean dressing, but I was loathed to offer my services.

What a fool's errand I set in motion that day in the Frynkish port. We could all be back at the River Exe, helping Blydh to rebuild our homes and fortify the defences against Duro attack. Tallack could be training up more youngsters to swell the warrior ranks and Jago would still be happy trailing Cryda's babe. Instead, we were cold, wet, hungry and in constant peril. The trade agreement was looking more remote every day as

Suliaman's health declined and Maleek retreated from my nephew's advances.

I wondered if Maleek also regretted his actions, the day he agreed to accompany his father into exile in search of a cure to lift the curse. He would sit at his uncle's side, learning the wisdom of great leaders in a civilised city of culture and written words. He would command great fleets of vessels, most being larger and deadlier than Tallack's fine ship, patrolling the shoreline to protect their trade routes. Maleek would be a man of great prominence, rather than the wretched creature I saw before me.

Him, I pitied. Him, I wanted to protect. It was not his fault that we were in enemy waters surrounded by hostile clans. Maleek did not make the decision to offer himself as a tribute to an evil god from far off lands. He saw it as his duty to do all that Suliaman demanded of him, even if that meant relinquishing his happiness, or perhaps his life.

I took a little willow bark from my kit and held it out in my palm for Maleek to see. He understood that I was trying to help him. He gave me a defeated smile. Closing his eyes and holding his hand up. "Thank you." He muttered, opening his eyes and taking the bark gently from my hand. A moment later, he saw me looking down at his father. "Can you help him too?"

I was taken aback at his request. Considering all that Suliaman had subjected Maleek to, I thought that he'd be content to let the man suffer. I sighed deeply, but did not feel that I could refuse. What good would it do any of us to let the Prince rot away in his chair before our eyes?

Looking at the state of the bindings, I knew that cleaning and redressing the stump would cause him great pain. There was the possibility that the numbness from his cursed state could have travelled to his arm before the hand was severed. I tested my theory with a calculated prod. Suliaman stirred with a whimper. There was still some sensation from around the burned flesh.

"I need to give him poppy resin." I said to Maleek. I knew not whether the raiders had made off with the large Frynkish pot of resin, or whether he had supplied Tallack with some from a separate source. Neither did I want to find out. I unsealed the wax from the little jar I had been given and took out a small quantity for the Prince's cup. At least if he stayed addled, he was less likely to feel anything. The clean-up was relatively straight forward once Jago had built a small fire and I could see from the light of the flames.

As I cleared away my kit and filthy bindings, Suliaman's warriors returned with a large black seabird with a graceful neck. It did not fight, nor flap as they carried it along the beach to our camp. My stomach sank at the thought that it might already be dead. Never before have I wanted a hunted creature to be alive more than at that moment. Without a sacrifice for their statue, Suliaman could insist that Maleek open his veins over the idol all over again, or worse. As they drew level with the fire, it was startled by the sparks and flames. It strained against his grasp, trying to peck his hand. My relief was profound. We had averted catastrophe yet again.

What I couldn't understand, was why some days it was sufficient to kill a bird while another day required a horse and another something as precious as the nobleman's son's blood. How did the old man decide what should be offered in appeasement? The only way I could discover this peculiar state of affairs was to ask Jago, and I was not about to upset him again after seeing him smile for the first time in days.

I slept ill that night, pondering the discrepancies between Suliaman's health and the size of the sacrifice offered to their god Melkarth. Even at our most sacred gatherings at midsummer around the great cursus before entering the grounds at Stonehenge, our gods only expected a few drops of blood freely given by our own hand. What kind of wickedness would expect a beloved child to bleed out over the statue?

In the morning, Renowden set to work with his bone hook and line. Jago gathered what branches and dried reeds he could find to rekindle the embers to cook a few small fish. Suliaman ate nothing. The water bladder containing the hop tonic was tucked at the side of his legs, and every so often he would grumble at one of the warriors to help him remove the stopper so that he could drink. From his poor temper and snappy responses, I figured that the resin had fully worn off and he was feeling its absence. I went to make water of my own in the dunes, and returned to find him peaceful and with drooping eyelids. He must have taken another dose.

We set sail soon after we'd eaten some of Renowden's catch, letting the ocean current sweep us along the shore in a northerly direction. By mid-afternoon, we'd drifted and paddled until the coast was barely visible on our starboard side. Huge peaks rose into the cloud in the distance in shades of dark green and grey. Ahead of us, the skies were black with winter weather. The rain held off until it was almost dark. The fishermen in the lead boats insisted that we pulled into a narrow cove, allowing the storm to pass through during the night.

As the warriors lifted Suliaman and his chair onto land, I heard Renowden arguing with the fishermen. Idina rushed to his side to smooth over any tensions, but within moments, she too raised her voice to them.

"What is all this fuss?" I yelled above the clamour, holding my arms up to silence the lot of them.

"They are demanding their payment now." Renowden told me.

I turned to Idina. “Didn’t you say that they would get their tin when we were safely delivered to the Skotek Isles?”

She exhaled a noisy breath and stuck her hands on her hips. “I did, but they are refusing to take us any further.”

CHAPTER TWENTY-FIVE

"What possible excuse have they got for breaking their word?" I fumed.

Idina narrowed her eyes at the tallest of the fishermen. It was obvious that this was the fellow with whom the bargain was struck. "This one says that he couldn't understand my accent, reckons that his deal was to get us this far only."

"And how much are we expected to hand over to get us the rest of the way?" I too fixed the man with my most evil glare.

"Nothing. They refuse to sail any further north than this point. Apparently, it is risking life and limb both from the currents and in meeting up with the Skotek tribes." Idina was infuriated. She clasped her hand to her forehead and wandered off, overwhelmed with the whole debate.

"Give us what you owe, old woman, or we'll take it from you." The tallest fisherman said, emboldened by the presence of us women.

Renowden snarled, unsheathed his dagger. In a flash, he grabbed the back of the man's head and held the blade against his throat. "Just you try it, you lying kyjyan!"

Cade and the warriors saw the scuffle, each of them drawing their blades and bearing down on the fishermen. Those that were not held captive by Renowden, fled. They ran down the beach to their boats and pushed them into the surf. We'd lost our transportation and guides.

Maleek called the warriors back to the Prince's chair. He'd slumped to such an extent that his back was arched over the seat, his legs folded beneath him and his knees embedded in the wet sand. Between them, they lifted him up. One of the warriors gestured to Suliaman's nose, it ran with red humours across his mouth and down his neck.

The Prince raised a claw hand to his nostrils, and examined the blood soaking into his sleeve. He was declining at an alarming rate. Even in the poor light, I could tell that his skin had thickened on his face and took on a strange yellow hue. That was a known sign that the bad humours were pooling inside him.

Tallack approached Maleek. "I can carry him down to the water's edge and we can bathe him together?"

The Prince's son barged past him, connecting their shoulders with some force. "I don't need your help." His rebuff could not have been more forceful. Tallack's expression fell from bubbly and hopeful into dejected and hurt. To my knowledge, my nephew had never experienced the loss of affections from a lover before. It had always been he who rejected others.

We all stood and watched as Maleek ordered one of his men to carry the shivering Suliaman to the breaking waves. The second warrior scampered off in search of driftwood and kindling.

"We cannot build a fire, Maleek." Tallack ventured, his tone gruff and tetchy. "The smoke would give away our position." Maleek turned away without rescinding the orders and followed his father down the beach.

Renowden blew out his cheeks, letting the captive fisherman flee. “I suppose I’d better see if I can catch us something to eat.” He didn’t wait for our answer, but wandered off towards the rocks at the side of the bay.

Jago stood in front of the statue. He was not much taller than the object as he stared down into its hollow eyes. What power baked clay has over his people is a mystery to me, but it is stronger than any tale of woe our tribe could relate regarding our own gods.

Idina, Cade and the maidens walked towards the cliffs in the hope of finding caves in which we could shelter for the night, leaving me alone with my nephew.

“I’m sorry, Tallack.” I said leaning my face against his shoulder as he gazed at Maleek in the distance. “I should never have asked you to come on this ill-fated quest.”

He thought for a moment, tipping his head onto mine. “You were not to know.”

“What shall we do now?” I asked, genuinely stumped as to how to solve our current dilemma.

“There is nothing to be done. Whichever Skotek tribe owns this territory will see the fire. We’ll be dead or slaves before daybreak.” His defeated attitude stunned me. This was not what I expected from the ever cheery Tallack. His ocean adventures and tales of the strange were just the tip of his exuberance. What had the foreigner done to him to lay him so low?

“Then you must stop them from lighting one.”

As I said it, he pulled away from me and wandered up the slope. “How?” Without a backwards glance, he walked over the ridge, and out of my sight.

My anxious state had me turning in all directions, trying to make sense of everything that had happened, and failing to think of a way out. We could not walk and carry that stupid idol, the Prince and our belongings all the way through the peaks of Skotek to an island crossing point.

We had little enough tin on us to pay for the boats as it was. The Prince looked to be in the final stages of his illness, the curse had taken his senses, his strength and now filled him with bad humours. It would be less than a quarter moon before death.

We were so close to the top of the world; I could almost taste the victory. If only those Cornovi fishermen scum had kept their word, we'd be there in just two days. Tallack was right. We could do nothing but surrender to the inevitable and pray that Cernonnus would be merciful.

I sat at the high-water mark on a rock, watching, waiting and growing accustomed to the idea that I would soon join my ancestors in the Between Lands. There I would stay, until the gods decided whether I should sink into the Underworld, or rise with my noble blood into the fringes of the Summerlands. Either way, it was too late for me to right any wrong doings over the span of my long life. I can't grumble about my lot. My sadness stemmed from the fate of my nephew, young Jago and to a certain extent, Idina and Cade. From what I hear about Skotek Tribes, a quick death was unlikely.

Against our advice and judgement, Maleek's men lit a fire and dried off the Prince next to the warmth of the flames. His spine could no longer support his weight. As soon as they sat him upright, he crumpled in the middle, squashing his ribcage and inducing a wheezing breath. Within a short while, the warriors had fashioned a stretcher from pine branches and bedding furs. A second contraption was created so that Maleek could carry the bloody idol on his back come dawn. They fully intended to walk all the way to the stones.

There were no caves, and no overhangs to shelter us from the strong winds and rain that night. Our only bright moments, were when Renowden returned to camp with a clutch of plump lobsters from the rocky shallows along the cove. They sizzled and cracked open from the hot rocks on which they rested in the fire.

Maleek tried to feed the Prince with a few soft flakes from the tail of his lobster, holding his feeble frame up to aid swallowing, but he choked every time. At that moment, I thought that our last meal in this world was fit for a Prince, and yet he of noble blood would have to resort to a thin grain porridge, baked in a beaker with a little of his hops water. He was even too sick to demand a sacrifice for the statue. Maleek didn't seem to bother about ordering the warriors to find a creature to kill in his father's fragile state, and we certainly didn't encourage the practice.

Since our fate was almost a foregone conclusion, I slept well that night. The rain pushed through before we all bunked down for the evening, and the lobster filled my belly. I was content to leave the world as soon as the tribe discovered us, in the knowledge that I had spent a lifetime trying to do the right thing at every opportunity. What now became of my kin, was in their hands.

Jago jogged me awake when the sun was high enough to filter through the grey clouds. He handed me some of the reheated porridge that the Prince had not eaten. Our stuff was packed into bundles ready to strap to our backs. Bless him. He must have risen early to do all the chores while I slept. Rubbing away the salted crusts from my eyes, I blinked until I could clear my blurred vision.

The warriors were sliding Suliaman back into his stretcher furs under Maleek's watchful glare. Cade, Idina and the girls were still sleeping on the other side of the fire. Renowden, was away from camp. I suspected that he was looking for more lobsters. Stretching and yawning, the elation hit me. I was alive, fed, warm and most of all, free. Our luck had held.

I handed my furs to Jago for packing and wandered up the beach towards a layer of shrubs. There was still a chance for us after all. Lifting my tunic and skirts, I squatted over the dead grasses and pissed. I tipped my head back and surveyed the high cliffs all around the bay, they stood sheer and imposing, silhouetted against the silver clouds.

As I straightened up, I saw them. More warriors than could be counted, lining the tops of the rocks. Every one sat on a horse, and all bore weapons of war. My elation was short-lived. Tallack was right all along. I hurried back to camp to warn the others, although there was no hope of escape, they had us fully surrounded with our backs to the sea.

I found Tallack laying across a small bolder with his eyes glazed and drool trickling down his chin. Kicking his feet, I yelled at him. "Rouse yourself, my Chief. We are under attack." He moaned and rolled over until his face was fully embedded in the sand. My little pot of resin fell from the crook of his elbow. He'd taken enough to knock out a whale. Further kicks to his shins gained little response.

I shook Cade and the women awake and alerted Maleek to our predicament. His warriors stood guarding the Prince with spears and swords as he lay on the ground, not that they would stand a chance against such opposition.

"Maleek, tell your men to stand down and surrender. There are too many to fight." I took the moments before the tribe reached us, to slip the poppy resin into my medical kit, and hide a blade in my cloak pocket. I could see their Chieftain and his stocky protectors, riding into camp. With a little sea water collected in my beaker, I emptied the lot onto Tallack's head to waken him to our unwanted visitors. He sat up as the Chief and his men encircled us around the fire.

The man in charge took a slow trot around us all, analysing each of our faces and state of wellbeing. His long hair and beard were braided with gold beads, his chest covered in a shaped plate of bronze. It was a simple but ingenious way to stop fleet arrows piercing his heart. The value of the metal alone was easily equal to the shield and long sword Aebba the Wild had made to pay his entry into the Summerlands. Only a Chieftain could afford such luxuries.

Those following him, seemed to have a similar confidence and swagger. By the way that they looked and spoke to the Chief, I surmised that they were his sons.

Cade stood up in front of the women to speak. "Great Chief, we come here in pilgrimage to the Skotek stones on the isles at the top of the world."

The Chief listened for a moment or two and then pulled on the reins to halt his steed at Cade's feet. Leaning forward over the pony's neck, he squinted at him, but said nothing.

Cade took a stumbling pace backwards. "We paid all our metal to Cornovii fishermen to take us directly to the island, but we were duped. They dumped us here on your land. We would never have trespassed without consent or tribute otherwise." Cade held up his hands in surrender. The Chief kicked the horse's flanks, urging it closer to Cade's face and hemming him in against the fire.

"Forgive us, merciful Chieftain. We bear the flag of truce." Cade's arms flailed about as he hopped over the flaming branches and embers to safety.

The Chief almost smiled. Yanking the reins, he closed in on our foreign companions. He took in their strange clothes and dark skin with raised brows. The warriors moved in unison, aiming their spears and taking a battle stance. This provoked a full chuckle.

He turned to his sons on horseback behind him. "Kill the men, take the women as slaves. Burn that sickly one over there and carve the rest up for the pigs. Can't waste good meat like that."

Two rangy men hopped down from their ponies and shoved Cade out of the way. More warriors joined in the struggle to capture Idina and the girls, while pointing their spears and swords at Maleek and his men. Tallack, to my utter disgrace, still lay in the wet sand in a permanent addled haze.

Idina fought against a warrior who tried to wrestle her to his horse. She scratched his face as he tried to bind her wrists with leather strapping. He clouted the back of his knuckles across her face, almost knocking out all her senses. She fell to the floor holding her reddening cheek and opening her jaw to see if it was broken. Her maidens rushed to her side, fussing and crying and squealing with fear.

Something had to be done or we were all likely to end up on the funeral pyre. "You'd be wise to treat that one with some respect, Chief. She is the daughter of a wealthy southern tribal Chieftain. You could ransom her for a cart load of metal, provided that she is unspoiled and unharmed." I had nothing to lose in my outburst. I fully expected to lose my life within moments, but if I could preserve one or two of them, I'd go to the Between World satisfied with my lot. "You'd get even more if you treat her maidens with honour too."

From the way that the Chief snapped his head around at me, I figured that he was not used to being gainsaid, let alone by an old woman. He did to me, what he'd tried to do to Cade. The stinking hot breath of his horse covered me in vapours he pulled in so close. I fanned the stench away with my hand, but I held fast to my spot next to my nephew.

The Chief peered at me, as if he was considering his options. I hoped that he might think my suggestion wise and agree, but that was not uppermost in his mind. "I know you." His voice was almost a whisper. Although I heard it, I doubt others from his tribe did, as they were still yanking the arms off the women.

"Truly, I am sincere. Those women are valuable to their kin. If you harm them, they will gather the clans across all the midland and the south to come to their aid." I aimed my attention at the young men who seemed more interested in lifting the skirts of the women to examine the spoils of war.

The Chief's horse flared its nostrils in my face. He would not back away, neither would he take his focus off my features. I turned to face him, squinting up against the brightness from the sky. What did he want from me?

"I never forget a face." It was another low murmur, but loud enough for me to hear. He was sure that we were acquainted, but for good or evil, I could not say. I have always tried to do what's right by those who cross my path, but there have been testing times over the seasons, this being one of them. I feigned a confidence that I could not support inside. My stomach roiled about with the kind of bellyache that comes from an intense fright. His sons swung their weapons, cracking through their flimsy spears and beheading Maleek's men without a second thought. Stepping over the bodies, the Skotek tribesmen approached Maleek. One crossed his arms over his chest to perform another swinging blow to the back of the foreigner's neck. Maleek clasped his hands together in front of his chest and began to chant a prayer to his god.

"Wait, please..." I shrieked, hoping for a last-minute change of heart. "I beg you, do not kill this man. I gave him my word that I would take him to the healing stones at Callanish to lift a deadly curse from his father."

CHAPTER TWENTY-SIX

I reached out to the Chief, imploring him to stop the bloodshed. "Please…"

"Healing stones. That was it. You're a healer." The Chieftain waved at his son, who in turn lowered his blade. "That's where I saw you… the midsummer gathering at Stonehenge when I was a boy. You healed my father." The Chieftain dismounted from his massive horse and patted its neck. His accent was so strong, I had to pay close attention to what he was saying.

Still quivering inside, I chose my words carefully. "I am a healer and I have attended many midsummer gatherings in my time, but I cannot claim to remember every person that I tried to help." I shrank back from him as he moved towards me. How could I recall all those summers ago, or whether I was able to save his father from whatever laid him low? "I am an old woman and my memory is not good. Forgive me."

All I could fixate on was how his teeth looked a lot like wolf fangs when he beamed at me. "Nothing to forgive. You did my father a great service that day, even though he was not able to pay you for your troubles."

For one horrifying moment, I thought he was going to strike me. His arm settled instead across the back of my shoulders. He squeezed me as though we were kin. His warriors and sons looked on with baffled faces.

"I'm glad I could help him." I said meekly, hoping to Cernonnus that it was not some trick to gain our favour.

"A brawl when the old Chief was half done in on ale and hemp. You stitched him up and bound his wounds. I remember my mother and I carrying him back to our shelter dying with embarrassment. We had nothing to offer you for your service." I was still tucked beneath his shoulder and he didn't seem to want to let go. I made no attempt to escape for fear of riling him. "Boys, come and meet the healer from Stonehenge." His sons sheathed their blades and wiped the blood from their hands. The shorter one stood before me and took hold of my limb at the elbow. I gently wrapped my fingers around his muscular forearm.

"Good to meet you, healer."

"Indeed, as with you." I said, lengthening my spine at the formalities. I repeated the process with his younger brother, and then looked to the state of my nephew laying on the ground. The embarrassment was all mine this time. Instead, I chose to explain the presence of Maleek and Suliaman, Cade and Idina, and finally apologise for Tallack's behaviour.

The Chief roared with laughter. "Nay, lass. That makes us even on that score. Nay trouble yourself." He let me fidget free from his grasp for a moment while he gave his tribesmen orders. Some of his men gathered up Tallack and slung him over a horse. Other's suspended the Prince from a wooden frame attached to the rear of a cart pony. Maleek, Cade, Renowden and the girls were given their own beasts to ride.

The gruesome idol still sat by the fire, stained brown with aged layers of blood. “What in the name of all the gods is that?” The Chief asked me, pulling a disgusted face.

I explained the importance to the Prince and that it was a part of their religion from far off lands. The grinning masks lay next to the idol, wrapped in fine purple cloth. On my say so, the Chief commanded that his men should transport the clay goods with care back to their compound a short way inland.

Filled with a mixture of relief and suspicion, I helped Jago onto the back of the horse I’d been given, and followed the long procession of warriors to their stronghold. I could feel Jago trembling against my back and knew exactly what was coursing through his mind, for I had the same notion. It was too fortuitous to be sheer luck, unless the Goddess Cerridwen favoured us and led the Chief to our fire. We had next to nothing left worthy of stealing, and our number too few to warrant a ruse to get us into the camp. If they had truly wanted us dead, it would have already happened on the beach, where the sea could wash away the mess.

“Fur Benyn, do you really know this man?” Jago whispered into my ear as we rode. I shrugged. For some reason, my slave wanted answers. I had few to give him, other than a faint recollection of the symbol burned onto the hindquarters of their horses. It jogged a memory of their tribal name, the Novantae.

The further along the track we rode, the braver and more inquisitive I felt. Sons of the Chief rode alongside me, as though I was a prized possession to be guarded. Not sure if this was usual, I turned to the shorter, and I assumed, the elder of the two and asked if it was permitted for me to ride alongside the chief. They both found my request hysterical.

"Aye, you can try, but he's a mean ole bastard." The younger of the two said.

Unperturbed by their jovial warning, I tapped my heel into the horse's belly and caught up to the front of the line.

The Chief gave me another wolfish smile. "I don't blame you. My boys are dull at conversation. Have you come to check that I won't have you slaughtered when we get to ma' home?"

I'd underestimated his intelligence. That wouldn't happen again.

"The way I see it, my kin still owe you for your kindness. You don't remember, aye, but I do. You even found him the following day to check up on his bindings and redress his wounds. We never did know your name or your tribe, but I ne'er forget a face."

"Tallack and I are Dumnonii, Cade is Cantii and Idina is Catuve-Llaunii." I told him, expecting his raised brow look of confusion. I didn't offer an explanation.

"Dumnonii of the tin mines?" Definitely sharper than he looked, that one. I nodded, watching his response keenly.

"Then I am very glad that I didn't have you killed. What do they call you? We should talk trades you and I."

"My name is Meliora, but I have more nicknames than I care to admit." I was bashful about telling him that my tribe, and some other folk insisted upon calling me a wise woman.

The Skotek wolf snuffled. "I can imagine. And your dark friend behind you? Can't be your kin, surely?"

"He is to me, Chief. This is Jago. Saved my life more times than I can count."

He pulled a face that seemed to say, *fair enough*, but at the same time indicated that he thought I was addled in the brain. It mattered little what he thought, Jago was family to me and that was a fact. After all my years of avoiding formal hierarchies, it felt odd to refer to this huge Skotek man as Chief. "May I ask what people call you?"

"Aye, it's Faolan." He grinned at me.

"But isn't that Skotek for wolf?" Now I was chuckling too.

"Aye, lass. It is that." He seemed to understand my amusement. It was plainly not the first time he'd been likened to the animal. As I thought about my aversion to the creatures, since the incident on the estuary, I realised that it suited him. He was a different kind of wolf, one which led a full and respectful pack. It reminded me of Blydh. He too was named for the wild hound. He was more like a lone wolf than Faolan, but equally devoted to honour and kin.

"The one behind you trying and failing to grow a beard is Ealar. My eldest on your right is Greum."

It was not a long ride to their compound, but in that time, the old wolf had wheedled every bit of information about our trip and the Prince's curse from me. Initially, I thought he might use Suliaman's illness to banish us from camp, just as Idina's father had done, but Faolan was shrewd. He knew the ease with which they, or we, could ship tin up to their region from ours. Having a solid alliance with our tribe would not only raise his fortunes, but would allow him to distribute tin to the whole of Skotek. It gave us a significant bartering power.

That evening, Chief Faolan welcomed us into his home and his heart. The ale flowed as freely as their tongues. They sang and drank and feasted to our health, and made us all comfortable and refreshed. All except Maleek and Suliaman, for the Prince's health continued to decline faster than ever before, and with it Maleek's temper too.

Tallack sobered up from his shameful bout of resin abuse, and apologised to Faolan's wife for not presenting himself sooner. He paid tribute to the red-haired beauty, and that of his daughter, with a few tin beads and a shark's tooth necklace he kept about his neck. It was a paltry offering compared with our usual tributes, but it was almost all we had left to us. Neither ladies seemed to mind, especially since we'd all pushed the incident on the beach aside, where the heirs to the Novantae beheaded two of our party and let their bodies wash out to sea.

The most surprising aspect of the feast was the way in which Jago and I were treated. I sat in the most prestigious seat next to Faolan, with my slave right next to me, on their high table. Tallack, Maleek, Cade and Idina sat on the bench below us with Faolan's sons and his daughter, the handmaidens lower still. That did not go unnoticed by Maleek. He sat with a stern scowl across his face all night. His poor attitude might have been because he was outshone by a humble slave and a silly old woman, or it could have been due to the fact that the grinning idol and masks were in Faolan's possession. Maleek was unable to pay tribute to the ugly god while we sat as the Novantae's guests.

Faolan sent for his own healers and wise women to take care of all Suliaman's needs. He was so weak now, that he remained in his fur stretcher supping what little he could take of broth and ale and poppy resin, but it took considerable help. When I went to check on him, his nose was bleeding, his eyelids were raw, and his stunted, claw hand prevented him from helping himself. His face was a mass of dry, raised lumps and the sores spread across his body. He was a pitiful sight.

He called out to me to come closer. "Fur Benyn. Please, can you bring my son to me." I did as he asked, clearing the women out of the hut where he lay and fetching

Maleek to his bedside. The Prince spoke too softly for me to hear his words. Maleek's forehead puckered up in deep concern. When their discussion was completed, the Prince called the women back to ask for more resin water.

"What did he say to you, Maleek." I asked, following him back to the feast.

"It was between father and son. Not for your ears. Go back to your fawning Chief and slave."

That was a low blow. I only enquired in case I could be of use to him. He was becoming as changeable as his father. He returned to his seat next to Tallack, and I to mine next to the Novantae leader. For the rest of the night, I watched Maleek and my nephew closely. Tallack attempted a reconciliation between them, pouring them both cup after cup of ale, and telling as many funny stories as he could remember. Maleek, on the other hand, appeared to be sulking. He stared at those of us on the top table, directing his fury towards me and Jago. Perhaps we should have insisted that someone as proud and noble as he should have taken our place next to the Chief.

At long last, when the singing quietened, and the ladies took themselves off to bed, Faolan stood and announced that he had ordered his ships to be made ready at the harbour, and that he himself, intended to accompany us to the stones at sunrise. We could not have asked more from this generous man, with his eye to our tin.

I slept like a Ruvane in furs and woollens, and a blazing fire to toast my feet. Jago had his own bunk on the opposite side of the hut I was given for the night. This was more than anyone could've expected.

In the morning, Jago and I were fetched when all the horses and provisions were packed ready for our departure. Faolan's daughter brought us fresh milk and salted pork to see us through to the harbour. I'm not sure what I was expecting, but the Novantae ship was bigger and sturdier than I anticipated. We all fit on his largest vessel, with his sons and some of his tribal warriors following us in smaller boats.

I crouched down next to Maleek and the Prince at the bow. “How is he?” I asked, assuming that Maleek was in a better mood since we had set sail.

He shook his head, all his facial muscles slackened, and I thought he might produce a tear. He held it at bay, sniffing and blinking. Suliaman lay at our feet, wrapped in layers of fur. His nose was less than half the size of when we had first met him in Frynk. It was as though the curse was eating him from the inside. The bone of his brows seemed to be caved in too, although he’d sustained no injuries to his skull during the enemy attack.

I’m sure that I was not alone in thinking that the best outcome for this poor creature from a civilised and noble family, would be to join his gods and leave his broken body behind. I couldn’t understand why Maleek was so intent on dragging his father to the top of the world in search of a cure. Even if the holy men could lift the curse, his flesh was too weak to recover from such a brutal ailment.

We set off at a brisk pace. The skill of the Skotek tribe in navigating their waters gave us a sense of relief. They knew the wild changes in weather, the fierce currents and the rocky shores better than we could guess them. Tallack sat with the Chief, making plans for the tin trade up the western coast between our two tribes. Even if the agreement with the Prince collapsed, we had forged an alliance with this honourable Chief.

Suliaman coughed and spluttered, choking. Maleek lifted his father by the shoulders until he could cradle him across his lap. As far as I could tell, the Prince was not conscious or aware of our discussion.

With the favour of the Novantae leader just a few steps away to protect me, I ventured the question which seemed to be resting on all our lips, but had remained unspoken. Faltering at first, I cleared my throat and caught the gaze of Maleek.

"You know, it is still not certain that the holy men at the stones will be able to lift the curse. They are, after all, of a different faith to yours." A leading question, skirting about what I really wanted to say.

Maleek did not answer. He wiped the cold sweat from his father's brow and returned his gaze to mine.

"I can see that he suffers greatly, every day." I continued. "Would it not be merciful to allow Suliaman to die in peace and be with his ancestors?" It had been building in my mind for such a long time, I felt its burden lift from me as soon as the words left my mouth. I hadn't expected his reply or the eloquence of his speech.

"I know that you won't understand, Meliora. How could you? You have done all you can to ease his suffering on this quest, and now that we are so close to achieving our goals, you want us to give in now?"

I tried not to be annoyed at his supreme grasp of our language after pretending his ignorance for so long. It was hard to avoid raising it in discussion, but I wanted to know what drove them both to go to such lengths. "Of course, we will not abandon the quest, but you ought to prepare yourself for what may come next."

"He has to make it to the Black Rites Ritual. He cannot die before the curse is broken."

"But won't it be broken when he dies anyway?"

Maleek misted up, his eyelids filling with tears. "I knew you hadn't understood. If your holy men cannot cure him before he dies, it will pass directly to me."

CHAPTER TWENTY-SEVEN

The stakes were higher than I thought. No wonder Maleek had given up the life of luxury in his homeland to spend it in exile with the Prince. He had a vested interest in finding the cure, or else he'd suffer the same fate.

We sailed in virtual silence for the rest of the day and moored at a settlement on an island for the night. Faolan and his sons provided us with every comfort, but our entire party were on edge. The cold and damp seemed to speed Suliaman's decline. His moments of lucidity, where he could speak to his son, were few in number and reducing every moment.

Our second day at sea took us along the outer edge of the isle at the top of the world, until Faolan could steer us into a sea loch close to the stones. The islanders saw our sails long before we docked. Some went to warn the holy men, others stayed to greet us. Their visitors were few, making every occasion a chance to trade.

I was grateful that Chief Faolan took charge of the entire event, since we were too exhausted by our journey to think clearly. Tallack handed over the last of our tin to pay for the ritual preparations and priests. We rested until nightfall, waiting to be summoned to the stone circle. As luck would have it, the clouds parted at sunset, affording us all a stunning red sky over the loch.

One of the islanders gave us warming broth and fresh bread. I had no idea what meat it contained. Suliaman perked up a little as soon as we were back on dry land. "Meliora. You are a woman of your word." He croaked to me from his fur-lined bedding. "Maleek will see to it that our agreement is kept, whatever happens this night."

Tallack beamed when he heard this. We had held up our part in the bargain and survived. The Prince asked for a private word with his son. We left them in the cosy, stone and thatched house, and went in search of Faolan. Cade and Idina had slipped away to the jetty next to the loch. She carried the votive panel with Phoenician script almost everywhere she went these days. It would appear that Idina had overcome her indifference to Cade and was happy to be in his company. They might make a fine couple after all.

Jago and the handmaidens laughed and giggled at Renowden's antics, juggling pinecones around a fire. Faolan ordered the unloading of the statue and masks from the other boats. I looked on in amazement.

"How come they have followed us here?" I asked the Chief.

"The Prince requested that they be brought to the stones. He said that if they were not present, he could not undertake the Black Rites Ritual."

My heart sank. "And I was thinking we were finished with all that bloodshed."

Faolan looked at me and frowned. "Should I go and trade for a sacrificial animal?"

"If it's not too much trouble. Better make it a big one, an ox or a cart horse or something of similar size."

As I said it, Maleek appeared in the doorway of the stone house. He saw Tallack and I standing next to the

Chief and made his way over to us. I noticed that he did everything in his power to avoid eye contact. "My father has asked to speak with the highest of the holy men. He is too weak to go himself. Can he be brought here before the ritual begins?"

Faolan whistled his son Ealar, who was sent to fetch the priest from the stones. "Was there anything else your father needs?"

Maleek flicked his eyes in our direction and then reverted to gazing at the ground. "He said that you have already arranged for the transportation of the statue. Faolan nodded. Maleek gave us a half smile. "We are in your debt." He bowed, turned about and walked back to his father inside the house.

Something was not right. I prodded my nephew in the arm. "Have you said something to offend him?"

"No, of course not." He side-stepped my insistent bony finger.

"Well something must have happened to make him this way." I said, narrowing my beady eye at him.

Tallack shrugged. "I did all I could to please him, but he won't have anything to do with me. He just mutters stuff about belonging to Melkarth."

Faolan pulled a quizzical face at me.

"That's their god of gods. Like Cernonnus, but from what I've seen so far, much nastier." I explained.

I sat on the rocks next to the fires while Faolan's men fetched and carted all that was needed from the settlement to the standing stones at Callanish. The holy man visited Suliaman on his own. Not even Maleek was permitted entry to the house while they spoke. When their meeting was over, I watched the Skotek priest leaving. He had a harrowed look about him, wrinkled with anxiety and shaking his head gently from side to side. Perhaps he saw the need for urgency in his task.

Fires burned across the rolling hills next to the loch, and yet not at the stones closest to where we landed the boats. From the rising moonlight, I could see the huge rocks casting mystical shadows on the frozen ground. Turning to Faolan, I asked, "Are we not using the largest circle over yonder for the ceremony?"

The Chief was surprised. "You have not heard the tale?" When I shook my head, he continued. "That circle is forbidden. No one has used it since my grandfather's father's time. According to legend, a red demon from the underworld escaped through the burial cairn chamber in its centre. Twelve of the thirteen priests were killed. The one who survived cast an enchantment on the stones trapping it within. By daylight, he had a capstone sealed across the cairn and buried it with earth to close the rift between here and the underworld."

"Kyjya! That was quick thinking on the priest's part. How is it that he managed to survive to tell the tale?" His story intrigued me. The circle was the largest and most impressive I'd seen other than Stonehenge.

"No one knows. Just lucky, I guess. The demon drove stakes through their hearts and smeared their blood over the guardian stone in the middle. Perhaps it kept him alive on purpose, to warn others to stay away."

I thought about Faolan's account for a while. How would a demon find enough stakes to kill that many priests if it was trapped within the circle? Did they just stand there and take their final blows without running away or fighting back? I asked these preponderances to the Chief, but he had no answers for me.

When the moon was full and high in the night sky, we ate around the fire and then we were taken to various houses in the settlement to wash, the men went one way, us women another. One by one, we were collected by different holy men and taken to our allotted spaces for the ceremony. Idina and her maidens were collected a long time before they came for me. I was starting to think that I would not be required for the ritual, when the high priest himself knocked at the door and bowed to me. His white beard was long enough to cover most of his chest. With that and his black robes, he was utterly colourless. Even his skin seemed grey.

"Fur Benyn, please, follow me." He handed me two crystalline rocks, placing one in each palm with such gentleness it was hard for me to think of him ever having to battle demons and curses. I slung my cloak around me and fastened the front together to keep out the cold. I wore almost every item of clothing I had to ward off the weather. As chilling as it was, the effect of the hoarfrost on the landscape was spectacular. Light from the moon and the fires surrounding the stones gleamed across the rolling hills in the distance, and the gigantic rocks glistened in silvery hues.

The holy man had long legs. I could barely keep up with him as he paced along the avenue of blazing torches that directed us past the closest forbidden stones and up a mild incline. Even at a distance, I could see a massive pointed stone, flanked either side by two thinner pillars. Another looked to have a face of its own, peering up towards the stars. The ground inside the circle was lined with cobbles. Half the space was covered by a wooden platform. This was where the holy men stood.

Maleek and Tallack stood facing the wooden structure, with Suliaman on his fur stretcher at their feet. As I approached, the priests began quietly chanting and banging drums in a rhythmic fashion. My nephew opened his fists a little to show me that he too carried white rocks in his hands. His brows raised in comedy at the scene before us. It was no laughing matter, but my love for him made me smirk at his irreverence.

The priest shot us both evil scowls. I concentrated immediately on his speech. "Stone priests hear us. We have come this night for your help." The drums rattled off a thunderous round. I took it to mean that he believed the myth that the rocks were once giants of men, trained in the priestly arts, who gazed for too long at the skies.

"Before you, stands a man in desperate need. His father weakens under an unholy curse. Together they have crossed vast lands and oceans to seek your wisdom and healing skills." There was a moment filled with more drumming and hand gestures towards the stars. I looked about me. There were no more than five or six holy men on the platform. Where were the others? Where was Cade and Idina, Faolan and Jago?

A cracking noise brought me to attention as the priests behind us smashed two of their white rocks together. As the next one did the same, I saw the flashes of light shining in his hand. Each holy man wrapped the stones together in turn, creating a little arc of light between them.

"You must join in if we are to create a sacred light worthy of Lugh." The High Priest said. We raised our hands and tried to coordinate with the holy men's sparks. The flickers of light danced in the darkness, leaving trails behind my lids whenever I closed my eyes. I am not a righteous person, nor a devout one, but I prayed that Lugh, The God of Light, would see our signal and come to our aid.

We worked up quite a sweat, smashing the rocks together in the circle, until the priests suddenly stopped. Maleek, Tallack and I did the same, and watched as a woman walked from behind one of the pillars carrying a bowl of steaming water. I could tell from the smell that it contained the root of burdock. She knelt on Suliaman's furs and uncovered his face and head. She gasped at his appearance, for even in the low torch and firelight, he was ravaged by the curse.

Those red-rimmed eyes were so sunken that his brow had flattened and his cheeks hollowed. His nose was no more than a stub of thin skin with enlarged nostrils. The woman dipped a cloth into the bowl and hesitated, afraid to touch him. Even though I had much longer to grow used to the sight of him, I could understand her reluctance. Whether she feared giving him further pain, or worried about the curse jumping to her, she did not move.

I tucked the white rocks into my cloak pockets and knelt beside her. “Here, let me.” It took only a moment for her to agree. She scrambled to her feet, threw the clippers to the ground and hurried away. I washed his face with the cloth, and then poured a little from the bowl over the top of his head and hair. His remaining hand was gnarled into a claw, and each finger shortened by a considerable amount. I picked it up and dunked it into the burdock water and dried it on my tunic. “There. That’s better isn’t it?”

Suliaman tried to raise his head, his eyes straining to open. “You’re a good woman, Meliora. I’m so sorry.”

Frowning, I struggled to my feet. It was only a warm wash. He couldn’t help it if the ailment laid him so low that he couldn’t clean himself.

The High Priest stood central on the platform and faced the hills in the distance. The silhouette on the horizon looked like a reclined woman. This, Skotek tribes believed, was the Earth Mother herself. “Mother and Goddess Cerridwen, we beseech thee. Look upon this man with your favour and grant him a pardon from the strife of this wicked curse.” The priest glanced in my direction and nodded to the clippers on the ground. I must have given him my best screwed up face, since he bent over and whispered, “Clip some of his hair and burn it in the flames.”

Why this was my job, I couldn’t tell, but Tallack and Maleek seemed to be preoccupied in a stare off of their own. Sighing, I did as the man asked. There were not many strands of hair for me to cut. What little I found at the back of his head, I clipped carefully, stepped up to the platform and threw the hair into the closest fire.

The drums fell silent. The priests stopped their chanting and two heavy men set among them, walked to Suliaman and picked him up on the stretcher.

“What happens now?” I muttered to Tallack. He shrugged, taking my arm as we turned to follow the priests so that I would not fall on the icy ground. “Was that it?”

Tallack leaned into my ear. “Considering we’re heading up the hill towards more fires, I’d say that was just the start.”

I blew out my cheeks. When I first agreed to bring the Prince to the top of the world, I never imagined that I’d be expected to play such an active part in the ritual. Puffing and blowing with exertion, I dragged myself up the hill to another contorted set of stones – a circle within a circle.

Every rock had something unique about it, a different colour, or shape or angle at which it was positioned. It all felt very deliberate and staged, as though the pillars had special meaning and powers.

To my eyes, the most noticeable was that of a huge pintel, towering into the sky as though it could get every woman in the world with child. Tallack saw it too and sniggered. Bless him, sometimes I forget how young he is, considering he is one of our tribal Chieftains. As we drew closer, I saw some of our friends and travelling companions already at the site. Standing on a slab of stone dug into the grass, was a tethered ox chewing on the cud in the moonlight. At least Faolan managed to trade for a large beast at the last moment. How fortunate we are having met him and his tribesmen.

The other shadowy figures came into view shortly after. Idina and her maids, Renowden and Cade, some of Faolan's men stood next to him and his sons. It was a relief that the whole fraught ordeal was almost over. The priests lay the stretcher down in the centre of the inner circle and joined others as they spread out to stand next to a pillar. Thirteen tall stones, with thirteen priests in front of them, one for every full moon in the solar cycle.

The chanting resumed. It was louder than ever. The holy men lifted the hoods of their robes over their heads so that their faces were obscured in the darkness. I could not tell them apart. One stepped forward and took Renowden by the wrist, leading him to a pillar on one side of the misshapen circle. Before they reached their destination, another performed the same movement with Ealar. A third collected and positioned Faolan, until all but three stones were represented by one of our party. There were five of us left, barring the Prince, and only three stones remaining, Maleek, Tallack, Idina, one of her maidens and myself. I looked all about me for Jago, but he was nowhere to be seen.

A sharply pointed white stone stood at one end of the circle with a red rock on its right and a tall black stone on its left. I had seen and heard about such combinations within god temples. It gave me an inkling of why we were left until last. Another hooded priest stepped quickly and grabbed hold of Idina, pulling her to the red stone. She giggled at the attention, setting down her wooden votive panel to stand in pride of place. The priest turned to face us, announcing, "Mother," in a loud voice.

Next was the turn of her young lady friend. She bounced and skipped up to the white pointed rock, touched it surface and then faced us with a twinkling smile.

"Maiden." The holy man said and stood to one side.

I knew I'd be next. "Yes, yes." I sighed. "I get the picture." Grumbling and muttering, I navigated the holes and bumps of the grassy circle and stood in front of the black pillar.

"Crone." Came the proclamation.

Tallack bit his lips to halt a grin when they finally came for him. Two priests manoeuvred him to stand with his back against the enormous phallus. Maleek stayed in the middle next to his father, his hands cupped over his mouth.

Thirteen of us were to play a role in the ritual. Thirteen priests stood behind each of the stones. In a flash of chaos, they ran around each of us with a thick cord of rope, binding us to our respective pillars. We were helpless and vulnerable.

One priest knotted my bindings tightly, the rope cutting into my ribcage. He walked into the centre and crouched beside the Prince on his stretcher. I recognised his voice; it was the High Priest himself.

"Are you sure you want to do this? There is still time to revert to our ways."

CHAPTER TWENTY-EIGHT

Suliaman nodded. He was content with the ritual thus far, and had no intention of altering whatever plans they'd agreed to in private. The High Priest shook his head. He was not pleased with the situation, but cared more about his payment than our comfort.

Maleek waved at two of Faolan's men who had carried the grinning statue all the way from the boats to the stones at the top of the world. They positioned it next to Suliaman on a flat slab of rock. Maleek ducked behind a wide pillar and gathered up the fine fabric bundle, which I knew contained the grotesque masks.

My stomach belched vile humours up my throat, my heart thundered in my ears. Every part of my skin was hot enough to cook eggs. I wanted to throw off my cloak and several layers of woollen fabric. Maleek rose from his crouched position, carrying one of the masks. He turned about, peering at each of our friends tied against the glistening rocks. I could feel the emotions stinging the back of my eyes and nose. His gaze swept past Faolan and Cade, Greum and Renowden. He did not even look at the first handmaiden. His vision slowed when he reached Idina.

"Mother." Maleek said. "Or soon will be while you hold my father's enchanted votive panel." His eyes looked on to the girl bound to the pointed stone. "Maiden." He said, through necessity. When he got to me, he started walking closer. "Crone."

All that passed through my mind, was the lingering thought that I had lived a good long life. It was my turn to save the younger ones, who still had memories to make. It wasn't my desired outcome, but better me than any of the others. My pulse calmed as I came to terms with my fate. Maleek stepped up to me and held out the binding string over the back of my head, slipping the clay face down over mine, until I could just see through the half-moon eye slits.

"I am sorry that it has to be this way, after all the kindness you have shown me and my father." He said, his voice cracking, making him clear his throat to finish his sentiments.

"I understand, lad. I have no blame for you. Just make it quick." I said, surprising myself at my capacity for forgiveness.

"The mask is so that our God Melkarth cannot see your tears. A life must be given freely and with joy, if it is to lift the curse, although he will not be used to the age of the offering."

Even at this tragic moment, I had to laugh. Not only was the cad going to kill me, but he had the audacity to call me old too.

Maleek looked deeply distressed by my laughter. "You think it funny that Melkarth insists on us offering babes younger than five cycles? He is only satisfied with those of pure spirits, but we cannot wait for Idina to birth a boy."

"What? Babes, you slaughter babies?" I was still yelling my questions as he walked away. With a short detour, Maleek scooped up the second mask and ambled to the giant phallus at Tallack's back.

"Hey! No! Maleek, I've already said I will give my life freely. Don't touch him. You cannot have my nephew. Stop this!" The more I wrestled against my bindings, the more the ropes dug into my ribs and belly. My cries and moans of distress were muffled by the hideous mask. "Please…" I begged; the sound of my own pitiful sobs distorted by the pottery.

"I am sorry, my friend." He said as he attached the mask to Tallack's face. He too struggled to free himself, but the knots held firm. The chanting grew louder along with the drums. The wolf lady's words, from the estuary on Canti lands, came back to me.

"Heed my warning, Fur Benyn. He'll take that which you love most. Don't let him turn your heart to stone."

We should have paid more attention to her warning. I'd dismissed her as a fraud, and now her words were coming to pass. I may be old but I am far from wise. My beautiful, brave nephew stood tall and proud. I could tell that he was dry eyed and stoic behind that mask. It was the Dumnoni way.

The chanting became louder for a few moments and then ceased altogether. The High Priest nodded to Maleek. It was time.

The more I wriggled the more the ropes burned into my flesh. Nothing I could say or do would stop Suliaman and Maleek from taking their chosen life. I called out to the High Priest to stop the madness. His response was to pull his hood further down, blocking his face.

Maleek took a pace closer to Tallack and another towards the wide pillar to his left, and yanked a skinny dark boy out from behind the rock. A thrumming in my chest increased my panic. A cascade of tears clouded my sight. Frantically blinking until the blur shifted, Jago came into focus. The gag choked him, the binding at his wrist looked to have dislocated his arm at the shoulder.

"Please, don't do this. I'll give you all the gold I have in the world, Tallack will give you tin, more than his body weight. Please..." I offered much more besides, but Maleek would not listen.

He held Jago by his good arm, and dragged him to the sacrificial slab by Suliaman's stretcher. Every organ inside my body trembled, my fists clenched with powerless fury and I cried like a babe. Maleek untied the gag and thrust Jago down on his knees.

The boy turned to see me clad in the gruesome mask and smiled. "Do not weep for me, Fur Benyn. I'm grateful for the love you have shown me, but I knew this day would come."

All the time he'd known. The statue was a stark and daily reminder of his forthcoming sacrifice. The more I loved him, the greater the target he became. What ruthless religion thrives on killing those who are loved the most?

I couldn't keep the sobbing quiet. He was the closest I had ever been to having a child of my own, and now some cruel ruler with his vicious gods were taking him from me.

"I go now to be with my wife. Thank you, Meliora, for all that you tried to do for me." Jago closed his eyes and faced Maleek with his head held high. Suliaman started his feeble incantation to Melkarth.

"Forgive me." Maleek cried, taking out his curved blade and slashing it across Jago's throat in one swipe.

The wound was vast and deadly. Jago's life force and soul poured through it and out onto the ground. His body toppled sideways and crashed to the grass.

"No!" My body sagged against the ropes; my despair complete. The pain inside my chest radiated out to all parts of me, enveloping me in a sadness beyond description.

Every person there fell silent, my cries and wails filling the void. The High Priest seemed reluctant to go on, but Suliaman barked at him to continue before the connection to the gods was lost. The man in the low hood approached me carrying a cloth of fine green material. Slowly, and with tenderness, the holy man removed the mask and stacked it against the black pillar behind my feet. He dabbed the fabric to my eyes and cheeks, mopping up my tears before turning to face the centre of the circle.

“God of our Phoenician friends, Melkarth. You have received your tribute. Lift the wicked curse from Byblos and set loose this man from its deadly effects.” The priest bent low and wiped the tear stained cloth over Suliaman’s brow. “We call on Airmed, Goddess of Healing and Herbs, to imbue these tears with the soothing balm of all health and happiness. May he be blessed.”

In that moment I am not proud of all the wicked and evil thoughts I had for the Prince. I wished him a curse of my own, sentencing him to die over and over again in the Underworld in the most hideous and brutal ways that I could imagine. If I was not strapped down, I would have gladly scratched out his eyes and fed them to ravens.

Try as I might, I couldn’t tear my sight from poor Jago’s body. His buckled limbs and protruding windpipe bubbled and frothed with blood. Those images etched themselves in my memory. Barring a few more incantations which I neither listened to nor heard, the ritual was over. Maleek knelt next to his father and flattened his hand in Jago’s blood. With the palm positioned on the grinning idol’s chest, he transferred the print onto the clay man. Melkarth took his fill, the pottery absorbing the blood in moments.

Those around the circle were freed one at a time, but none spoke nor moved from their spot next to the stones. I suspected that one false move might render them the next in line for the curved blade. Suliaman lifted his quivering arm in search of Maleek. Father and son held hands for a moment, until Suliaman raised Maleek's hand to his lips, depositing a kiss. "Thank you, son."

It was the last words uttered from the man of the east. All the damage that man had done, all the heartache and misery, and he passed into the Between Worlds moments later. Maleek stayed on the ground, clutching his dead father's hand. There were no tears, no laments, just a stillness amid the flickering flames of the surrounding fires.

The collection of priests started their procession back towards the settlement. One led the oxen. Its blood deemed unworthy of sacrifice. The High Priest gestured for us all to follow, but I couldn't bring myself to leave Jago. I hovered over his twisted corpse, fresh tears stinging my face in the frigid temperatures. Tallack surrounded me with his cape, rested his arm along my shoulders and steered me away.

Word must have spread among the settlers, as a kind woman from the house in which I had washed earlier in the evening, gave me honeyed valerian tea and placed furs across my knees. I sat and rocked myself next to her fires, oblivious of the discussions surrounding me. All I knew was that a young life, filled with love and laughter and the sharpest mind I'd ever known was stolen from me.

I stayed like that until daylight broke over the Earth Mother hills in the distance. Tallack carried me from the jetty onto Faolan's boat, and stayed by my side until we made it back to Novantae lands. Suliaman and Jago's bodies must have been stowed on an accompanying boat behind us, since Faolan approach me to ask what funeral rites I would prefer. Even considering my options pained me. I couldn't think straight.

Tallack took charge and organised everything with Faolan as part of their trading agreements. They were becoming fast friends, which would benefit both our tribes. Faolan's golden rivers and streams would see all our fortunes improve. The Chief arranged for Jago to have a full pyre with a mourning supper for all those in his family, alongside our friends.

Maleek declared that he would need to take his father's bones back to Tyre, to prove to his family that the curse was lifted. That meant defleshing and storing the remains in a sealed travelling jar. I was not about to volunteer my services in the accommodation of his wishes. My family had sacrificed enough.

The following morning, Faolan ordered that Suliaman's body be broken into limbs, torso and head, and then boiled until only clean bones remained. At first, when I heard this, I feared that Faolan's tribe might have some disgusting custom which insisted that we must all partake in this Princely stew. My relief was quite evident, when the resulting meaty remains were turned out to the pigs. Nothing gave me more pleasure than seeing that selfish man scoffed by kept boar.

When the skull was clean and dried, Faolan presented it to Maleek in his feasting house. I sat at the top table, next to the Chief, feeling the loss of my young friend keenly. Tallack sat in Jago's seat, regularly jogging me alert from my reflections with a jab of his elbow.

The offensive article lay along the table not far from where I sat. The curse had ravaged Suliaman's bones. Where the skull should be smooth, with fine grooves where the regions met, his was rough and worn away. The holes for the eyes and nose were no longer separate, but joined by ragged channels into deformed shapes.

Maleek took one look at the odd-looking skull and pinched shut his eyes. “My people must not see how this curse ate his face thus. It would cast a taint on all my kin.”

Tallack piped up. “Would they tell the difference if you took a different skull home instead? I’m sure that Faolan would have some slave bones fresh enough to dig up.”

Before Faolan could agree, Maleek shook his head. “That would never work. Melkarth would know and would punish me for the sin of falsehood.”

I kicked Tallack under the table for trying to help someone who had betrayed us both. He yelped more in surprise than pain.

Faolan had the solution. “Then coat it in gold. I have some of the finest smiths in all of Skotek. They will dip the article in molten metal and then build up the missing areas. By the time they are finished buffing, it will look like the skull of a god.”

Maleek nodded his approval. “I like this idea.” His hand reached up to the golden torque around his throat, handed down through the generations of his family. “Please, ask them to reuse the gold from this.”

I was shocked at how readily he gave up the necklace, knowing how he treasured the jewel. “But it belonged to your ancestors.” I hadn’t meant to say it out loud, but I couldn’t stop myself.

Maleek glanced up with the doleful eyes of the bereaved. “A small sacrifice compared to yours.” His acknowledgement of my suffering was too little, and too late. At that time, I prayed to Cernonnus to take him and all his family down to the Underworld, and to torture them for all eternity. What use was all that kindness and healing if all it brought me was the death of Jago.

It was more than I could take in one sitting. I thanked Faolan for his hospitality, pushed passed my nephew and sought out my bed for the night. Back in the same bunk as I was given before we set sail for the top of the world, I lay awake with a growing numbness shrouding my thoughts. Not the same lack of feeling Suliaman experienced with his curse, but an all cried out kind of ache. I had lost many people over the course of my life, and I grieved them all in my way. None were as painful as losing the boy who had overcome so much adversity and still brought joy to an old tired woman.

All through the night, I heard Faolan's slaves carrying and building Jago's funeral pyre. Every dropped log and shout to watch out jarred my senses and quickened my anger. By daybreak, I'd slept no more than a dog nap.

True to his word, the pyre was enormous and laid with holly, ivy and heather on the plinth, ready for Jago's swaddled body at sunset. Tallack hovered over me all day, watching and waiting for me to explode, or to wreak my revenge on Maleek thus spoiling their trade alliance. I did neither, for the Phoenician noble stayed out of my way.

Faolan's family were a blessing during those brief days of meeting them. Their capacity for hosting troublesome guests unlimited and undiminished. My only regret was that I had little to give them in tribute. I offered them my largest bronze knife, after Brea had made off with my best, but they declined. Their justification made sense. What good was a healer who had no tools with which to heal. I was not sure that I deserved the title anymore. A healer who wanted to do harm was not a trustworthy one.

At sunset, Tallack came for me. He led me by the hand as the honoured guest of the Chief and his family. We stood side by side as Faolan handed me the torch to light the pyre.

"Would you like to say a few words about the departed?" Faolan enquired.

I shook my head and sniffed. Jago's entire body was wrapped in furs and skins. A privilege reserved for the family of Chieftains, and never for lowly slaves. I was glad of it. Seeing his face would have undone me completely. "No, thank you." I said, trying to keep my voice from wobbling. "Those who knew him well, understand what has been lost." Idina's maidens erupted in tears. She patted their backs and shushed them. At least I was not the only one who loved him.

Dropping the torch into the dry straw at my feet, I watched it catch fire and surge along at speed from the oils and fats Faolan's slaves had laid down. When it reached the pyre, the flames spread to four clumps of thin kindling before igniting the oil coated wood under his body.

Black smoke filled the compound, billowing in whirling eddies about the settlement huts. Through the crowds, I could see Maleek standing on the opposite side of the pyre. In his hands, lay the shining golden skull of his father.

My fury boiled over into rage. With a disturbing calmness I issued a direct order to Faolan's sons, and clapped my hands together to speed their return. Within moments they appeared, carrying the bloodied half-god Melkarth and his treacherous masks. Stepping forwards, I dislodged a long log from the pyre, its end fully ablaze.

"This is what I think of your kyjyan gods!" I yelled at Maleek, drawing my arm back and smashing the log across the torso of the idol. It cracked into several parts, making it easier for me to crush it under my feet. Stamping my wooden pattens down on the grinning faces, I took out all my bitterness and hatred on the clay items, before picking up the shards and tossing them into the fire.

With a final hocked spit on the pot remains. I stuck my fist into the air in defiance. “You can tell your baby killing god, that he’s not welcome in my homeland. Keep your uncivilised practices to yourselves.” As I stormed off towards the guest hut, the sound of rhythmic foot stamping filled my heart anew. The Novantae supported me. I hoped that my nephew would too.

CHAPTER TWENTY-NINE

Come daybreak, I expected some sort of retaliation for my actions with the Phoenician deity. There was none. The Novantae treated me with the same, if not more respect than they had shown me previously. Whether Chief Faolan had spoken to his family or Tallack, I have no idea, but the whole matter was forgotten as though it had never taken place.

Faolan himself came to my hut in the morning, bringing fried pork and fresh bread and cheese, along with more sweetened valerian tea. I knew that it was his wife's doing, but in truth, I was glad of the calming effects of the herb. He sat on my bunk while I ate his food, and explained all that he'd agreed with Tallack. He intended to sail with us on our return journey, to exchange gold for tin. It was such a relief to know that I would not have to ride all that way back to the Dumnonii.

The preparations took two days, with me keeping much to myself in the hut and leaving the arrangements to my nephew. I occupied my time stitching some decorative motifs on fabric to give to Faolan's wife. A small tribute in thanks. She was such a comfort to me in my grief, I couldn't begin to repay her compassion. Their compound was peaceful, and it did give me time to reflect on all that had happened, but I was eager to return home regardless of what we might find there.

Blydh's battle plans would be well and truly underway by now. The signs of spring buds and a winter thaw would have the Durotriges keen to invade our lands. Tallack collected me when it was time to leave for the ship, carrying my bundle and kit as though I was too weak to manage it myself. "Give it here." I jostled him to hand me my medicine bag. "I'm not that fragile."

Tallack grinned at me. Perhaps he thought I'd already bounced back from the turmoil. I hadn't, but wallowing in self-pity was no use to anyone. Maleek stayed at the front of the ship, clutching his repulsive golden skull, while I spent my days near to the tiller with Tallack and Chief Faolan. He was good company and had fresher tales to tell than those of my dear nephew. Cade and Idina, Renowden and the maidens sailed with us, along with Faolan's younger son, Ealar. Greum, his eldest, was charged with maintaining Novantae affairs and protecting their woman folk. It was a bit of a squeeze granted, the ship being considerably smaller than Tallack's fine Phoenician vessel, but we managed.

Faolan could only take my mind off Jago for a short time. While he and Tallack were busy navigating with Renowden, or drinking ale and laughing at their bawdy japes, I was left to ponder on our homelands. I was more convinced than ever that Cernonnus had visited me in the Catuve-Llauni forest that snowy day in the form of a stag - that warning of death that Tallack persuaded me to ignore.

So many opportunities to abandon the quest, all of them dismissed as nonsense. If only I had stayed at the mining settlement at Bentewyn, maybe Jago would have lived. There was also the possibility that Brea could have slaughtered us both in our sleep the moment Tallack set sail. I shall never know now. What is known, is that Brea escaped us all on Cade's horse, with my tin pouch and best knife.

My trip to the Frynkish port only succeeded in providing enough herbs for part of our journey. Even the supplies I traded for from the wolf lady had not lasted long. If I was to be of any help in the coming few moons, I would need to forage widely and with care.

None of us slept well on the journey home. Idina came down with a bout of sickness, using up the last of my hops. She attributed the nausea to the rolling waves, but I knew better. That devious Prince put the notion of having a child into her head when he gave her the carved wooden panel. No doubt she did all that she could to make the idea come true. Not that Cade seemed displeased by her change of attitude towards him. Perhaps that evil old man did something worthy by bringing them together after all. She even seemed content to have kept her hair, which could have a lot to do with the fact that Cantii women never shave.

After a full day of sailing against the current, Renowden suggested we made port at a tiny island off the headland of Kembra. None of us knew which of the Kembran Tribes laid claim to the land, but Renowden assured us that it was so remote as to be deserted. We all hoped that he was right. After all that trouble with the copper supplies from the Ordoviches, and the subsequent nuptials of Tallack's sister to the Ordo heir, the last thing we wanted was to upset any alliances forged.

A roasted fish supper and a chilly night's sleep on soft grass meadowland and we were good for another day of rip tides and tacking. When at last we hit the prevailing currents from the massive western ocean, Faolan and Tallack struggled to maintain our course. Renowden kept his eagle eyes landward, waiting to spot a safe place for us to make port. The tide dragged us into a bay which Renowden recognised.

"This is on the edge of our borders. The moors are just over yonder." He pointed east from the estuary where we dropped anchor. Cade and Tallack swam ashore in search of a smaller row boat to carry us all to dry land.

Idina sat with me while we waited for the men to return. "Cade and I will travel over land from here with my ladies. We have no axe to grind with the Durotriges and so with a small tribute, we'll be safe enough to pass. It's no trouble for Maleek to journey with us too."

I grabbed her hands and squeezed them tightly. "Thank you and bless that child growing in your belly." She blushed, but did not deny my claim.

Renowden shuffled closer. "You know, it's not a bad idea to let the Chief keep his ship here for a time. A little gold would pay for a whole bunch of trusted settlers to help Ealar guard its safety. Better here than on the southern coast. The Duro's will be keeping watch down there if Blydh has rebuilt the compound."

I gave it some thought, and then relayed the plan to Faolan. "This bay is almost due north of our place on the River Exe. We can walk the borderlands and get there quicker than sailing around Land's End and back east again. What say you?"

The Chief was not keen on the idea of leaving his ship in the hands of strangers with his youngest and most inexperienced son. I don't blame him. There was enough gold on board to warrant betrayal from even our most trusted warriors.

When the men returned with a row boat, a compromise was reached. Faolan would sail around the edge of our land and meet us at the mouth of the Exe. Renowden agreed to stay aboard to direct them into safe harbour.

We were almost home. Weary, and with little food in our stomachs, we scrambled up the rocky cliffs to seek out horses with the little gold Faolan had given to us. Some homesteaders allowed us all to spend the night in their cattle shelter and were only too willing to trade for their horses and a few meagre bundles of food to see us all on our way. At a hill on the borderlands the next morning, we stood and said farewell.

Tallack made a lunge at Maleek, thinking that he would break his faith in order to embrace him. He did not. He stepped back, making my nephew a fool for ever loving such a man. I could hardly bear to look at him. This was a person who condoned the killing of infants for a malevolent god. With his father gone, and him set to inherit the entire city of Tyre, I'd hoped that we had made an impact on his beliefs, perhaps allow for a little leeway in their brutal practices, but I was wrong.

He turned to me and made eye contact, the first time in days. "I know that you will never understand, nor will you ever forgive me for carrying out my father's dying wishes, but he would want you to know this. You restored his faith in people from Inglond, and showed him that women are equally shrewd and intelligent as the tutors who came to our city to teach my father and I." He held out his hand to me, urging me to take it in mine. "We are bound together through Melkarth. I shall never forget you, Meliora, and I thank you for all your kindnesses."

I wanted to be the bigger person and forgive him. I wanted to say that he was acting through duty and honour to his father, but I could not get the memory of Jago's slashed throat from my mind. In a form of truce, I shook the man's hand, not as we do, with our forearms aligned on top of each other, but as they do, palms together and locked with fingers.

Before I let go of his hand, his sleeve slipped up his arm, revealing a circular patch of pale skin. It took all my powers of self-control not to betray what I had seen. The earliest stages of Suliaman's curse had passed onto Maleek.

After all they had done to appease their despicable god, to lift the bane of Byblos. They had sacrificed my most beloved Jago, and all for nothing. Maleek would die in the same agonising, face eating and limb numbing way.

I didn't know whether to laugh or cry. Was this Cernonnus' way of redressing the balance? Had he heard all my prayers to seek vengeance on these mild-mannered foreigners? These people who appear so civilised and learned, while thinking nothing of killing babes in arms?

I tried to think with a cool head and a lighter heart about our own priestly practices. We too could be equally barbarous in the dispensing of justice or the offerings to our gods. Were we any different? Maleek mounted a pony with his golden skull and set off towards the moorlands with Cade, Idina and her maidens.

Tallack and I rode south along the borderlands. We didn't get far before Tallack spotted several smoke trails coming from the next valley. Kicking our heels into the horse's sides, we pushed them hard to the top of the hill, and were shocked by what we found.

As far as the eye could see, were rows of tents and shelters and smithies. Lines of young men faced woven targets as they practiced their aims with longbows and arrows. Boys lunged at one another with wooden swords and spears, horses were broken in and made used to noise and fire. All manner of battle preparations were underway, and all under the Durotriges banner.

The most disturbing of all, was how close we had ridden to the Chieftain's tent. He stood on a platform outside, supping ale from an antler cup and bellowing orders at those before him. This was the grizzly husband of Tallack's sister, Wenna, who lost her life in a skirmish over our mines. This was the man who hated the very thought of us. This was the man, whose tall chair sat next to a familiar woman from the Ordoviches Tribe. Brea had joined our enemy.

My breath left my body and anxiety took its place. She knew everything about our tribe, where our boats docked, when settlements would be most vulnerable and much more besides. I admit that a small portion of me rejoiced in her betrayal. She no longer posed a threat to me for my mistake regarding her treachery.

A fleeting thought passed across my brain, urging me to confide my knowledge about her killing Aebba the Wild, but I pushed it back into the dark corners of my mind. It had been too long since his murder and of the punishment inflicted on the wrong woman in response. Tallack would know that I had kept this from him for all these moons. No, this was not the time to divulge all that I knew about the traitor.

"Is that… it can't be Brea, can it?" Tallack said, pulling his horse back behind a thicket of shrubs.

My mouth hung open and I was silent for a long time, absorbing all that I could see. Standing next to Brea's chair was another of our family, one with a greater claim to vengeance than I.

"More importantly," I gasped. "What is your half-brother doing there, and with the sword I found at the lakes near to Stonehenge?"

***

If you enjoyed this novel, and have a moment spare to express your opinion, **a review on any of the distribution sites would be greatly appreciated**.

For more information on the rest of the series, please go to: https://www.carantocpublishing.com

The next book in the series is entitled **Pagan Revenge**

About the Author

Sam Taw is the pen name for fiction author Sam Nash. Sam is committed to delivering novels in two distinct genres, historical thrillers and a unique blend of science fiction and international espionage stories.

She lives in a small market town in the south of Leicestershire, in the UK but dreams of one day owning a woodland on the Cornish coast.

For information regarding the work of Sam Taw, please visit:

https://www.carantocpublishing.com

For information regarding the work of Sam Nash, please visit:

https://www.samnash.org

Made in the USA
Coppell, TX
28 September 2021

63179869R00164